"Ja"

Hard Times, Good People

Kurt D. Thelen;
Illustrated by
Kelsey Thelen Klages

America Star Books
Frederick, Maryland

First printing

This is a work of fiction. Names, characters, places, and incidents either are the product of the author's imagination or are used fictitiously. Any resemblance to actual persons, living or dead, events, or locales is entirely coincidental.

America Star Books has allowed this work to remain exactly as the author intended, verbatim, without editorial input.

Softcover 9781683943402
PUBLISHED BY AMERICA STAR BOOKS, LLLP
www.americastarbooks.pub
Frederick, Maryland

For Dennis and Joni

PREFACE

The pages ahead contain the narrative history of a generation placed in the midst of The Great Depression, World War II, and personal hardship as seen through the eyes of two kids growing up in rural Michigan. From a historical perspective, early to mid-1900 was a most trying and fascinating transitional time in American History. The children, Dennis and Joni, like many of their childhood contemporaries, worked behind teams of horses on their parents' farms. And both, just a couple of decades later, again not unlike their adult contemporaries, flew across the country on modern jet airliners and watched on television as an American astronaut took the first steps on the moon.

One of the most significant differences in the day-to-day life of rural America in the early twentieth century and today is the earlier reliance on physical labor, both in the home, and on the farm. Today's relatively simple tasks such as preparing lunch or mowing the lawn took considerably more effort in the 1930's and 40's. The multitude of technological conveniences we take for granted today were not available in the world of Dennis and Joni's young generation. The physicality demanded by the outside world also helped to forge the interior toughness required to endure the daily hardships imposed by economic instability, war, and personal loss associated with the era. Hard physical work was the only real means by which a farm family could directly affect their lot in life. And, sometimes even that was not enough to overcome the adversity of the times.

In addition to the many daily and seasonal tasks that could be conquered by hard work and determination, early farmers were also confronted by many factors over which they had absolutely no control. A primary example of this is the weather, which had an immediate and significant impact on the day-to-day life of early farmers like the families of Dennis and Joni. In the pages ahead, the reader will notice a reliance on historical weather data to frame the background and hopefully draw the reader further into the context and experience of the story. To a large extent, seasonal and daily weather determined what activity was attempted on a given day and for better-or-worse, often determined one's financial success or failure. This complete dependence upon the ebb and flow of the natural world and reliance on factors outside their control, fostered a strong, resilient, religious faith within the rural communities of early America.

Language was another primary difference between now and the time period in which Dennis and Joni grew up. The central Michigan area was prominently ethnically German in the early 1900's and consequently German was the language spoken in local households, particularly in the rural areas. In fact, Dennis and Joni spoke only German at their homes until they were taught English by the nuns at St. Mary School. The transition to English was hastened by the onset of World War II. Nevertheless, throughout their childhood, the local dialogue was a mixture of German, English, and often a hybridized version with sentences consisting of words from each language. The stories ahead are peppered with some of the more common German phrases and words that persisted in the local culture.

One such word that persevered through the transition from German to English in the rural Michigan settlements was the common affirmative response of "*Ja.*" The local pronunciation, despite the spelling was "Yah," with the "J" pronounced more like the consonant pronunciation of a "Y."

If you look "*Ja,*" up in a German to English dictionary, you'll find direct translations to English words such as "yes" or "aye." However, in the cultural vernacular of rural areas the word was often used in a more philosophical context. To be sure, the translation was still an affirmative response, used for emphasis, somewhat like we might now use the word "Indeed." However, in contextual terms, "*Ja*" could be taken to mean an acquiescence to the hard truth of the situation, almost a surrender of sorts to a fate controlled by a higher power. Perhaps the closest representation my poor linguistic acumen can compare it to is the French "*que sera sera*" which of course in English lyrically translates to "whatever will be will be."

It has been said that life is ten percent what happens to you and ninety percent how you react to it. I hope you enjoy Dennis and Joni's stories ahead and ponder the resiliency and integrity their generation portrayed in reacting to the adversity of the fascinating times into which they were born.

TABLE OF CONTENTS

PREFACE 5

BORN IN A BLIZZARD 11

A NEW BEGINNING 23

FR. GUTHA IN THE CONFESSIONAL.............. 30

HEAT WAVE 35

LITTLE FARMER GIRL.................................... 44

CENTENNIAL 49

SUNDAY CHICKEN DINNERS 56

NEW TRACTOR.. 62

FIELD WORK 69

CANDY BARS 75

SELLING PIGS 79

EASTER.. 85

SCHOOL GIRL 95

A CHANCE MEETING...................................... 99

WAR AND APPREHENSION 103

FAREWELL VISITS 105

THE ULTIMATE PRICE.................................. 108

POW'S ON THE FARM 111

MAKING HAY 115

A SENSE OF DIRECTION 123

RACCOON HUNTING 129

MARKIE 139

VE DAY 149

BITTERSWEET 153

VJ DAY.. 160

THANKSGIVING 164

CHRISTMAS 169

EIGHTH GRADE GRADUATION 175

WHEAT THRESHING...................................... 181

GROWING UP 188

BUTCHERING 198

DAVID... 210

TRIP TO LANSING... 219
WORKING FOR A LIVING 226
BASKETBALL.. 236
CONSCRIPTION... 240
WORKING GIRL.. 252
SETTLING DOWN 256
DENNIS AND JONI... 264

BORN IN A BLIZZARD

With the evening chores finished, Raymond muscled the red-painted wooden barn door shut, latched it tight, and turned his face directly into the icy wind. He didn't notice that the iron caster wheels on the door mount had frozen in place causing the door to skid and drag across the iron rail rather than roll effortlessly as it was designed to do. Brute force was often sufficient to overcome the little challenges that cropped up around the farm, even though it too, was helpless, in the face of the more complex matters in the circle of life. Matters like the one that now loomed large inside the farmhouse.

Raymond's mind was not on his work. A large, barrel-chested man, a notch over six feet in height, with high, weathered, ruddy cheekbones, and still just in his late twenties, Raymond Wieber cast an imposing appearance. Despite the burly packaging, Raymond usually projected a facial expression suggesting good humor. That wasn't the case however, on this Sunday evening in mid-February, 1936.

The cold Michigan wind raged in hard from the west now, swirling the foot of snow that was dumped earlier in the day when the erstwhile weather drove in equally hard from the northeast. The subzero temperature left the snow grainy textured and abrasive as it cut across Raymond's face. The previous night the low temperature had reached -6 ^{0}F and tonight, Sunday, February 16, the thermometer read a meager 1^0. This evening, Raymond didn't notice the snow either.

Making his way from the large barns in the direction towards the cut brown-stone farmhouse, he first stopped at the woodshed that sat just east of the house. The wind slammed the hinged entrance door shut behind him and Raymond paused for a minute to let his eyes adjust to the fading light inside. The west part of the woodshed, closest to the house, was used to store firewood for heating and cooking. The eastern end of the woodshed comprised the *"beck house"* which was the German slang for outhouse toilet. Feeling his way along the wall in the dark, Raymond worked his way over to the stacked cord wood. He grabbed an armful of split, dried hickory logs, retraced his steps and kicked open the door with his left knee. The woodshed was only about fifteen feet from the house, and Raymond covered the distance with a few quick strides.

The entrance to the house opened straight into the basement stairway. Raymond scaled the basement steps and dropped the hickory logs next to the wood burning stove in as quiet a manner as he could. These logs combined with what he'd brought in before chores, would heat the house through the night. He shed his boots and barn coat, leaving them next to the wood burning furnace so they'd be dry and warm for tomorrow's morning chores.

Raymond hesitated. Upstairs his young wife, Florence, lay in bed, struggling through the pangs of a difficult labor. Raymond had brought Martha Fedewa, Florence's aunt, over to the house a few days earlier when the labor pains had begun. Martha was an experienced mid-wife, but Raymond could sense Martha's increasing anxiety as the labor continued to languish slowly without result. Their first child, Eddie, now a year and half old, was born in the summer, and it seemed, with no problems whatsoever.

Shaking off the fear, which kept clinging to the corner of his mind, Raymond focused his attention on the task at hand. He grabbed two pieces of firewood and carried them upstairs to the kitchen. With his right hand he popped one of the four stove lids off using the iron handle that fit neatly into a small notch in the lid. The stove lids looked much like a smaller version of today's manhole covers, and collectively they formed the top surface of the stove. A metal tank appended to the side of the stove, served as the water heater for the house. Martha had instructed Raymond to be sure the water tank was full and that the stove remained hot. Raymond was diligent in his duty, relieved to have at least some small measure he could contribute to the difficult birthing process transpiring over the past few days in the first floor bedroom.

Finally, after days of anticipation, later that evening, Aunt Martha called Raymond into the bedroom with Florence. Conversing in their usual German, Martha informed Raymond that the baby was a girl, "*Es ais frau.*" Martha's demeanor was stern and her voice was somber, "The baby is very weak," she informed Raymond. "I can baptize her now, but we should get her into town as soon as possible to have Father Gutha baptize her proper." Florence was holding the baby, too exhausted and spent from the protracted labor to say anything at all.

Aunt Martha prayed over the two of them, reciting a layman's baptismal prayer for the baby, giving her the name Joan Eleanor Wieber, the name Martha and Florence had discussed earlier. According to Catholic doctrine, a lay person can perform a licit baptism in cases where the person is in imminent danger of death and no priest or deacon is available. Baby Joan was weak, and in Aunt Martha's opinion, in imminent danger of death, at least to the point where she felt compelled to take it upon herself to do the emergency baptism. "Pray for us sinners now and at the hour of our death, amen," Raymond and Florence whispered the end of the Hail Mary Prayer, numbed by Aunt Martha's disconsolate prognosis, the urgency of her ad hoc, in-room baptism, and the very real prospect of facing the loss of this new child.

Outdoors the Michigan winter raged. Raymond cringed when a sudden burst of wind rattled the glass in the bedroom window. The thought of taking this new helpless, weakened baby out on snow-drifted roads the four miles to St. Mary's Church for baptism left him uneasy.

Historical weather statistics from the National Oceanic and Atmospheric Association show that for the next full week, nightly low temperatures would dip below zero, culminating with a low of -20^0 F actual temperature, on Saturday, February 22. Combined with steady winter winds and periodic snowfall, the country roads were left impassable. Many speculated that the dustbowl, a protracted series of droughts that ravaged the Great Plains during the early 1930s, was adversely affecting the weather across the U.S., even in the Great Lakes Region. The lack of rain parched the earth and killed vegetation, especially across the Plains states over which many of the Great Lakes Region's weather systems formed. The bitter cold of 1936 completely froze over Lake Michigan, one of only a few times in recorded history that the lake was completely iced over.

Raymond looked at his new daughter, cuddled tightly now by Florence. Her eyes were blue, like his, and it appeared she would have his fair, but ruddy, complexion, different from Florence's brown eyes and darker complexion, which Edward had inherited.

"We better get the baby to church tomorrow," Florence meekly asserted. His wife's first words since the difficult birth jolted Raymond back to his senses.

"*Ja*, sure, get some rest now, I'll make arrangements for church soon enough," Raymond said, again remembering the foot of blowing snow that had fallen earlier in the day.

"Get some rest now," Raymond repeated, as he exited the room and went dutifully back down to the cellar to tend the wood burning stove.

The next morning Raymond finished chores with a cold-numbed but hurried sense of urgency. Carrying two full cans of milk, he retraced his route back into the house. The tracks he had made going out to the barn two hours previous were completely filled in, erased in the cold by the relentlessly blowing snow. The wind slammed the basement door shut behind him instantly relieving the stinging sensation of the grainy snow pelting against his cheeks and the rushing noise of the wind in his ears.

The heat from the well-stocked wood furnace rolled up the basement stairs to meet him. He didn't mind having to run the milk through the cream separator, a task usually done by Florence. It kept his mind off the looming decision of whether or not to take the baby into town for an emergency baptism. Earlier that morning, at 5:00 am, when Raymond was leaving the breakfast table for chores, Aunt Martha had once again reiterated her concerns for getting the baby to town for baptism at St. Mary's Church.

"The baby is not well," she reminded Raymond. He had no answer for her. He knew that getting to town now without getting the car stuck and trapped in the snow was an almost certain impossibility.

As a young adult, Raymond had not felt threatened about weather, or, for that matter, just about any adversity life could throw at him. His father, Edward, had passed away three years previous, and like any man of that place and time, Raymond had a healthy respect and fear of death. Since his mid-20's Raymond had taken over the Wieber homestead farm and the daily privation and challenge of farm life had hardened him physically and mentally to the point where he was confident that he could take, head-on, anything in his path. That all changed when baby Eddie was born. The stark contrast of a totally helpless baby, a formative version of himself, obliterated any air of invincibility he had once held. Life was fragile. And now, with baby Joan struggling through her first week of life, Raymond was once again confronted head-on with that helpless sense of fragility. And, unfortunately, baby Joan still did not appear to be gaining strength.

Raymond slogged through the rest of the week in a cold stupor. Aunt Martha's prognosis on the baby was unchanged. "The baby is not doing well," was the daily report. The words struck Raymond as coldly as the weather outside. On Tuesday night the low had reached -16^0 F followed by -12^0

F on Wednesday with more blowing snow. Raymond busied himself with the twice daily chores of feeding the cattle, sheep, horses, and chickens, and the constant tending of the wood stove. At dinner that evening, Martha again reminded Raymond of the urgency in getting Joan baptized. Florence was confined to bed, a medical practice for the time period which mandated that new mothers stay bed bound for at least a full week following childbirth. Silently, Raymond wished that Florence was somehow up and able to free him from Martha's grip. The tension was palpable. Raymond did not know what to do.

In a more modern context, the decision to risk an already health-compromised, newborn infant's life by taking her out into a blizzard may seem absurd. However, in 1930's rural Westphalia, matters of faith were accepted unequivocally and without exception. The fragile thread between life and death was often left exposed, unprotected by the power of today's modern medicine. Although great improvements had been made since the turn of the 1900's, infant mortality rates, including stillborn deaths, in the early 1930's still approached 10% of all live births.

The constant, tangible proximity to death, combined with an unquestioning belief in baptism-dependent sanctity, rendered rudimentary the decision to risk everything on a dangerous trip to town. Now, at midweek, and in the midst of a terrible winter storm, the Wieber family was on the precipice of making that risky decision.

On Thursday morning, February 20, 1936, the thermometer read -12^0 F when Raymond pulled his barn coat over his bib overalls. With his head down and his body pitched forward, he trudged against the wind through the snow to the barn. He knew the northeast direction of the wind meant more snow. With more than just a hint of anger, he shoved open the corner entrance door to the barn. In the darkness, the draught horses, stomped their feet against the cold, demonstrably demanding their morning hay.

"*Ja*, Prince, Freddie, yer feed is coming," Raymond muttered in the general direction of the horses in the two stalls nearest the door.

Paint, and Lady, the other two draught horses in the next two stalls snorted impatiently for their turn to be fed. Perfunctorily going through the motions, without thought of what his body was actually doing, Raymond finished the morning chores. He dreaded going back into the house. Now the fourth day since baby Joan's birth, a cold routine had evolved whereby Aunt Martha would join Raymond for his "after chores" morning coffee and bring him up-to-date on Florence and baby Joan's health. So far, the news was never very positive. It seemed the pall cast over baby Joan's health was as relentless and unforgiving as the winter storm outside. Something had to give, and, brimming with frustration, Raymond hoped it wouldn't be his temper.

He wanted to head the three quarters of a mile down Tallman Road to his brother Robert's house and have a glass of cider or maybe even a beer and talk about the weather or the stockyard's paying price for cattle. Bottled beer was always served in a glass back then and Rob would stick a spearmint soaked toothpick into your beer to give it a unique, minty flavor. Rob kept a small bottle of spearmint, in which he would submerge the toothpicks, in a narrow corner cupboard in his wife's kitchen. A minty beer would be good about now, Raymond thought.

"The baby doesn't seem to be getting much better," Martha's words broke in and sucked away the pleasant thought about minty tasting beer. Once again today, the news from Martha was no different.

Thursday blended seamlessly into Friday. The snow clouds brought in by yesterday's northeast wind had actually pushed the temperature up slightly. The thermometer only read -6^0 F this morning. Raymond permitted himself a chuckle as he caught himself seeing -6^0 F as an improvement in the weather.

Once outside, Raymond noticed the wind had subsided and the lack of wind brought with it some relief to the livestock.

After milking and feeding the cows, Raymond released the stanchion locking mechanism for each cow, turning them loose in the outdoor barnyard for a little morning exercise while he tended the sheep and forked hay down for the four draught horses. By the time the feeding was done, the wind was picking up and it had started to snow again. The cows were impatiently standing by the barn door, eager to be let back in. When the door was opened, the cows, right on cue, ran quickly into the barn, each one placing her head through her own stanchion. To one not familiar with stanchion milking barns, it would seem remarkable how each cow always returns to its own stanchion. Walking around to the front of the single row of stanchions, Raymond one-by-one, slid the locking mechanism of each stanchion into the closed position.

By the time Friday evening chores were finished up, the blizzard had again reached full force. With the wood supply in the basement replenished and the basement furnace and kitchen stove restocked for the evening, Raymond settled down at the kitchen table with a glass of cider which he had drawn from the barrel downstairs. Martha appeared from the bedroom, and skipping over the usual polite greetings, launched into a frustrated outburst on how the baby just wasn't making any improvement.

The situation had gone on long enough. Raymond, and obviously Aunt Martha, had reached the point where waiting was no longer a prudent option. Turning his head to his right, Raymond repositioned his glare through the east facing kitchen window. The narrow area between the house and the woodshed created a wind tunnel effect, and the swirling winter wind had deposited a huge, five-foot-high snow drift there which was now barely visible in the dim light emanating through the kitchen window.

"If there's no improvement in her health by tomorrow morning, we'll take the baby to church," Raymond stated not averting his attention from the window. Quietly, and with more doubt than hope he added, "Maybe by then this storm will finally be blown out."

"My brothers can help with opening the road up" Florence volunteered, when Raymond walked into the bedroom.

Florence had overheard the earlier kitchen conversation between Raymond and Aunt Martha. Sensing Raymond's apprehension about getting through the four miles of snow clogged roads into town, she suggested having her brothers work eastward from Grange Road, where they lived, shoveling their way with their car up Pratt Road. Raymond listened. He was relieved to finally end the waiting game with the winter storm.

"I'll call your mother and make plans for tomorrow morning," Raymond responded in agreement.

In the kitchen, Raymond's thick fingers cranked out the four character phone number, 87S2, and waited for the connection to his in-law's phone. With carefully chosen words, he explained to his mother-in-law, Eleanor Fedewa, the situation. After an initial moment of silence on the other end of the phone, Eleanor assured Raymond that they would be over tomorrow morning to help Florence and him get the baby to church for baptism. For good measure, Eleanor reminded Raymond that baptism, preferably by a priest, was of utmost importance and a prerequisite to obtaining salvation. "Eternity depended upon it," and by shear will power Eleanor was committed to making it happen that Saturday morning for her new granddaughter, Joan "Eleanor."

Saturday morning arrived without respite from the winter storm, in fact, the historical weather records show the low was a bone chilling -20^0 F, the coldest yet for the February, 1936 blizzard. After finishing morning chores, restocking the firewood, and replenishing the wood stove water heater, Raymond, with much trepidation, went in to check on Florence and baby Joan.

The baby's condition hadn't changed and neither had Aunt Martha's opinion regarding the urgency for a church baptism. Right on cue, the telephone party line rang the requisite three short rings. Raymond answered and was immediately connected with Eleanor. Florence's brothers: Harold; Isadore; Art; and Leon; were ready to begin the repeating process of shoveling snow and pushing and pulling the car east up Pratt Road from the Grange Road intersection. Eleanor would ride along to help with the baby. The going would be slow, but the men expected they would reach Tallman Road in about an hour. Eleanor indicated that she had tried to reach the church rectory by phone but was not able to get a connection.

"We'll find Father Gutha when we get there," Eleanor's voice crackled through the phone line, abruptly concluding the conversation.

Raymond hung up the ear piece, passed along the news to Aunt Martha and went back down to the cellar to put his heavy chore coat back on. Grabbing a shovel and starting at the shed door that held the family car, he began shoveling out the snow drifts, working his way out the drive and south on Tallman Road towards the Pratt Road intersection about a quarter mile away. With gusto, Raymond welcomed the work and shoveled with tenacity sufficient to obliterate the menacing worries spinning about his mind. The wind direction had switched late Friday and the now westerly wind had quadrupled the snow in the north-south running Tallman Road relative to the lesser amount drifting across Pratt Road. The Fedewa's car, frosty white from having traveled four miles, reached the intersection before Raymond.

With his chin resting on his hands which were clasped to the upright shovel handle, Raymond exhaled as he momentarily watched his brother-in-laws energetically attack a snowdrift with three shovels while the trailing car lunged forward before the wind could reclose the drift. He briefly felt a sense of triumph at having conquered the winter storm, reminiscent of his carefree younger days. However, the short break in his own physical activity allowed the spinning thoughts of Florence, baby Joan, and the emergency baptism to cascade back into his consciousness. He shuddered against the cold and quickly resumed shoveling.

With the Fedewa's car now safely in the driveway, Raymond headed to the house to get dressed for town. Eleanor hastily followed Raymond into the house and after conversing with her sister-in-law Martha, entered the bedroom to see her daughter Florence, and, for the first time, her new little granddaughter, Joan Eleanor.

Martha and Eleanor agreed it was out of the question for Florence to travel. As per the labor and delivery protocol of the time, she would be confined to bed rest, especially given the length and severity of this particular delivery. Aunt Martha agreed to stay behind and tend to Florence and little Eddie. Finally, it was agreed that the rest of the crew would all ride along to town, counting on the extra man-power, should the car get hung up in the snowy roads which were rapidly drifting shut again despite the wheel tracks just made by the Fedewa's car.

While the car waited with the engine running in the driveway, Eleanor wrapped the newborn baby in two blankets and handed the bundle to Raymond who had just emerged from the other room wearing his Sunday suit, his only non-work clothes. For a split second Raymond froze in his tracks. He had grown accustomed to toting the hefty Eddie around the house and outdoors while checking on the livestock or crops. He wasn't prepared for the seemingly weightlessness, despite the two blankets, of his new baby daughter. With a renewed appreciation for Aunt Martha's anxiety, he shuffled out to the waiting car.

Packed into the car, the anxious group made the four mile trip into town, retracing the Uncle's shoveled path down Tallman, Pratt, and finally Grange Road, miraculously without incident.

"I'll drop you off at the church door," Raymond said to the entourage with a sigh of relief upon arriving safely, adding "No sense in walking the baby in all the way from the parking lot in this weather."

A NEW BEGINNING

Around the Tallman Road corner and down Pratt Road a mile and a half east of the Wieber homestead, Norman and Mary Thelen moved their own family of three boys; Dennis, age three; Markie, age two, and Clair, age six-months to what was a fairly typical farm for mid-Michigan. The farm was an upgrade from the Jones Road farm near Portland, Michigan where Norman and Mary first started farming. Little Dennis' first cognizant memory was one of leaving the Portland farm.

"Where chairs go?" he asked his mother suddenly noticing that the contents of the house had been moved away.

The new farm was only two miles south from Mary's parents' farm. And, the farm was contiguous on the west border with a farm Mary's brother, Henry, would eventually buy and homestead. The closest town to the new farm was Westphalia, where Norman and Mary were married in the only church in town, St. Mary's, just five years prior on October 12, of 1931. The proximity to relatives was important to farmers of that time period, especially younger farmers with children too young to help much. Having relatives nearby facilitated the sharing of manual labor and farm equipment.

Just twenty-six years of age when he moved his young family to the new farm, Norman was relatively short and had a stocky build, not long and lean like his father Joe. The children called their paternal grandpa, "*Reicha* Joe," pronounced in German, with a rolled "R," inferring a tall, proud, well-to-do mannerism. Mary's father, also named Joe, was known as

"*Dika*" Joe, which denotes a more, stout, or rotund physique. Despite not inheriting his father's height, Norman did inherit *Reicha* Joe's stoic demeanor being a man of few spoken words.

Norman's shorter stature, about 5' 9" was inherited from his mother, Catherine, who, unfortunately, passed away when Norman was only twelve. As far as physical features, Norman was a product of his work environment. His hands and forearms were thick from manual labor. His forehead was pale in color relative to the rest of his face, which without the protection from his straw hat, was darkened by direct exposure to the sun. By his mid-30's Norman already had the beginnings of a slight portly profile, undoubtedly from Mary's good cooking. The portliness was further emphasized by the then contemporary fashion practice of cinching one's dress trousers up with the belt clasped high above the belly button.

Mary was an inch or so shorter in height than Norman. She had dark brown hair, which was cut short, above her shoulders, and she wore dark framed glasses that gave her a serious look which belied her always cheerful personality. Mary's oldest daughter Jane, who was born the summer of 1937, the year after the family moved to the farm, described her mother as follows: "I always felt proud of my mother; I thought she was pretty and always looked so nice. I also thought of her as being a very prayerful person. Several times when I came downstairs after we children had gone to bed, she would be sitting in the rocking chair with her prayer book, deeply engrossed in prayer. When I was on the choir in Church, I would look down at her and think she looked so holy—her head would be kind of bowed to one side in prayer."

Norman purchased the 150-acre farm from Oscar Schafer, Mary's brother-in-law, with financial help from his and Mary's parents. In the early 1900's, farm families were typically quite large. Generally, farms were passed from generation to generation. However, in cases where there were simply too many grown children to sustain as successors on the homestead, it was a common practice for families to help establish children in farming operations of their own by loaning money or purchasing farms outright and mortgaging them back to their children. These arrangements were especially practical in the Great Depression era of the 1930's when bank failures were common. Norman was born the sixth of nine children, and, being in the middle of five boys, it was practically a given that he would branch off the homestead and someday be starting a farm of his own.

Like most of the population in the Westphalia, Michigan area at the time, both Norman and Mary's ancestors were farmers. Norman's Grandfather Peter, immigrated to Michigan from Langscheid, Germany to start a farm of his own. Similarly, Mary's grandfather, Johann, immigrated to Michigan from Eifel-Rhineland, Germany to start a farm of his own in the New World.

Norman and Mary's new Westphalia farm had flatter, heavier, clay loam soils, which held nutrients and water better than the more rolling, coarse textured soils from the old farm near Portland. Like much of the farmland in the mid-Michigan area, parts of the land, particularly in the northwest corner of the farm, were still inadequately drained. Norman worked and invested heavily, both financially and personally, in a persistent struggle to drain and improve the land.

The new farm had two hip-roofed hay and cattle barns, a hog barn, a machine shed, chicken coops, and a couple of other smaller out buildings. The solid wooden frame house was square in shape, with light tan colored slate siding and a shingled pyramid style roof that peaked at the center with identical sloping angles on all four sides. There was no electric power line down that section of Pratt Road when the house was purchased, but when the utility company finally established a line a year later, Norman had the house and main barn wired for electricity.

Like most farms in the area, the new farm had a windmill for pumping ground water and also had a buried cistern for collecting roof runoff for potable, non-consumptive water use. The furnace was a wood and coal burner located in the basement. In the early 1940's, Norman had an electric water pump installed to pump water from the well beneath the windmill to the house which brought running water to the kitchen and backroom sinks. However, indoor bathrooms were not an option in most rural Michigan farm houses until the mid 1940's brought an end to World War II, and with it, an end to county board rationing of construction materials and plumbing fixtures. Therefore, Norman wasn't able to build an indoor bathroom until after the summer of 1945, when he was able to procure the necessary county permits to purchase a toilet and tub. To ease the transition back into production of consumer goods, the war rationing for some items remained in place for a year or so after the war ended.

The driveway for the farm was pretty much exactly the half-mile point on Pratt Road between Wright and Bauer Roads. The house was set to the west of the driveway and a huge fenced-in garden occupied the area on the east side of the driveway. A long farm lane, which was a running extension of the driveway, served as a transect along which the farm fields were splined off, with the side fences running in an east-west orientation perpendicular to the north-south oriented lane. Page wire fence lined the fields, and, for the time period, Norman kept the fence lines exceptionally clean and free of brush by periodically grazing livestock along the field edges.

Starting a new farm in the midst of the Great Depression brought with it many challenges. There was little margin for error with regard to crop or livestock losses. US Bureau of Labor statistics showed that crop prices plummeted by 60% during the 1930's. Without money to spend on inputs, farmers basically went into a self-sufficiency mode throughout the depression. Self-sufficiency then carried over throughout the duration of World War II when the availability of raw materials, such as metals and synthetic fertilizers was scarce to nonexistent.

By necessity, farms had to be fully integrated with regard to livestock and crops with each enterprise synergistically supporting the other. Manure was the primary nitrogen, potassium, and phosphorus fertilizer resource on the farm. Harvested crops were used to feed livestock directly and crop residues, such as wheat straw, were used for animal bedding. Farmers also capitalized on synergistic opportunities within crop and livestock enterprises. Out in the field, legume cover crops and crop rotations with legumes provided nitrogen fertilizer for rotational corn crops. Milk that wasn't sold whole was run through a cream separator with the condensed cream being sold off the farm and the whey serving as a high protein feed for hogs or veal calves. Poultry often followed behind livestock scavenging for partially digested grain. Most of the food that ended up on the kitchen table originated from the farm itself.

On a daily basis, Simon Brothers Trucking from the nearby town of Fowler, picked up ten-gallon cans of milk from Norman's small dairy herd with a flatbed truck. The milk was poured into the ten-gallon milk cans immediately after twice-daily milking chores. The cans were kept cool by being submerged in well-water stored in cut-in-half oak stave cider barrels which were kept outdoors near the windmill while they awaited pickup.

During the spring time, when most of the cows freshened, (gave birth to a calf to begin a new lactation) Norman sold extra milk, above his quota for whole milk, to the creamery in Westphalia. This cream, also sold in ten-gallon milk cans, was picked up twice weekly by the creamery's flatbed truck. Another truck stopped by the farm on a regular route to pick up eggs which were collected, cleaned, and stored in the basement until pickup.

Corn and wheat grain was sold to the elevator in Westphalia in two-bushel, one-hundred-twenty-pound burlap bags. Norman and Mary also kept a good sized flock of crossbred sheep. Wool from the sheep was sold annually to Snitgen's Store in Westphalia. Fattened lambs and steers were sold primarily through the livestock ring in the nearby town of St. Johns, but occasionally cattle were shipped directly to the slaughter houses in Detroit.

The apple trees, located on the west side of the homestead between the house and the hog barn supplied fresh apples for eating and drops were used for pressing cider. Norman kept a couple of repurposed whiskey barrels in the basement of the house for drinking cider and a separate barrel for apple vinegar. Hogs and cattle were butchered for meat and the huge garden on the east side of the house produced tomatoes, snap beans, peas, for canning, salad greens, and cabbage which was fermented in large crocks with vinegar in the basement for sauerkraut. Additionally, Norman grew oats, hay, sugar beets, and corn as livestock feed and as cash crops.

The physical labor requirements of farming in the 1930's cannot be overstated. The milk alone in a milk can, most of which were ten gallons in size, weighed 86 pounds with the can adding another 20 pounds. These were handled twice daily during milking and cream separating chores and then loaded daily or at least twice weekly onto trucks for transport. Two-bushel grain sacks for wheat and corn, weighing approximately 120 pounds each were handled primarily at harvest but also throughout the year for feeding livestock. Daily manure handling was also done by physical labor. Gutters behind stanchions in the milking barns were cleaned out twice daily. In addition, horse stalls and cattle pens in the huge hip-roofed barns were mucked out by hand held pitch forks.

Tractors were just finding their way onto farms in the 1930's but secondary tillage operations such as field cultivating were still mostly done by draught horses. The animals were controlled by heavy leather reins. It took considerable strength and stamina to work full days, weeks on end, controlling a team of hulking draught horses. Older, more mature horses were often paired with younger "green" horses to help break them into the routine of draught work. Once a pair was established they often stayed paired together in harness and once they were old veterans they were often trusted with younger children to do the driving.

The brute force approach to the physical labor requirements of the farm could also be used to describe the mental attitude embraced by the early rural culture in the area. Reduced to its simplest form, the harsh, austere, early farm life often demanded a willpower sufficient to carry on physically when mentally and emotionally you wanted to shut down.

"Put your feet on the floor and get up," Norman would say to his young sons, when still half asleep, they reluctantly had to leave their warm bed and get up for morning chores.

The process of getting up in the morning could not be delayed by any foolish notion of wanting to stay wrapped in the warmth of the blankets and rest a little longer. Rather, it was expected that one would, by sheer willpower, raise yourself out of bed and put your feet squarely on the floor, despite physical or mental desires to the contrary. In later years, the concept of the modern day snooze alarm seemed absurdly foolish to Norman and his generation. Any effort less than rigid adherence to strict mental toughness and discipline was a weakness that could not be tolerated.

That same willpower and mental toughness was relied upon to persevere and survive the many adversities associated with the era, including economic depression, world war, personal hardship, and heartrending bereavement.

FR. GUTHA IN THE CONFESSIONAL

The small group, Grandma Eleanor, Raymond, and the uncles: Harold; Isadore; Art; and, Leon; and of course, baby Joan, huddled together in the back vestibule of St. Mary's Church. With their initial shoveling and pushing, they had conquered the snow filled roads and successfully delivered baby Joan to the church, but, they weren't quite sure what to do now that they had safely made it to their destination.

Eleanor had not been able to reach Fr. Gutha by telephone, but being familiar with the weekly Saturday confession schedule, she knew right where they would find him in the church.

It must have been a particularly sinful week in town that cold February in 1936, as the line of penitents kneeling in the pews along the confessional seemed unusually long despite the harsh winter conditions outdoors. To Eleanor's way of thinking, it didn't seem appropriate to have her fragile little granddaughter wait in the cold church for the hour or so it would take for confession to be over. Uninhibited, due to the urgency of her mission, Eleanor jumped into decisive action.

"Leon go and get Father out of the confessional," she ordered, much to the shock of Raymond and the other uncles.

Incredulous, Leon's eyes widened like saucers. Pointing to the confessional, Leon stuttered, "Yyyyyou want me to...?"

Leon didn't finish the question. He didn't have to. The glare emanating from his mother's stern face obliterated any supposition he might have of protesting. Harold and

Art simultaneously glanced at Leon with equal measures of remorse for the mission upon which he was about to embark, and relief that it wasn't their name that Eleanor had uttered.

Raymond, who was now holding baby Joan, quickly cemented his own alibi with, "Well, I'd go get him myself but I should probably hold the baby."

There was no way out. Leon was going to have to walk into the confessional and extract Fr. Gutha while he was in the middle of hearing confessions. In the small rural conservative Roman Catholic community of 1936, Westphalia, interrupting the pious Fr. Gutha during the holy sacrament of confession was akin to a mouse sassing a lion. The confessional was a hallowed sanctuary of avowed secrecy, the contents of which priests took sworn, sacred oaths of nondisclosure.

Eleanor again pointed to the confessional, and, for good measure, shot Leon a second glare that doubled the intensity of her original look. Leon dutifully began walking down the side aisle holding his hat in his hand as he kept his eyes on his feet, lest he make eye contact with the long row of piously waiting penitents which he was walking past in a horrendously rude breach of church protocol.

Leon could sense the indignant, burning glare of the waiting people, who peered up from their kneeling position as Leon shuffled past them like he was cutting in front of them in a lunch line. Not knowing the proper etiquette in which to interrupt someone pouring out their sins to a priest, Leon stalwartly marched forward, and trying his best to look like an authority figure who knew precisely what he was doing, rapped his knuckle on the outside of the priest's confessional compartment. Not eliciting a response from his knocking, Leon glanced back at the five-some of relatives still standing in the doorway at the back of church. Absent any further direction from them, Leon knocked again on Father's confessional door, and this time, without waiting for a response, Leon pulled open the door, exposing a completely shocked Fr. Gutha. The disbelieving priest squinted his eyes through his wire rimmed glasses as light rushed into his darkened cubicle through the now open door. Simultaneously, the kneeling church patrons gasped aloud in disbelief of what they had just witnessed. Meanwhile, completely oblivious to the disruption occurring outside his enclosed cubicle, the poor confessor on the other side of the veiled screen prattled on with his itemized list of sinful indiscretions.

Reaching up from his chair, Fr. Gutha quickly pulled the door shut again. The blood quickly and effusively rushed into Uncle Leon's face, and with the door now shut in front of him, he instinctively turned to look back towards his mother. All down the aisle, he noticed the shocked expressions on the single-file line of faces occupying the pews in wait for their turn to enter the confessional. An elderly woman, who happened to be closest to Leon, and next in line for confession, gasped loudly, and dropped her hard-covered prayer missal, landing it with a crash on the tile floor. The crashing prayer book elicited a second round of gasps from the other waiting patrons which reverberated through the high cathedral ceilings of the church, further exacerbating the embarrassment of poor Uncle Leon.

Eleanor's steely glare at Leon intensified, and, for a second, Leon didn't know whether to run away forever or to open Father's confessional door again. Since Eleanor was blocking his egress out of the church he had no other option than to open the confessional door again.

This time Fr. Gutha was ready for him. "Leon, what do you think you're doing?" Father Gutha stated without inflection in a tone that revealed saintly restraint on his part.

Before Leon could answer, the poor fellow behind the veiled screen of the confessional wall answered, "Uhmmm, I'm not Leon."

Without breaking eye contact from Leon, Fr. Gutha reached over with his left hand and slowly closed the sliding barrier across the veiled screen, effectively ending the conversation with the confessor on the other side of the confessional wall.

"Sorry about the interruption, Father," Leon responded meekly. "My sister Florence's new baby isn't doing well and they would like you to baptize her."

Fortunately, for everyone involved, the baptism went off without further incident and was duly recorded in the St. Mary's Church baptismal records, dated February 22, 1936. Historical weather records show that the record setting winter storm broke the very next day, and, in fact, a winter thaw occurred with temperatures reaching above the freezing mark for the entire next week.

The health issues of baby Joan's tumultuous first week also subsided and although she remained a relatively small child, she grew as strong and feisty as the time period of the late 1930's required. And, to friends and family, little Joan's spunkiness quickly resulted in the loss of her baptismal name for the more appropriate nickname of "Joni."

HEAT WAVE

"I wonder if it's raining back in Portland," Norman quipped to Mary at supper.

It was only late June but already the crops were wilting in the dry heat. Mary laughed. She was happy to be settling into the new farm, closer to her and Norman's extended families.

"Probably flooded out," she joked and returned to de-capping the strawberries their neighbors to the east, Joe & Irene Pung had brought over last evening when they had come to visit.

Joe Pung was proud of his strawberries. He grew them near the barns on the south side of Pratt Road, across the road from the farmstead's brown cut-stone house. Joe had developed a system in which every year he would establish a linear row of composting manure in a trench laid out adjacent to the last planted row of existing strawberries. The next spring, he would plant a new row of strawberry seedlings right over the previous year's compost row. A new row of compost would then be created for the following spring's planting. Since the strawberry plants would generally remain productive for about 5 years, Joe maintained a 5-row strawberry patch, with each row established in successive years.

In 1930's rural Michigan, it was common for neighbors to visit on evenings when the chores were done. Occasionally, Joe and Irene, along with their son Jim, also known as "Pete," and Pete's sister Mary Louise, would walk the half-mile distance down Pratt Road and pay Norman and Mary's family a visit.

Sylvester "Vessie" Hengesbach and his wife Odelia, moved into the Farm just to the west of Norman and Mary later in the 1930's, and they, too, would occasionally walk over for an evening visit. Vessie rented the farm from Jackie Gutha, Fr. Gutha's bachelor brother, who lived and worked in Detroit during the week but drove or bussed the over three hour trip out to the farm most weekends. Jackie Gutha maintained his own bedroom on the second floor of the Hengesbach's rented house. Being a bachelor, it was said he had an affinity for Odelia's cooking, which kept bringing him back to the farm on most weekends.

Norman and Mary, and their young family, would reciprocate and visit the Pungs and Hengesbachs on occasional evenings after chores. To be sure, these visits were primarily social but they also served a practical function for exchanging information on farm pest scouting, making arrangements for equipment sharing, and working out details for borrowing a bull, ram, or boar to service a prospective mate. Farms of that era were truly integrated into a web of social and practical reliance with neighboring farms.

Like most families of that time period, Norman and Mary also socialized frequently with their extended family, primarily their respective brothers' and sisters' families. This was especially the case between Mary and her closest-in-age sibling, Pauline Armbrustmacher, who lived about ten miles away near Fowler, Michigan. Pauline and her husband, Clemens' children lined up in age remarkably close to Mary and Norman's. The three eldest Armbrustmacher children, Jim, Mary Ann, and Joseph were all born within a year's time of the three eldest Thelens, Dennis, Markie, and Clair. Coincidentally, the pattern would hold consistent for their future children. The strong sisterly bond between Mary and Pauline had definitely carried over to the cousins of the next generation.

***

In addition to the fiscal challenges of the Great Depression, Norman and Mary could not have picked a worse climatological year to start their new farming venture. The summer of 1936 turned out to be the driest, hottest summer in Michigan since weather records had been kept. It was the same throughout much of the nation. In the Plains States the dust bowl was at its very worst. The heat constituted one of the deadliest weather disasters on record. About 5,000 people are estimated to have died from the effects of the heat in the U.S. during the summer of 1936, most of them during the especially scorching hot week of July 8-15th. According to the National Weather Service, the period is likely the most severe heatwave ever experienced in Michigan, and one of the worst ever recorded in U.S. history.

Weather records from a federal weather station located in Charlotte, Michigan, about twenty miles from Norman & Mary's farm, recorded consecutive daily highs in excess of 100^0 F, for the entire week. To make matters worse, the temperatures did not abate overnight with temperatures ranging from the mid and upper 90s at the start of the evening (6:00 to 7:00 pm) to hovering still in the mid-80s at midnight. The heat was especially deadly in large Midwestern cities such as St. Louis, Minneapolis and Detroit. With nowhere to go to escape the heat, the urban death tolls mounted. A Chicago newspaper reported the Detroit death toll at 365 (570 total across Michigan) for the week with the following description: *"The Detroit morgue is typical of other stricken cities. Dead lie in long rows with weeping relatives seeking to identify them. The supply of shrouds has been exhausted."*

Norman wiped the sweat from his brow with the linen handkerchief he kept stuffed inside the left front pocket of his bib overalls. It was midday on Tuesday, July 7th. Very warm air had rushed north into Southeast Lower Michigan, causing the mercury to rise up to 97 degrees, but this was just a mere harbinger of the oppressive heat to come.

"Let's go in for dinner," Norm said to Ves, the hired man.

Ves, a.k.a. Sylvester, was Mary's younger brother who was staying with Norman and Mary and working as their farm hand.

"*Ja*," Ves, responded.

A steady dripping stream of sweat drizzled from the tip of Ves' nose as he looked up from the new milk house foundation trench he and Norman were digging on the west side of the main barn.

The mid-day meal, which was called "dinner" was served at noon. Like "supper," which was the evening meal, dinner usually consisted of boiled potatoes, beef, pork, or chicken as the meat, gravy made from the juice of the meal's meat and in-season or canned vegetables from the family garden. Interestingly, although most of the farms in the area raised sheep, mutton was seldom on the menu. Rather, finished lambs were sold through the stockyards with the meat finding its way to urban butcher markets in Lansing and Detroit.

Norman leaned over the backroom sink and splashed the cool, well-drawn water, over his face. Using the residual water remaining in his hands, he methodically slicked his hair back. The water felt refreshing and the coolness of it regenerated his thoughts. As Ves cleaned himself up, Norman turned towards the kitchen and watched as Mary scooped the potatoes out of the kettle on the stove and placed them in a ceramic serving bowl destined for the table. Dennis, Markie, and baby Clair were already seated around the table. Dennis and Markie giggled when Uncle Ves sat down on the chair next to Markie. They were still getting used to the idea of having their twenty-year-old uncle live and work with them in their new home.

Mary put the platter of pork down on the table and sat down next to Norman. Norman began the blessing for the meal with the sign of the cross followed by the traditional "Bless us our Lord…" prayer. The kitchen was hot, and as the food was passed around, the conversation immediately turned towards the weather.

"Hot out there," Ves said, looking directly toward little Dennis. Dennis didn't know quite what to make of this. The old adage that children were to be seen and not heard, was standard protocol at meal time.

"*Ja*, the hay is drying quickly," Norman replied, rescuing Dennis from his conundrum. "If we can get it turned after dinner, we'll start bringing it in yet this afternoon."

"I'll have the boys bring some cool water and cider out when you get back to the barn," Mary offered.

In their first few years on the farm, consistent with the technology of the time, Norman harvested the hay exclusively as loose hay, meaning it wasn't tied into bales. Rather, it was gathered up from drying windrows in the field and hauled to the barn on wagons. At the barn, it was elevated into the barn loft on a rope sling which was hoisted to the peak of the gable roof by a series of ropes and pulleys. A metal track, hung just beneath the peak of the roof, traversed the length of the barn. The sling mechanism was pulled along the track to carry the loose hay to whichever loft was chosen for storage. Once above the designated loft, a tagline rope was pulled to trip the sling mechanism, releasing the hay to the loft. Just prior to

World War II, a few tractor-driven hay balers were purchased in the area and Norman would custom hire some of the hay to be baled.

That particular hot afternoon in July of 1936, Norman and Ves put up half of the downed hay before supper time. By supper, the kitchen had grown even warmer, having absorbed the warmth from the afternoon sun and the added heat from the preparation of another full meal. Despite all the hard work endured during the afternoon, no one had much of an appetite. It was quiet around the table, too hot for conversation. Mary cleaned up the supper dishes as Norman and Ves headed out for the barns to do the evening chores.

On Wednesday July 8th, the temperature soared to 104 degrees, setting the stage for the most severe heat wave ever recorded in the Midwest. For the next seven consecutive days, the mercury would exceed the 100 degree mark.

"I think Ves and I will try to sleep outdoors tonight," Norman said to Mary.

Mary nodded her approval. She would stay indoors with the boys. She could see the toll the heat was taking on her husband and brother as they struggled to put up hay during the day, and suffered through the twice daily chores with the sweaty, surly, heat-stressed livestock. Working outdoors all day in the blistering heat was taking a toll on their usually unlimited stamina and on their dispositions as well. This kind of heat had a way of bringing out the worst in both man and beast.

Air conditioning was not available on a household level. There was no escaping the heat, but, sleeping outdoors would at least afford a couple hours of tolerable sleeping conditions after midnight. Inside the house, it just never cooled down. The walls and contents of the house absorbed heat during the 100 plus degree days, heat which was constantly radiated back out into the ambient room air, keeping an uncomfortable elevated equilibrium with the surrounding airspace. The few hours of cooler outdoor air temperatures during the pre-dawn early morning hours were not sufficient to bring down the indoor temperature. Norman yearned for his youthful days when he and his brothers were free to cool off in Muskrat Creek that crisscrossed their old homestead on Jason Road.

Norman and Ves sweated through the remainder of the week, even managing to finish the haying. Although milk and egg production were down significantly, the livestock were gradually acclimating to the heat and the farm managed to get by so far without losing any animals. Much like the farm work, Mary continued on as best she could with the household chores and gardening. Regardless of the weather, the work had to continue. Survival depended upon work. The ability to persevere and continue working through hardship and adversity, with limited relief from modern conveniences, is a testament to the fortitude and resiliency of what some historians have termed "our nation's greatest generation."

Sunday was Ves' day off, and following chores on Saturday evening, Norman would drive Ves the two-and-a-half miles over to his parent's farm, located on the corner of Wright and Price Roads.

All through the evening chores, Norman was looking forward to his Saturday evening bath. The farm's well, over which was perched a twenty-five-foot-tall windmill, was located about twenty feet off the northeast corner of the house. Before going out for evening chores, using two five-gallon metal buckets, Norman carried water from the well and filled the washtub which Mary had brought up from the cellar and placed over the woodstove. As Norman finished chores, the bath water in the tub warmed to a level comfortable for bathing. First the boys, and after they had finished their baths, it was time for Mary to bathe.

After chores, Norman, as usual, entered the house through the north facing door which opened up to the cellar. He could hear the boys splashing in the backroom as he closed the door behind him. It would be a while before it was his turn in the tub so he headed down the steps to the relative coolness of the cellar for a glass of cider.

When Mary had finished her bath, Norman decanted two pails of lukewarm water out of the tub and replaced it with two pails of cool, fresh water from the well. Norman thought about how the well water, drawn from a depth of about twenty feet, was always a constant 54^0 F. It didn't matter if it was January or July, the groundwater was always 54^0 F. Norman didn't mind being the last one to bath, which usually meant bathing in less than pristine water. But, this evening, he was going to take advantage of the well system's geologically based cooling to lower his own core body temperature.

Norman chuckled to himself as he thought how much colder the same water seemed in the winter time. Mary would add piping hot water from the kitchen stove to heat the bath water in the winter months. And here he was this evening, adding well water to the tub to cool it off.

"You will make yourself ill, Norman," Mary scolded as she reentered the backroom to retrieve the boy's clothes.

"*Ja*," Norman replied, and submerged himself into the cool water, escaping for a few minutes at least, the suffocating heat of 1936.

The next morning Norman rushed through chores in an attempt to beat the encroaching heat. While he cleaned up in the backroom sink, Mary put breakfast out on the table.

"It will be hot in church today," Norman opined, his shirt already completely drenched and adhering uncomfortably tight to his skin.

Norman's forecast turned out to be accurate. According to US historical weather data, on Sunday, July 12, the local temperature reached a scalding 104^0 F. To make matters worse, the temperature would increase from there, reaching 105^0 F on Monday and culminate at 106^0 F on Tuesday. On Monday July, 13, 1936, the all-time hottest official air temperature ever experienced in Michigan, 112^0 F, was recorded in the town of Mio.

Climatologists theorize that several factors contributed to the Midwest's extreme weather experienced in 1936. The poor soil conservation practices that led to the dustbowl in the plains states resulted in a parched landscape devoid of much of its usual vegetation. Lacking the infra-red reflectance and heat retaining moisture normally contributed by a lush green canopy of plant foliage, the vast western plains, laid barren by the dustbowl, soaked up the sun's scorching heat by day and continually conducted it back out, acting in much the same way as a giant blast furnace. The perfect storm was made complete during that fateful mid-July week of 1936, when a strong ridge of high pressure set up over the West, funneling heat northward across the Midwest and Great Lakes states. Hot air from incident radiation, and dust, originating in the west, rolled across the country to the Great Lakes Region and as far as the Eastern Shoreline.

LITTLE FARMER GIRL

Back on the Wieber homestead, Raymond and Florence's family had grown as well, however, not in number to the level of the Thelen family down the road. In May of 1937, Florence gave birth to a healthy baby girl, whom the couple named Janice. Like her older brother Eddie, Janice had inherited Florence's pretty brown eyes and darker complexion.

Little Joni had overcome her auspicious start and diminutive size with spunk and zeal. As she grew up there was no question that she preferred to be outdoors working in the fields, doing chores, hunting, shooting, and trapping in the creeks and woodlots surrounding the farm. She also liked working with the two teams of draught horses, Prince & Freddie, and Paint & Lady. As soon as she was capable of wielding a pitchfork she took on the chore of mucking the draught horse stalls.

Raymond had a hired man, Simmy Smith, but during the depression years, thin profit margins on farms necessitated using as much family labor as possible. Unemployment was rampant in Michigan and throughout the U.S. during the 1930's. Nationally, unemployment peaked in 1933 at nearly 25%, and by 1938 it was still at 19%. The federal government did not keep state level unemployment statistics specifically in the 1930's but rather, for statistical purposes, relied on Bureau of Labor Statistics indices, the United States Census of Occupations, and the Census of Unemployment. Michigan ranked among the highest states in the nation for unemployment with an astounding 43% unemployment rate for the 1932-33, time period.

As a consequence of the Depression era high unemployment, it was not uncommon for vagabonds to wander the village and rural roads of Westphalia looking for day jobs or perhaps a meal. At the conclusion of a long day of harvesting while Raymond and Simmy were putting up the last load of hay, a gentleman who had walked up Tallman Road, approached Raymond asking about possible farm work. Raymond reluctantly informed him that unfortunately, he did not have the wherewithal to hire another worker. However, they did leave the man with some food before sending him on his way. The next morning when Raymond was forking hay into the cattle's manger, he uncovered the poor fellow, half asleep and tortuously hungover, buried in the haystack. As per usual, Raymond had a crock jug of cider in the barn for refreshment during the previous day's haying work. After the long day of work, Raymond had forgotten and left the jug of cider in the barn overnight. The vagabond had later snuck back into the barn and helped himself to the remaining cider!

Joni also helped with the milking chores, at first by hand, and later on with an automated milking machine. Unlike Norman Thelen's farm which sold whole milk to the dairy cooperative, Raymond ran all of his milk through a cream separator located in the cellar of the big cut brownstone house. The cream was sold to the Westphalia Co-op Creamery, which was known for its rich tasty butter. Raymond retained the whey fraction of the milk which he used as feed for calves and hogs on the farm. Twice weekly, a flatbed truck from the Creamery would show up at the farm to pick up the cream.

The fresh cream, which was separated daily by Florence in the farm house basement, was stored in ten-gallon, tin milk cans. The full cans of cream were temporarily stored in a small cut-stone building, called the milk house, with thick walls and an earthen floor. The milk house sat between the house and big hip-roofed barns. The front of the milk house was where the ten-gallon cans of cream were stored in tubs of cool well water. In the rear of the building was a separate room, which was used during butchering time as a smokehouse to preserve meat.

As a youngster, Joni's fondness for the chickens eventually landed her the responsibility of taking care of the chicken flock. On a daily basis she would feed and water the chickens and gather the eggs. The eggs were washed in the basement and stored in a cool room in the back of the cellar. Once a week, a truck would stop by the farm on a regular route to pick up the eggs which were sold in Lansing. During winter months, the chickens were confined to the coop, but during warmer weather they were free to browse the yard and scavenge for insects. Chickens were dual-purpose providing both eggs and meat. Because farms back then did not have refrigerators, chickens were often butchered minutes before ending up in the frying pan.

***

One summer morning, soon after Joni had been given responsibility for taking care of the chicken flock, Florence and Joni set out to catch and clean a chicken for supper later that day.

"Grab the hatchet out of the shed," Florence advised, as she carried a bucket of steaming hot water which she had drawn from the heater mounted on the side of the kitchen wood stove.

"OK Momma," Joni replied, feeling quite grown up and important now that her chief chicken caretaker job had expanded into helping with the butchering.

The two would-be-assassins ambled past the woodshed over to the chicken coop, beside which Raymond kept a twelve-inch diameter oak stump that had two large ring-shank nails, sunk about half-way into the stump and spaced about an inch apart. This handy tool, referred to as the chopping block, was ideal for stretching out the unfortunate chicken's neck so it could be cleanly severed by a deftly swung hatchet. One would simply slide the chicken's neck between the two nails. Then, with your left hand firmly grasping the chicken's feet, you would pull back gently until the chicken's neck was nicely stretched. "Whack," you'd then swing the hatchet down with your right hand, aiming for the midpoint of the stretched out neck. The end result was a clean kill, and a headless chicken carcass that once the nerves settled down to the point where it stopped flopping around, was ready to be dipped into scalding hot water and plucked clean of its feathers.

"Why don't you grab that one right over there," Florence suggested pointing to a nice plump Leghorn cockerel that was stalking a grasshopper in the lush grass outside the coop.

"You mean Fluffy?" Joni asked her voice trailing off.

"Well how about that one over there then," Florence redirected, sensing a bond of attachment between Fluffy and her daughter.

"You mean Stevie?" Joni winced.

"Good grief child, do they all have names?" Florence asked incredulously.

"Uh huh," Joni replied, adding, "That one's Buttercup, that one's Brownie, that one's Chippy…"

"OK, OK, just get Stevie and let's get this over with," Florence retorted, not liking the direction in which the chore was going.

Obediently, Joni chased after Stevie, eventually cornering him against a bottom plank of the outdoor hog lot fence. With both hands firmly wrapped around Stevie, she carried the surprised bird over to the chopping block. Having seen her parents and the hired man, Simmy Smith, do this many times, Joni knew what to do next. Bending over, she placed Stevie's neck in between the two ring shank nails.

Stevie looked at Joni, and Joni looked up dejectedly at her mother. Florence began to draw the hatchet back, but after looking at Stevie, who was now looking up forlornly at her, she began to equivocate and said, "Joni, how would you like to do the chopping since you are in charge of the chickens now?"

Shocked at the unexpected offer, Joni paused for a moment and then answered truthfully and matter-of-factly, "No, I can't do that to Stevie."

"OK, I'll do it," Florence responded back, somewhat embarrassed at herself for having asked her daughter to do the dirty deed in the first place.

Once again Florence drew the hatchet back, and once again Stevie looked up from his compromised position, directly and sadly into Florence's eyes. At the top of her backstroke, Florence hesitated.

"Oh, I suppose we can boil up a soup bone for supper," she blurted out and turned back to the house leaving Joni to liberate Stevie, at least for one more day.

CENTENNIAL

"The Parish Centennial Mass of Thanksgiving is this evening," Mary reminded Norman on a comfortable Thursday morning.

The date was August 26, 1936. The record setting heat wave that enveloped the area in July had broken and the weather, at least for the time being, was actually a little on the cool side. St. Mary's Parish, established in 1836, was hosting a four-day, centennial celebration beginning with Mass on Thursday evening.

"The parade is planned for Saturday and Grandpa *Dika* Joe, has a covered wagon decked out for the parade. He'd like Dennis and Markie to ride with the other little cousins," Mary directed.

"*Ja*," Norman responded.

"Henry and Norman M, will be playing ball on Saturday, and Sunday, too," Mary added, referencing two of her younger brothers who played on the St. Mary's baseball team.

"It will be good to take it easy for a couple of days and enjoy the festival," Norman concluded.

Saturday, August 28, arrived as another uncharacteristically cool day for the summer of 1936. The sky remained cloudy, occasionally spitting out an unseasonably cool rain. The overnight low the night before had gone down to a chilly 52^0 F.

"Dennis, Markie, get your dress clothes on," their mother fussed as she tussled with baby Clair, changing him out of his messy overnight diaper.

Before she could finish, the wall phone rang with three short bursts which Mary instantly recognized as an incoming call intended for them on the party line, probably her Mother, Theresa. As Mary rose to answer the phone, the eight-month old Clair escaped on all fours, dragging the half attached clean diaper along behind him. Upstairs, Dennis, who was now three and half years old, managed to pull his knickers on and his Sunday shirt, although it was on backwards.

Proud of himself, Dennis now turned his attention to his two-year-old brother. "Here, Markie, I'll help you get dressed."

Mary sighed as she hung up the phone. The caller was her mother, calling to let her know that Pa, *Dika* Joe, didn't want to take the parade horse and wagon into town because of the rain.

"If this rain keeps up they'll for sure end up rescheduling the parade for tomorrow," Theresa assured her daughter Mary.

Disappointed, Mary turned her attention back to the boys as she scooped up the now completely naked Clair and stuffed him back properly into a clean diaper.

"Dennis, Markie, it's too rainy for the parade today," she submitted. "Go ahead and get your regular clothes back on."

On Sunday morning, the sun was bright in the eastern sky but the air was still on the cool side as Norman returned to the house from morning chores in the barn. With the sheep and cattle turned out to pasture, the daily chores took less time, basically the time it took to round up, stanchion, and milk the cows, and water the stock.

"I wish we'd have gotten a little more rain yesterday for the parched crops," Norman volunteered although no one was listening in the bustle to get ready for the Centennial Parade.

As it turned out, the parish had started the parade on Saturday, as scheduled, but ended up aborting it midway through due to a sudden rain shower. As it was, the threat of rain had kept many of the parishioners, especially those with younger children, from attending in the first place. So, just as Grandma Theresa had predicted, the parade was rescheduled for the following day, Sunday, with an assurance from Fr. Gutha that the weather would cooperate.

"Did Ves mention when Grandpa *Dika* Joe was planning to leave with the buggy?" Mary asked.

"*Ja*, if the weather held out he was planning to leave by 9:00 o'clock" Norman responded, adding, "We're supposed to have Dennis and Markie in town and ready to ride by 10:30."

***

"Dennis, keep an eye on Markie," Mary ordered as she handed her two older sons off to her Mother, Theresa.

Grandma Theresa picked up Markie, and with Dennis and a couple of her other grandchildren surrounding her, began to walk over to the parade staging area which was located in the part-time pasture, part-time Westphalia baseball field, located on the John Pung farm, north of the church and festival grounds. While walking to the wagon in which the children would ride in the parade, Dennis noticed that one of his cousins, a year older than he, began to jump, with both feet, on cowpies appearing along their path.

The cattle had been removed from the part-time pasture, part-time baseball field a few days earlier in preparation for the big Centennial Parish Festival. The cowpies had aged sufficient to have a thin crust over the top that covered a still moist and green-colored inside. When the not-to-be-named cousin would jump on a cowpie, it would spontaneously explode, sending a stream of liquid green mortar streaking out in every direction, not to mention over the offending boy's feet and legs. Shocked by the audacity of his elder cousin, Dennis, looked up at Grandma Theresa. One look told Dennis that another cowpie wasn't the only thing about ready to explode. Before Dennis could turn around, in less than patient German, Grandma Theresa shouted out, "*AUS DAS!*" which put an immediate end to the stinky transgressions.

The streets were lined with smiling spectators as Dennis' grandpa, "*Dika* Joe," snapped the reins across the horse's rump lurching the covered wagon onto Westphalia Street, in step with the rest of the parade. Discreetly, Dennis peered out from under the canopy of the Conestoga wagon. He had never seen so many people. The parade route began moving south past the parish grounds, stopping briefly near the church for the parade announcer to introduce each entry to the crowd. When *Dika* Joe's wagon stopped, the horse pulling a similar style parade wagon right behind them kept moving forward and placed his head inside the Conestoga canopy startling Dennis, Markie, and the other children inside.

Jerome, an older cousin, smacked the horse across the bridge of his nose, "*Dummkopf*," he swore in German.

Dika Joe turned around on the buckboard seat and peered into the wagon canopy. "*Dummkopf?*" he repeated with inflection.

The children giggled and as the wagon resumed moving forward they scrambled to positions in the front and rear of the wagon where they could watch the crowd. The parade continued south past the main crossroad in the center of town, turning west at the next block on Oak Street. When the parade reached Heyer Street, *Dika* Joe slightly pressured the right side rein and the horse responded by turning to the north circling the block and following the parade back to its origin on the Pung farm.

After the parade, Mary and Norman collected Dennis and Markie from the parade staging area while Grandpa *Dika* Joe found a place to temporarily stall the horse until one of his sons could drive it the three miles home. Across from the pasture parade staging area, the St. Mary's baseball team was warming up for their game against the team from the nearby town of Fowler.

"Why don't we eat first?" Mary suggested. "It'll be a while before the game gets started and I think the boys are probably getting hungry."

Norman nodded in agreement. The smell from the chicken dinners, being served family style in the parish hall, had wafted across the parade route and Norman was more than ready to eat. After a delicious meal, the family returned to the Pung farm baseball field to watch a few innings of the game and cheer on Uncles Henry and Norman M. Following the game, Mary suggested it was time to take the boys home.

"Dora is coming over at 5:00 pm to watch the boys," Mary reminded Norman.

Dora was Norman's sister, who the kids referred to in the German vernacular as "*Mama Hanshin*" for reasons unknown. After Norman finished chores, he and Mary drove back into town. Norman headed over to the beer garden while Mary joined a group of ladies waiting outside the raffle booth to hear the names of the raffle winners. A new car was the top prize.

Back home on the farm, Dennis and Markie were ready for bed as soon as Norman and Mary had left. Clair was already fast asleep. It had been a good day.

***

Norman and Mary's family grew quickly. On July 6th, of the next year, 1937, the family welcomed their first girl, Jane, to the fold. The St. Mary's Parish Picnic had returned to its regular traditional date of July 4th that year, and being just two days prior to when Jane would be born, Mary was not feeling well enough to attend. Parishioners were required to work a shift at the Parish Festival and Norman was scheduled to work later in the picnic beer garden, so, after evening chores, he left Mary and the boys behind and headed into town.

After finishing his shift serving beer to thirsty parishioners, Norman stopped by the spinning paddle wheel game booth and bought three of the foot-long, paddle-shaped wooden panels, each of which had four of the spinning wheel's numbers engraved on its face. He placed the wooden paddles face up on the 2"x6" board that framed the booth for the spinning wheel game. When all the paddles were sold, the booth worker gave the wheel an aggressive spin. The wheel buzzed and whirred as the spokes separating the numbers on the perimeter of the spinning wheel clicked across the demarcating stiff leather finger that would eventually determine the winner.

When the spinning wheel stopped, the number matched the "6" stenciled in black paint on Norman's paddle. Handing the paddles back to the booth worker, Norman pointed to the blue-eyed, black-haired doll perched on the top shelf of the booth. It was no secret that the entire extended Thelen family was hoping Mary would have a baby girl, someone to provide Mary with feminine relief from the roughhousing three older brothers. Norman thought the blue-eyed doll was a providential sign their prayers would be answered.

When Norman returned home, he greeted Mary with, "*Es ais frau*," meaning "It's a girl."

Mary looked at Norman like he'd been drinking too much beer. Sensing trouble, Norman quickly gained his composure and presented Mary with the little girl doll.

Laughing out loud, Mary said, "I sure hope you're right."

Two days later, on July 6, 1937, Mary gave birth to their first daughter. The couple named the baby Jane. Mary would later tell Jane how much she looked like the little doll, which soon belonged to Jane, with blue eyes and a full head of black hair.

SUNDAY CHICKEN DINNERS

"Put the card in the window Joni, we'll need ice for Uncle Harold's party on Sunday afternoon," Florence said as she wiped the last remaining remnants of freshly made strawberry jam off of Janice's face.

Joni jumped up from her seat at the kitchen table, reached into the bureau drawer, and pulled out the Ice Company's card. Carefully she placed the card in the window facing the driveway, just to the east of the house's side entrance door. Florence had an ice box in the kitchen, the predecessor to the modern refrigerator. The wooden ice-box had insulated walls and a compartment inside in which the ice-man would place a block of clear, clean ice. When a customer needed a block of ice, they would communicate to the route driver by leaving the "ice card" in the kitchen window.

Homes in rural Michigan had electricity in the late 1930's, but mechanical refrigeration, which seems so essential to today's homes and farms, was not yet commonly available. Some of the kitchens in the area had an icebox, like Florence's, but, many others didn't even have that convenience. Without an icebox, families would still often purchase ice during the summer months, placing it in a galvanized metal washtub wrapped in blankets.

Well water was used to cool milk, but the process was labor intensive as the water had to often be hand carried, and continually replaced to effectively cool milk. To preserve meat without refrigeration, families would soak freshly butchered meat in salt brine contained in twenty-gallon crocks kept in the cellar prior to taking it outside to a smokehouse for curing. Additionally, butchering was confined to the fall and winter months to facilitate rapid cooling of meat carcasses which would be hung in sheds, out of reach from marauding barn cats. Less valuable cuts of meat such as soup bones, would often be stored outdoors in the winter months in old cider barrels. Most families also had "root cellars," which were simply earthen floored rooms within the house basement, or, sometimes dug outside the boundary of the home. These would be used to store root crops like carrots, potatoes, and beets as well as for temporarily storing eggs prior to pick-up. The buffering effect of the earth would keep the root cellar close to 54^0 F throughout the bristling heat of the summer and brittle cold of the winter.

***

With both hands cupped, Joni pulled her arms towards her midsection scooping out grain from the burlap feedbag, and sliding it into the metal bucket which she held in place by straddling it between her legs. It was mid-morning Sunday and ever since Raymond returned the family from morning Mass, Joni had been anxious to get her chores finished. A mid-morning breeze, sufficient to cleanse the last of the morning humidity from the air, refreshed the June sky, revealing the pleasant aroma of Florence's flower garden. Joni hummed softly to herself as she trudged along with her feed buckets, dragging them across the green grass between the hog-house corn cribs all the way over to the chicken coop.

After dispensing the feed and filling the flock's water receptacles, Joni skipped back to the feed room to return the feed buckets. She paused for just a second to pet one of the barn cats, who generally found it profitable to hunt mice amongst the grain-filled burlap bags stored upright in the feed room. Suddenly remembering it was Sunday, Joni quickly skipped back to the house. Inside, Florence was putting the finishing touches on a frosted cake at the kitchen counter.

"Let's go, Daddy," Joni urged.

With a twinkle in his eye, Raymond looked up from the newspaper he was reading in the living room. "Have you fed the chickens yet, Joni?" he asked knowing full well that she had already completed the job.

Jumping up and down, Joni emphatically spouted out, "Yes, yes, I have already."

"Are you sure? I just saw a chicken walk by the window and he looked pretty hungry," Raymond said, his shaking shoulders giving away his attempt to appear serious.

"*Ja*, go wash up, Joni," he reassured her. "I'll be ready in a minute."

"The cake is ready, Raymond. Could you chip some ice off the block to keep it chilled?" Florence spoke up from the kitchen, adding, "We probably should get going."

The family was heading to a Sunday chicken dinner, hosted by Florence's brother Harold. Harold, like his brothers Art and Leon, was still a bachelor and lived at home. Harold had recently purchased the "Esch" farm across the road from his parent's homestead. Florence's father Edward passed away when Joni was four. This left Eleanor's bachelor sons, Leon, Art and Harold to operate the farm. Harold would eventually marry later in life, but Leon and Art never did marry, remaining bachelors throughout their lives.

It was not uncommon in the early rural 1900's for unmarried brothers, and sometimes a combination of brothers and sisters, to remain single and live in a common household their entire lives. There were plenty of such households in the rural Clinton County area that fit this description. It is somewhat of a mystery why this type of household, that is so rare in today's society, was quite common in rural history. Viewed through the lens of modern times, this arrangement may have been predicated by the labor requirements it took to run a household and farm. Without modern plumbing and kitchen appliances, household tasks like cooking, preserving food, doing laundry, mending clothes, general cleaning, and tending the thunder jug (a.k.a. porcelain pail or chamber pot), was easily a fulltime job. Additionally, without modern mechanization, farming was extremely labor intensive. Perhaps the security of having the necessary labor required for the household to survive made it easy to just maintain the sibling family unit. Or, perhaps limited transportation and limited resources to travel, severely restricted the geographic area in which to find a suitable spouse.

On the Esch farm that Harold purchased, was an old abandoned house. Harold, with help from his brothers, would invite family and friends over for Sunday afternoon chicken dinners, served up in the old abandoned house. The brothers moved tables and wooden folding chairs into the empty house on which to eat. The fresh chicken, just butchered the day before, was fried in cast iron skillets on an old wood stove that was about the only useful thing left remaining in the house. Everyone brought a dish to pass, and, what Joni liked best, dessert was almost always cake and a crazy new-fangled dessert called Jello.

After eating, the adults played euchre, a locally popular card game, while the children played hide-and-seek, ducks-and-geese, or other made-up games outdoors. Florence's sister Beatrice and her husband Marcus would drive out from Lansing, with their kids, Bob, Alice, Bill, Kenny, and Janet. Florence's married brother and sister-in-law Isidore and Dorothy would be there from their farm in nearby Portland with their children Barb, Pat, Joyce, Denny, and Diane. Her younger sister Catherine and her husband Louie Bauer would also come over from Portland with their two young sons Jim and Dale. Occasionally the kids would cross Grange Road to play in Grandma Eleanor's huge barns. Needless to say, Joni always looked forward to the Sunday afternoon chicken dinners and playing with her many cousins.

Quite often on non-chicken dinner Sundays, the Wiebers would still visit Grandma Eleanor Fedewa. Grandma Fedewa had a huge Victorian style house with white painted wood siding and fancy sculpted wood trimming hanging from the front facing gables. The interior, contrary to today's open designs, had many claustrophobically small, four-walled rooms: sitting rooms; parlors; living rooms; and, of course, bedrooms. Outdoors, two identically matched, massive hip-roofed barns sat connected to each other end-to-end. Inside the barn, the Fedewa Uncles kept a hand-truck, also known as a "dolly," used for wielding around the 120 pound, standard size heavy grain bags. The hand-truck was ideal for racing down the length of the long wooden barn, with a couple of kids aboard, hanging on for dear life. Grandma's hog barn had an easily accessible roof, which the grandkids would often scale on the west facing side, out of view from the house and any potentially observing adult eyes.

***

In addition to visits to Grandma Eleanor's and the Sunday chicken dinners at Uncle Harold's abandoned farm house, the Wieber family, on every August 15, would travel to School Section Lake, up in Mecosta County, Michigan. Florence's sister Beatrice and her husband Marcus, owned a summer cottage on the lake.

August 15th is a Catholic holy day of obligation known as "The Assumption of Mary in Heaven." In addition to the requirement to attend Mass, Catholic doctrine states that on Sundays and holy days of obligation, the faithful are to refrain from engaging in work or activities that hinder: the worship owed to God; the joy proper to the Lord's Day; the performance of the works of mercy; and the appropriate relaxation of mind and body. Of course on the farm, the twice daily chores of milking cows and feeding the animals still had to be done. However, that was about the only work to be done on Sunday and the six annual holy days of obligation, unless of course, exception was made consistent with the biblical metaphor, "your ox was stuck in the mire."

No matter which day of the week August 15th landed on, the Wieber family would pack up after morning Mass and begin the seventy-five-mile drive in the family car up to School Section Lake. Most of the drive was over poorly maintained gravel roads, and in Joni's mind, it took forever to get there. However, the opportunity to spend a summer day on the lake with her cousins was well worth the misery of the long hot drive getting there.

The little cottage, one of the first to appear on the lake, was constructed by Marcus and his sons. It was built on the west side of the lake and painted a bright summer shade of mint green. The lot had about eighty feet of sandy beach. The August 15, patrons at the lake were the same group of children at the Sunday chicken dinners. And, somewhat similar to the Sunday chicken dinners, after eating the obligatory mid-day meal, the adults would settle down around tables set up under the shade trees to play euchre, while the children splashed around in the lake. By the time the last goodbyes were said and Raymond steered the car southward towards home, Joni, Eddie, and Janice were already fast asleep in the back seat.

NEW TRACTOR

It was Mid-March of 1939, and Dennis and Markie huddled together peering out the upstairs bedroom window to the driveway down below. It was still cold for mid-morning, but the boy's northeast upstairs bedroom, through which the chimney passed, was snug and warm. Downstairs, Norman's sister Dora, was busy watching over Clair and baby Jane. Aunt Dora, or "Mama Hanshin" as she was called by the children, often came over when Mary needed extra help. This was one of those times as Mary was expecting another child any day now.

The boy's room upstairs had one window on the north side and one on the west side, both of which afforded a view of the busy, growing farmstead below. The young boys liked to occupy the windows and watch as Norman and Uncle Ves went about the day-to-day tasks of the farm. Whenever a truck or other farm visitor would pull into the driveway, the two would sneak off to their upstairs windows for a birds-eye view of what was going on.

"Wow, it's a red tractor," Markie whispered in awe, as the new International F-14 tractor and two-bottom moldboard plow with 14" plowshares were unloaded from the implement dealer's truck. From now on, the heavy duty job of plowing would be done by the F-14.

Norman still kept his best team of horses, Rosie and Jake, to do the lighter work including fitting the soil, spreading manure, slinging hay to the haylofts, and hauling wagons.

But, the very next day, Dennis and Markie along with Clair and two-year-old Jane, were back at the upstairs windows, watching the commotion below. Joe Hanses, one of the local truckers, had pulled into the yard, in the very same spot in which the brand new tractor was unloaded the day before. However, this time, something was leaving the farm. As the truck stopped, Norman emerged from the lower south door of the main barn with Queenie, an as of yet unbroken filly that was foaled by Maude, one of Norman's older mares. Queenie was jet black with a blaze forehead and one white sock. The F-14 immediately lessened reliance on the stable of draught horses. Queenie had to go.

The arrival of the tractor and sale of Queenie was a telltale sign of the changing times. But, the Great Depression had begun to release its grip on the nation, with the national economy now growing at an annual rate of over 5%. The ugly scars from the dustbowl, characterized by experts as the worst ecological disaster ever incurred by the U.S., had begun to heal over, aided by rain and the implementation of much needed soil conservation measures.

***

The mixed breed sheep flock, housed in the east barn, was a significant part of Norman's livestock portfolio. In March, the sheep were shorn, just prior to the lambing season. Having a cleanly shorn underside on the ewes facilitated the soon-to-be born baby lambs' ability to locate mom's udder.

"Dennis, you can help with the sorting," Norman said matter-of-factly, that morning after Dennis and Markie had finished feeding the chickens.

Sheep shearing was a busy day on the farm and the day's work involved everyone, outside the house with the actual shearing and inside the house preparing food for the hungry shearing crew. In the spring of 1939, the inside work was particularly trying for Mary who was now in her ninth month of pregnancy, expecting the family's fifth child.

In the early days, Norman hired Urban and Lawrence Hengesbach, to do the sheep shearing. Urban and Lawrence were two local brothers who also owned and operated their own farms in addition to running their custom shearing business. Later, Mary's brothers, Norman M, Walter, and Henry started their own custom shearing business and they soon took over the job of shearing Norman's flock. When Dennis was old enough to shear, the uncles invited him to join the custom shearing crew, but more on that later.

Urban and Lawrence pulled into the driveway just as the morning chores were finished. Helping with the sheep sorting was an important job, and young Dennis was bursting with pride at being considered old enough now to help. Sorting sheep required patience and enough strength to hold your own when the sheep started crowding in your direction. A feed bunk, running in the east-west direction, split the barn down the center with the sheep occupying the north side of the feed bunk and cattle on the south side. Urban and Lawrence set up their equipment in the alleyway on the west end of the barn near where the wooden stave silo stood.

The clippers the men used were mechanically driven by a shaft which was powered by an electric motor. Long, mechanical arms, with several points of articulation in a universal jointed shaft, linked the clipper head and blades to the electric motor which was configured to power multiple clippers. The Hengesbach brothers also had a gas engine available to substitute for the electric motor in cases where electricity was not available. Norman also raised some sheep with Frank Pung, who farmed just east of his brother, Joe Pung. The barn in which Norman and Frank kept their jointly owned sheep was located on the opposite side of the road from Frank's farmstead and didn't have electricity available. When the Hengesbach brothers would shear sheep there they would use the gas engine to power the shears.

Feeding the sheep shearing crew was always a challenge for Mary and not just from the arduous, physical nature involved in preparing a large meal in the day of wood stoves and non-plumbed kitchens. Because of the practice of always shearing prior to spring lambing, the shearing would usually take place during the holy Lenten season. During Lent, Catholic families in the area were only allowed to have meat for one meal each day, unless it happened to be Friday, which of course meant abstinence from meat for the entire day. The shearing crew would be fed the mid-day meal, dinner, on the farm so invariably that would be the one meal for the day that Mary would serve meat. Being late in her own pregnancy, this particular spring was an even greater challenge for Mary and once again she was extremely grateful to have her sister-in-law Dora over to help with the work.

A skilled shearer could separate a sheep from its yearly growth of wool in a matter of minutes and keep the wool in basically one solid sheet. Norman and Ves would drag the sheep, one by one, to Urban and Frank for the shearing. The wool from each individual sheep was tied into a single bundle and tossed aside. Dennis and Markie would help load the bundles onto a trailer, which Norman would hook up to the family car and tow into town. Dennis enjoyed the trip into town to sell the wool since it usually meant he'd get a piece of candy, or maybe even a piece of chewing gum.

Dennis and Markie peered over the dashboard of the 1936, Ford, as Norman pulled the car and loaded trailer up to the wooden out-building located on the south side of Snitgen's General Store in Westphalia. The store was owned and operated by brothers Alfred and Hilary Snitgen, the third generation of the Snitgen family to operate the business. In the 1930's a large box of Quaker rolled oats cost a quarter at Snitgen's store, three bars of Palmolive soap could be purchased for twenty-three cents, and two large boxes of breakfast cereal also cost a quarter.

"Dennis, guide me back and line the trailer up with the open doorway," Norman directed.

"*Ja*, Pa," Dennis responded and hopped out of the car.

Motioning with his right arm, he guided Norman as he backed the trailer up to the white painted sliding door. Inside the shed, Alfred was busy with a crew of workers sorting through bundles of wool lying about the wooden plank floor. Like bundles of similar quality and color were stuffed into large burlap bags, destined to be sold off to clothing manufacturers further up the distribution chain of the wool industry. Dennis and Markie watched as the Snitgen crew weighed each individual bundle of wool, and since the trailer full of wool was found to be sufficiently uniform by Alfred, the bundles were tossed directly from the scales into burlap bags.

When the unloading was finished, Norman chatted with Alfred and Hilary briefly about the other two loads of wool still to be delivered. Motioning to the back door of the two-story red brick building that housed the general store, Norman told the boys to meet him inside after he moved the trailer to make way for the next load of wool, already waiting patiently in line.

Mary had asked Norman to pick up some fish while he was in town. Easter wasn't until April ninth that year which meant there was still almost half of lent to get through yet. Mary needed more fish or she was never going to be able to get the family through the last couple of weeks of Lent. Whitefish, which were packed in ice, were a quite common Lenten meal, but without mechanical refrigeration, the fish couldn't be bought very far ahead of when they were intended to be consumed.

Snitgens' Store also sold small wooden kegs, about two and a half gallons in size, of whole herring packed in brine. The brine preserved the herring, which still had their heads on yet, even though they had been appropriately gutted and cleaned. The herring could be purchased with or without the fish eggs included. Norman grabbed a keg of the "no eggs included" herring and also procured several pounds of whitefish. Finally, without speaking, Norman nodded at Dennis and Markie, providing the affirmation they had been waiting to receive. The boys each grabbed a piece of their favorite candy and placed it on the counter next to the herring and whitefish.

"C'mon Markie, let's get in the car," a weary Dennis said as Norman gathered up his groceries.

Dennis was spent from the full day of work and trip into town. And, unlike most days, he was more than ready to go to bed when the car finally rumbled into the driveway.

**

"*Ja*, Norman, you'd better get Regina over here, quick," Dora hollered out the east porch of the house in the general direction where Norman and Ves were repairing the barnyard fence the following morning.

Norman dropped his hammer, mumbled something incoherent to Ves, and quickly turned towards the family car. Regina Schrauben lived around the corner on Wright Road, about a mile away. She served as the mid-wife for Mary, since the family had moved over from the Portland farm. Later that March morning, before Norman had time to take the last two loads of wool into town to sell, the couple's fourth son, and fifth child, David, was born.

***

Throughout the summer of 1939, the local radio and newspapers began to trickle in reports regarding the saber rattling occurring across the ocean in Germany. Many feared the bold rhetoric and aggressive policies of Adolf Hitler and his Nazi party would eventually lead to war over in Europe. Later that year, in September, Hitler led an invasion into Poland. The news report bylines were thousands of miles away, and at the time, few Americans thought the European unrest could possibly lead to a war of sufficient scale to draw in the United States.

As the local economy began to emerge from the grip of the Great Depression, the people of rural Michigan focused their attention on pulling their farms out of poverty and returning their lives to a more normal rhythm. None could possibly have imagined that the onset of World War II, and all the dark, horrific atrocities associated with it, would soon, like the Great Depression, once again wreak havoc on their daily routine and for many, alter their lives forever.

FIELD WORK

At a very young age, little Joni was already helping with the field work. Raymond would plow the spring ground with his steel-wheeled John Deere model D, tractor, pulling a three-bottom plow. Going in the same direction in which the moldboard plow laid down the furrows, young Eddie would follow behind with the draught horse team of Paint and Lady, pulling a heavy roller to firm down the uneven plow furrows. Joni would then follow the roller with the second draught horse team of Prince and Freddie, pulling a three-section drag to break down the plowed furrows into smaller clods of earth. Because the soil was tilled clean, the occurrence of a hard rain could sometimes result in a firm, impenetrable crust forming on the surface of the clay loam soils. This was especially problematic if a crust formed before the tender shoots of the planted crop had emerged from the soil. Under these conditions, Raymond would have Joni drive Prince and Freddy across the field pulling an implement called a "weeder" to break up the crust and at the same time pluck out small weed seedlings.

Joni loved being out in the open air of the farm fields on spring days, particularly when helping out by driving a team of horses. Prince and Freddie, despite names suggesting otherwise, were both mares. They were born on the Wieber Farm back when Raymond's father, Edward, still owned and operated the farm. Prince and Freddie knew their way up and down each and every field on the property, and, they also knew enough to maintain exactly the right spacing from the freshly worked soil of their previous pass down the field to ensure that the implement they were pulling didn't overlap but was consistently dragging across new unworked soil. Her own thoughts to the contrary, Joni was basically just along for the ride. The horses knew what they were doing, and, they were experienced enough that they wouldn't spook and bolt at the sudden startled appearance of a woodchuck, or from a thunderous backfire from the model D tractor.

In the late 1930's through to the end of World War II in the mid 40's, the majority of farms in the area still maintained draught horses to share the workload with the farm tractor. The draught horses were generally used to pull the manure spreader, do secondary tillage to fit the soil for planting, and to haul crops from the fields to the barns. The early tractors were used for heavy work such as plowing and some were equipped with belt drives to provide mechanical torque for running grain threshing harvest equipment.

Despite obvious drawbacks, horses did have one advantage over tractors. In addition to being beasts of burden, the draught horses, at least the mares, would serve double duty and reproduce themselves. Because of their aggressive nature, stallions would generally not be used for anything other than, well, being a stallion. Draught horses were predominately mares or gelded stallions. Most farmers couldn't justify keeping a stud stallion around just to service a mare or two.

When the timing was right, Raymond called upon a local fellow who owned a service stallion and would travel with it from farm to farm. The gentleman would show up on the farm in a horse and buggy with the stallion tethered behind the buggy. Once the stallion was introduced to the mare, Raymond and the owner of the stallion would head down into the cellar to imbibe in a glass or two of cider, which was usually sufficient time for the stallion to complete his task. Then, after collecting his stud fee, the gentleman and his horse and buggy, with the stallion in tow, would head back home and await the next call.

***

"Dinky is coming! Dinky is coming!" Joni shouted as she ran into the back door of the house and into the stifling hot kitchen.

Atop the heat-radiating wood stove, the blue-metal lid of Florence's canning kettle rattled and hummed from the bubbling, boiling water contained within it, which by way of the escaping steam, was in the process of preserving eight glass Mason jars filled to the top with green beans that Joni and Janice had picked earlier from the garden.

"*Ja, ja,*" Florence nodded, in acknowledgement as she grabbed the galvanized metal bucket, half-full of more green beans from Joni.

"Is that it now for the beans?" Florence asked.

"Yup," replied Joni.

"Well, maybe we can get some peaches from Dinky to fill out the canner for the next batch," Florence said, wiping her hands on her apron.

Dinky was a travelling fruit peddler, who traversed the countryside, hawking fruit from his rickety, red, panel truck. He would come by the Wieber farm every couple of weeks or so, selling assorted fruit, and, on occasion, various kitchen utensils. Additionally, there was a "Watkins" man, and a "Raleigh" man who also peddled household wares from door to door. Dinky, however, seemed to stand out from the rest of them. He was quite diminutive in stature, especially relative to the burly Raymond. He was rail thin, quite leathery in complexion, and had a wiry composition. The local folks, who tended to be ruthlessly descriptive in their German vernacular, also referred to Dinky affectionately as "*Wrega Wurum*" which translates roughly to "Ring Worm."

The red panel truck pulled up next to the south facing side door, and as it rolled to a stop, the dust cloud, which had been trailing dutifully along behind it, quickly enveloped and then passed the truck's cab. With a dry hacking cough, Dinky emerged, slamming the panel truck door behind him. Little Joni and Janice were already standing on the side porch in dusty bare feet, peering curiously at Dinky.

"Your mum home?" Dinky asked in a strained, gravelly-parched voice.

In unison, the girls nodded affirmatively. Overhead, the prevailing summer breeze that just finished chasing away Dinky's dust cloud, now steadily wafted through the leafy green boughs of the tall, stately, silver maples that lined the driveway and framed the lawn. Right on cue, Florence emerged from the house with a tall glass of cool well water.

"Oh, that'll hit the spot, thank you ma'am," Dinky said, and he settled down on the comfortable grass with his back resting against the trunk of one of the silver maples.

"It gets pretty warm, tooling around in that old truck," he added.

The steady fanning of the maple leaves emanated a sleepy, hypnotic white noise, interrupted only occasionally by the late summer high pitched resonating hum of a cicada. Dinky set the now empty glass down in the grass beside him and with a relaxing sigh, leaned his head back against the tree.

Florence sat down on the edge of the side porch next to her two daughters. "Do you have any peaches today?" she asked.

Not hearing a response, Florence repeated a little louder, "Peaches, do you have any on the truck?"

After another long pause, Joni asked warily, "Is Dinky sleeping?"

"Well, I'm not sure," Florence answered.

The two girls looked at each other and simultaneously jumped off the porch to get a closer look. Stealthily, Joni and Janice approached the silent figure slumped against the tree. Not wanting to get any closer, but close enough to hear Dinky's rhythmic breathing, the girls leaned forward and peered closely at the old man's wrinkled face.

"Yup, I think he's asleep," Joni whispered in a tone just barely legible over the summer breeze.

The hours spent bouncing along the dusty gravel roads in the stifling hot panel truck had sucked the energy out of old Dinky and under the refreshing breeze of the silver maples, he was helpless to fend off the onset of an unplanned afternoon nap. Giggling, the two girls scampered back to the porch.

"What do we do now?" Janice asked.

"Well, I'm not sure," Florence answered once again, her voice uncertain.

She had never encountered such a situation before. Being a hospitable, very well-mannered lady, Florence didn't feel comfortable just walking away from the poor old vendor. They considered Dinky a guest, even though he was visiting the farm in a commercial, professional context rather than a social one. Folks in that era tended to treat anyone who showed up at their door, whether they be friends, family, or as in this case, a regular visiting salesman, as guests. If you showed up at dinner or supper time it was customary that you'd be invited to sit down at the table and eat with the family. If you showed up in the afternoon, and Raymond wasn't away out in the fields, he would certainly escort you down the cellar for a glass of cider.

The situation had developed into a conundrum.

"Can we go now?" Joni asked impatiently, having grown tired of watching the old man slumber restfully under the shade tree.

"No, wait with me here a while longer." "I'm sure Dinky will wake up soon." "We don't want him to wake up and find that we just walked away leaving him all by himself," Florence reasoned.

Florence, Joni, and Janice remained there, hands at their sides, sitting on the edge of the porch with their legs dangling above the ground. Every few minutes, one of the girls would re-ask the question, "Can we go now?"

And, every time, the answer from Florence was the same, "I'm sure he'll wake up any minute now."

There probably was not a more comfortable place to be on this warm summer afternoon. The abundant shade from the large silver maples and steady summer breeze made for a very soothing and comfortable environment. Nevertheless, Florence's thoughts wandered to the canning work being left undone in the kitchen and the girls were tortured by the thoughts of the million other things they could be doing on such a beautiful summer afternoon.

Mercifully, after about a half-hour, Dinky showed some signs of life. At first his right foot shifted a bit, followed by a snort that broke the cadence of his restful breathing. Then, abruptly his arms stiffened and he pushed himself into a more upright sitting position. He slowly shook his head, in an effort to chase away the last vestiges of sleep that still gripped his body. Then he slowly raised his right hand, and starting at his forehead, deliberately rubbed it down across his face.

"Yes, about those peaches," Florence cheerfully chimed in, deftly picking up the conversation at the exact point it was earlier interrupted.

CANDY BARS

"*Reicha*" Joe, Norman's father, was tall and lean. He always stood at attention, with an upright dignified posture and the German translation of his nickname, "*Reicha*," descriptively reflected his stately demeanor. Unfortunately, Norman's mother, Catherine, did not survive to see her 50th birthday. She had passed away seventeen years previous, in 1922, after having birthed and for the most part, raised nine children. Catherine was peeling potatoes, preparing the noon meal for a threshing crew on the farm when she suffered a massive stroke. Norman, the sixth born of the nine surviving children, was just twelve when his mother passed away. *Reicha* Joe never remarried.

"Guess which hand," Grandpa *Reicha* Joe chuckled as he pulled the bag of candy bars behind his back.

Jumping up and down with excitement, Clair and Jane tugged at his left arm. It didn't really matter which hand they chose. The candy was always in the other hand. However, that didn't matter either, for Grandpa *Reicha* Joe always gave the candy away regardless.

"Now, now, let Jane pick first you boys," Grandpa *Reicha* Joe said in a tone trying to feign seriousness.

"Pick one out for baby David too," he said smiling at Jane.

Quickly surveying the loot, Jane picked out two small candy bars, and jumping up and down with excitement, she politely thanked Grandpa *Reicha* Joe and stepped back to allow the boys access to Grandpa's candy.

Clair, closest in age to Jane and the youngest of the boys present, lunged forward and as any five-year-old boy would do, he quickly snatched up the single large-sized candy bar in the bag.

"Are you sure that is the one you want?" Grandpa *Reicha* Joe asked.

Looking down at the candy bar, with a sheepish smile, Clair said meekly, "Yessssss."

"*Du weist das ist diene mutters*" (You know that is your mother's) was Grandpa *Reicha* Joe's stern response.

Clair immediately felt overcome with shame for his impulsive and selfish choice. Reaching forward he attempted to put the large candy bar back into Grandpa's bag. Sensing a teachable moment, Grandpa *Reicha* Joe would not let him put the large candy bar back. Quietly, Clair stepped back allowing Markie and Dennis their turns to pick a candy bar. When they had made their selections, Grandpa *Reicha* Joe tussled the hair on the three boys' heads with his thick work-worn hands and went into the house to visit with Norman and Mary.

Under the windmill on the northeast side of the house, the children collectively tore the paper wrappers off of their candy bars. Jane saved baby David's candy bar to give to Ma later, since she didn't think baby David was old enough to eat one yet. Clair however, only stared at his large sized candy bar, unable to force himself to open the wrapper. Taking a bite of his candy bar, Dennis suggested to Clair that he might as well eat his large candy bar since Ma would likely not care that he had taken the big one leaving her with a small one.

Reaching over Clair's lap, Markie took the candy bar from Clair, carefully tore open the wrapper and peeled the paper back.

Handing the candy bar back to Clair, Markie said, "*Ja*, Clair, you might as well eat it now."

Clair examined the candy bar. Somehow it didn't look very appetizing. He thought about his mother. If anyone ever deserved a bigger candy bar surely it was her. Ma worked tirelessly all day long without complaint, always making sure that everyone was taken care of before considering her own welfare. Closing his eyes, little Clair bit into the candy bar. As he forced himself to chew, a single tear squeezed past the eyelashes of each of his closed eyes. The candy bar seemed to lodge in his throat, and, with much effort, he choked down the first bite. Feeling for his brother, Markie took the candy bar from Clair and assured him that it would taste better later that day after supper.

Grandpa *Reicha* Joe, who was a widower for eighteen years, was Dennis' godfather in addition to being his grandfather. It was a long standing tradition in the area that a couple's first born child would have as godparents, a grandparent from both the maternal and paternal side. The second born child would then have the remaining grandparent from each side as godparents, if they all happened to be still surviving.

Just before Christmas of 1939, Grandpa *Reicha* Joe came back out to the farm to give his godson, Dennis, a Christmas present. It was a fancy toy car. The car had real working headlights, an almost unthinkably exorbitant toy for a six-year-old boy to have during that time period. Unfortunately, it was the last present Dennis or his siblings would get from Grandpa *Reicha* Joe. *Reicha* Joe passed away peacefully in April of 1940, the springtime of year when the shrill evening calls of the first spring peepers usher in the re-greening of the fields.

SELLING PIGS

The sizzling sound of day old eggs frying in bacon fat atop the wood stove greeted Joni when she came down to the kitchen from her upstairs bedroom. She left Janice behind upstairs, still asleep, burrowed beneath quilted blankets on a surprisingly chilly fall Saturday morning. Eddie was already up, sitting next to Raymond at the kitchen table. The old wood stove warmed the kitchen and the satisfying glow of the oak fire within it wrapped around the smell of the bacon and eggs frying in the heavy cast iron skillet.

Florence emerged from the cellar with a bowl full of fresh home-made butter, soon to be slathered generously on top of thick slices of homemade bread which were now toasting on the surface of the wood stove, adjacent to the rest of the morning's breakfast.

"*Ja*, we'll be selling pigs today," Raymond said, breaking the sensory spell the early morning kitchen had cast over Joni.

"Joni, you and Eddie can help me get them separated," Raymond added as he drained the last swallow of his morning coffee.

Joni looked up at Eddie and smiled. Sorting and loading pigs was always an adventure. To be sure, Joni understood that her role would be limited to opening and closing swinging gates, she was just too small to be in the mix with the fattened hogs. However, the smile between Joni and Eddie was made in secret acknowledgement that they'd likely get a chance to drive Joe Bierstetel's livestock truck. Joe was a local livestock trucker who Raymond would hire to haul market hogs to a slaughter house located in nearby Ionia County.

The hog barn was situated on the west side of the large hip roofed barns. The west wall of the hog barn served as a built-in corn crib. The crib was six feet wide and ran the full length and height of the gable roofed barn. The side of the crib walls were slotted in the traditional corn crib functional design to allow ambient air to filter through and dry the corn, which was harvested and stored as whole-ears. The gabled end of the roof faced to the south, and a large drive-through door was placed in the center of the barn. The area in the center of the barn served multiple functions. It was used to store the farm's wagons, served as a butchering area for both hogs and cattle, and was also used as a feed room for chicken and hog feed. On the east side of the barn was a long narrow pen that opened up to an outdoor dirt-surfaced hog lot.

A cool October morning breeze rustled the brown and drying leaves of the corn planted adjacent to the north fence of the hog lot as Raymond and Eddie sorted out the finished pigs from the smaller ones. The undersized pigs still needed a couple more weeks on grain before they'd be ready for market. Perched atop the wooden board fence, Joni served as the gatekeeper allowing only the chosen hogs to enter. After about twenty minutes, Raymond was satisfied that they had achieved the perfect pen size of fat hogs and told Joni to latch the gate shut. The three pig sorters then broke off to do their morning chores while they waited for Joe Bierstetel to show up with his truck.

Interestingly, many farmers of the late 1930's to mid-1940's in rural mid-Michigan, did not own a now ubiquitous farm pickup truck. Farms used a tractor and wagon, or sometimes horses and a wagon as their basic hauling tool. Additionally, the family car was quite often used to haul seed, feed supplements, and even an occasional sheep or calf. There were a few larger sized trucks in the area such as the ones owned by Joe Bierstetel or Joe Hanses, and these were available for hire to truck livestock or farm commodities to more distant markets. It wasn't until several years after the war that pickup trucks became common on area farms.

Late morning, Joni heard the unmistakable sound of Joe's truck rumbling down Pratt Road. The wooden stake racks rattled loudly over the rumble of the gas engine as Joe made the turn from Pratt Road onto Tallman Road. Joni was shelling corn, gleaning it through a hand operated corn sheller by turning a heavy cast iron fly wheel. The wheel was geared down to torque heavy circular cast iron plates with protruding fingertip-sized knobs against a stationary cast iron plate with similar protruding knobs. The turning plate would rotate the ear of corn as it pulled it further between the spinning and stationary ledger plate, gradually separating the grain kernels from the cob. Once separated, the grain dropped out of the bottom of the shelling mechanism where it was collected in a bucket while the now barren cob continued out the far end of the shelling machine. Raymond kept the hand-driven corn sheller in the feed room area of the hog barn next to the corn crib.

Excitedly gasping for breath, Joni dropped her hands from the drive wheel, instantly forgetting about the two unshelled ears of corn in the throat of the sheller, and ran to the big barns where Eddie was mucking out the horse stalls.

"Joe's here," Joni squealed unsuccessfully trying to hide her excitement.

Eddie dropped his pitchfork and the pair emerged from the barn just as ol' Joe pulled the truck into the driveway. The truck made its way east past the house, woodshed, chicken coop, and followed the turn past the granary and toolshed. Making its way towards the big barns, it rolled to a stop. Joni and Eddie could hear the gears grind as Joe shifted into reverse and backed up to his usual loading spot at the front of the hog barn door. The smaller pigs left out in the lot quickly and in unison raced away to the far north side of the hog lot at the sound of the revving engine, all the while kicking up a cloud of dust that was rapidly dispersed by the cool fall wind. Inside the hog barn, the fat hogs jostled and squealed in response to the commotion going on outside.

"*Guten tag,*" Raymond emerged from the corn crib he had been prepping for harvest and greeted Joe in the harsh sounding but friendly mannered German dialect used in the area.

Joni and Eddie watched from the feed room access door as Raymond pushed the hogs towards the exit door and loading ramp. Raymond was a big man and he readily pushed the squealing, churning mass of a dozen, two-hundred-fifty pound pigs with the heavy oak plank gate. Eventually, with the incentive produced by a few sharply enunciated words of encouragement, the lead pig headed up the loading ramp. One by one the others followed and Joe quickly released the latchstring, loudly dropping the back gate of the stake rack truck shut as the last pig's rump cleared the threshold.

"*Das gute,*" Joe smiled, pleased that the dirty work was over.

"Do you have time for a cider?" Raymond asked, not even bothering to look up as he climbed over the wooden boards of the hog lot fence—he knew the answer to that question.

"*Ja, ja,*" Joe replied. "As long as the kids bring the truck up to the house," he added, grinning at the restrained reaction from Eddie and Joni.

"Let's get that morning cider," Raymond said and the pair ambled off on foot to the cellar for a cool glass of Raymond's crisp hard apple cider.

"Remember last time you said you'd let me try to drive," Joni blurted out to Eddie as they hustled scrambling into the cab of the old truck.

Even though Raymond gave his tacit approval by walking away, the children still had the mischievous feeling of getting away with something they weren't supposed to be doing. They knew their mother would never approve of them driving any type of motorized vehicle at their tender young age, much less a large truck loaded to the gills with pigs.

"I suppose," relented Eddie.

Joni hit the starter button and the engine sputtered to life.

"Push the clutch in, the pedal on the right," Eddie instructed. "Once you get it pushed down, I'll shift it in to first gear for you," he added.

Joni nodded eagerly. Clasping the large steering wheel with both hands for leverage, she pushed down with all her might on the clutch pedal. Joni's eyes sunk below the dashboard as the pedal lowered to the floor, taking her body down with it.

Shoving the shift lever into first gear, Eddie said, "OK, now release the clutch."

As she did so, the truck, and the ton and a half of squealing live weight in the back of it, lurched forward in one violent jerk, promptly stalling out the engine.

"No, no, you've got to ease the clutch out," Eddie chided, rubbing the top of his forward where he bumped it slamming into the dashboard.

"*Ja, ja*, I'll get it," Joni instinctively responded.

Joni may have been undersized but she wasn't about to let the truck get the best of her. If Eddie could drive it, she knew she could. The next time, Joni slowly eased off the clutch and the truck began to creep forward.

"That's good," Eddie said. "We'll just keep it in first gear, though," he reasoned out loud.

Joni pulled the truck forward and continued on the two-track drive west of the big barns. She approached the toolshed and swung the big truck along the curve in the drive that led around the granary. Continuing forward, she pulled under the now yellow-leaved silver maple trees lining the lawn adjacent to the house.

"OK, push both pedals down," Eddie hastened, suddenly worrying that maybe Joni wouldn't be able to engage both the clutch and the brake.

Once again, Joni gripped the bottom of the steering wheel for leverage and pushed down on the pedals with all her might. The truck promptly responded, and Eddie slipped the shift lever into neutral.

"I made it!" Joni beamed.

EASTER

In February of 1941, Regina Schrauben was back in the Thelen household to deliver Norman and Mary's sixth child, Rosemary. Dennis, the oldest, was just two weeks shy of his eighth birthday. During that time period, large families were very common in rural communities, especially those that were predominately Catholic. And now with six children eight years and under, Norman and Mary were doing their part to uphold that tradition.

The house was wired for electricity and had the benefit of electric lighting. However, the indoor plumbing was still limited to a hand pump in the backroom of the house, which delivered potable, but not consumable water to the backroom sink from the buried cistern located on the east side of the house. A large wood burning furnace located in the basement of the house provided ample heat. Nevertheless, in today's world of creature comforts and modern appliances, it is difficult to conceptualize the amount of work it took just to run a domestic household during that time period, much less a household with six young children.

By the time Easter came around that spring, Mary, now twenty-nine years old, was eager and ready to get up and out of the house after spending the winter carrying the family's sixth child. Mary held fast to a Holy Saturday tradition observed by many during that time period. Lent would end after morning services on Holy Saturday, the day before Easter Sunday. On Holy Saturday, the church services and liturgical Mass were held very early in the morning and Norman and Mary always made sure the barn chores were done and that the family was on time and in attendance. All the statues were still covered with their Lenten purple linens, holy water would be blessed, and there were many prayers and blessings, all prior to 8:00 AM when Mass would officially begin. At the beginning of the Gloria recitation, all the bells were rung, the organ played, the statues were uncovered and the Easter flowers were brought to the altar.

On Holy Saturday afternoon, Mary, in observance of a longstanding local tradition, would take all the children down the lane that basically split the farm in the north-south direction. At each gate in the lane that opened to a field, she would sprinkle holy water obtained earlier at Mass. She and the kids would then pray for blessings on the crops to be planted there that growing season.

Additionally, when the first wild flowers would start to bloom, usually around the last week of April to the first week of May, Mary would walk with the children down the lane that ended at the woods on the north border of the farm. There, they would pick purple colored hepatica flowers that would appear as a flowery carpet beneath the maple and elm trees that still had not fully rolled out their leaves. White trillium flowers were also bountiful in the woods. When the flower pickers returned home, Mary would place an aromatic purple and white bouquet in front of the Pieta where she kept a May alter on the bureau.

***

That Easter, the extended Thelen family celebrated at Norman's younger bachelor brother, Martin's farm. Dennis and the other children were excited to go to Uncle Martin's farm for the Easter celebration. They knew that all the other cousins would be there to play. When the Easter dinner was over, the children wandered outdoors while the adults settled into playing euchre in the house. It wasn't long before the children found their way to the large barn on the property.

"Come and sit in the sling, Agatha, and we'll give you a ride up to the hay mow," the older children encouraged Dennis' cousin, who was the same age as Dennis.

Dennis knew that this was not a good idea, but at just eight years of age, he dared not speak up against his older cousins. It just wouldn't sit well with them, and he didn't want to risk the chance that they might force him into the sling next!

The large hip roof hay barns that dot the landscape throughout much of the U.S. typically were equipped with a sling, trolley, and rail system to unload harvested hay from wagons, pull it up into the barn, and, deposit it into the specifically desired hayloft. The sling, as the name implied, was a web-like configuration of ropes and 2x2 boards designed to hold the loose hay in place such that it could be hoisted using a pulley system up to the hay trolley. The cast iron trolley ran across a steel rail that was suspended just below the very peak of the hip roof and ran the entire length of the barn. Heavy barn ropes would be used to drag the trolley along the rail. A system of rope tag lines was used to close the sling up around a load of hay and to trip the release which would then, of course, dump the hay.

After a little coaxing, the older cousin's lured Agatha into the sling. The older boys then pulled the taglines taught which pulled the ends of the sling up around Agnes, trapping her like a wild animal in a net. With the sling now closed, the older boys, including some of Agatha's own brothers, hoisted the sling along with Agatha inside of it, upwards toward the top of the barn roof. All the while with Agatha protesting vociferously. She began to tug at the sling ropes which only served to sway the sling violently to and fro.

Agatha thought that the boys would probably lift her to a height of about ten feet or so and then release the tag line to dump her out into a pile of loose hay. However, urged on by each other, the boys kept raising the sling. As Agatha ascended past twenty feet she began to increase her protestations, and the sling began to sway and pitch all the more. Dennis and the younger kids watched not knowing whether to laugh along with the older boys or run into the house and notify the parental authorities.

The more Agatha protested, the higher the boys hoisted the sling. Soon, the sling reached it's maximum height, and Dennis heard the familiar ratcheting sound as the brakeline on the lift pulley engaged. When the sling was used for its proper purpose, the braking action at the top was designed to remove the weight of the load from the team of horses that were engaged in lifting the sling full of hay.

Agatha was now perched about thirty feet from the floor of the barn, whence her wayward journey began. The sling was now swinging precariously, tucked right under the very peak of the barn roof. All Dennis and the other kids could now see of poor Agatha was her spindly legs sticking out from the ropes of the sling as she kicked and screamed. She was now pleading to be let down, and her threats of "I'm telling mom," had finally convinced her brothers and cousins that they had better relent and end the shenanigans.

"Release the pulley brake and let her down now," Gerald, Agatha's older brother told his cousins, his voice now decidedly more serious than when the escapade began.

"I'm trying to," was the response, "but the brake is stuck."

"Let me down, LET ME DOWN RIGHT NOW, THIS ISN"T FUNNY ANYMORE!" Agatha's pleas escalated from concerned to outright demanding.

At about the same time, the laughing and joking of the older boys diminished as they fidgeted with the tagline, trying to free the brake on the lift pulley.

"What's the matter with this thing," Gerald asked out loud as he continued to futilely jerk the tagline.

At that point, the escalating tension was more than the younger children could stand. Finally reaching the breaking point, one of the younger children bolted to the house, and the others instinctively followed. The younger children stumbled into the house like a herd of stampeding cattle, all of them shouting a jumbled, chaotic, message of panic.

Uncle Louis, Agatha's father, deciphered the word "Agatha" in the garbled jumble of words and quickly jumped up from the table and ran out to the barn. Norman, and Louis' other brothers, Julius, Frank and Martin, followed behind. The uncles were followed out to the barn by a beeline of the smaller children who initiated the rescue in the first place. The children were then followed close behind by the Aunts who had been busy talking in the parlor.

When Louis opened the barn door he was greeted by a shrieking Agatha, kicking her legs in a tirade straight above him swaying high above the barn floor. The lift pulley tagline, the sling release rope, and the trolley tow rope now dangled freely below as the older boys were now nowhere in sight. They had fled the scene of the crime as soon as they realized the younger contingent of kids had turned tail and ratted on them.

Louie jerked on the tagline trying to release the pulley brake to lower the sling, but he had no more luck than the boys had.

"That brake has been sticking," Martin said, matter-of-factly.

"Probably better pull the trolley all the way to the end of the barn," Martin suggested, adding. "We can climb up the wall ladder and get her down that way."

Agatha was sobbing now, but the sobbing turned back to shrieking as the trolley was pulled along the steel rail, suspended thirty feet from the barn floor, tucked under the peak of the roof. Norman pulled the trolley, slowly and carefully, all the way to the end of the barn. Louis climbed the wall ladder all the way to the top, and when he had a firm grasp on Agatha, he hollered down for Norman to pull the sling trip line. Norman did and the sling opened up releasing Agatha fully into her father's strong grip. As Louie made his way down the ladder with Agatha, Martin pulled the trolley back to the center of the barn. With a quick snap of his wrist on the pulley brake tagline, the brake released now that there was no longer any weight in the sling, and the sling quickly descended harmlessly back to the barn floor.

***

Later that spring, on a Friday night after chores were finished, Norman was tightening the drive chain on the two-row corn planter, when Teddy, the family dog, sounded notice that the neighbors were coming over for a visit. It had been a difficult spring, but Norman and Ves had finally planted the last of the corn crop that same afternoon, and Norman was now getting the corn planter ready for storage. Looking over his right shoulder down the road to the west, Norman confirmed his suspicion. Vessie and Adelia, along with their sons Alfred, Markie's age and Bernard who was Jane's age, were making their way down Pratt Road for a Friday evening visit.

"*Ja*, Dennis, hand me that grease rag over there," Norman instructed, adding, "It looks like we'll have company tonight, we better head in and get cleaned up."

Dennis eagerly handed the grease rag to his father and skipped over to the house.

"Ma, the Hengesbach's are coming," Dennis informed Mary as he burst into the backroom.

Reaching into the wash basin, Dennis scrubbed the evening chore grime from his arms and hands. By the time he was toweling himself off, the knock had sounded on the side door and Mary was welcoming in the Hengesbach family. Norman followed Dennis' procedure through the wash basin and clothes changing routine. He slicked his hair back and entered the living room to join in on the lively conversation.

The women had retired to the parlor while the men pulled up chairs around the living room radio. Friday night was fight night and Vessie particularly enjoyed listening to the live boxing matches. Dennis, Markie, and Clair would giggle out loud watching Vessie as he sat hunched forward in his chair, throwing right jabs and left handed hooks into the empty air, as he weaved and bobbed his head to the play-by-play call of the radio announcer's voice crackling over the ever present static emanating through the single radio speaker.

A few weeks later, on June 28, to be exact, Vessie and his family were over for a similar visit. At about 8:00 PM, the visiting party came in from the comfort of the front porch to hear the radio call of Joe Louis' title defense over Tony Galento, broadcast live from New York City. Vessie's jaw almost hit the floor when the champ was knocked down in the 3rd round. However, he jumped right out of his chair when

Louis pummeled Galento to a TKO decision in the very next round.

There were no other heavyweight bouts on that particular night but the men enjoyed a couple of light and middle heavyweight matches over glasses of hard cider and bottles of beer. When the conversation inevitably turned to farming, Norman mentioned that he was looking for a new sheep buck for the fall breeding season.

"Raymond Wieber has a couple of stout Suffolk rams that he's looking to sell," Vessie offered.

"*Ja?*" Norman answered inquisitively.

After a brief pause Norman concluded, "Maybe we'll have to go over there one of these days and have a look at them," and he drained the last swallow of cider from the bottom of his glass.

***

Summer had given way to fall and Dennis looked down at his shoes and with his right foot, scuffed at the loose pea stone on the playground surface. He didn't want anything to do with a fight. Nonetheless, on a school playground teeming with young life, sometimes it seemed, a fight or two would inevitably find you whether you were looking for it or not.

"There's some town boys that want to fight you, Dennis," Dennis' classmate and friend Joe Pohl chided him again.

Dennis didn't answer his friend but continued to look down at his foot which by now had displaced a significant amount of playground pea stone. He knew who these town boys were, a group of kids a couple of years ahead of him in school who liked to throw their weight around picking on younger boys on the playground.

"I'm going to get a drink of water," Dennis said looking for a way out.

The playground water bucket was kept on the concrete pad adjacent to the school. The handles on the two tin drinking ladles kept with the bucket had long since been broken off and discarded. Getting a drink meant submerging a grubby hand into the soiled water to retrieve the handle-less tin cup. Dennis looked into the bucket. The bucket was nearly empty and the rims of the tin cups were just visible above the murky water line.

"I changed my mind, I'm not thirsty after all," Dennis admitted.

At once there was a commotion on the far corner of the playground. A crowd of kids were beginning to assemble and the buzz in the air seemed to indicate that something was amiss.

"What's going on over there," Joe said turning his attention away from the grimy water bucket.

The hustle bustle and migration of more kids all flocking to that corner of the schoolyard looked suspiciously like a playground fight. Dennis was relieved. It looked like the bullies found someone else to pick on today.

"Let's go see," Joe added and the two made a beeline to check out the commotion. The boys were hoping to see some action before the playground monitor caught wind of the hullabaloo and put a premature end to the situation.

Dennis worked his way through the crowd formed around a couple of the town bullies who were about ready to claim another victim. Pulling his head over a classmate's shoulder to get a better look, Dennis couldn't believe his eyes.

"Markie!" Dennis whispered under his breath.

Dennis could see his little brother, a year behind him in school, confronting one of the older town boys. Next to the older boy, Markie looked like a little Irish leprechaun prancing around with his arms cocked and his fists clenched. This wasn't going to end well. The agitator was older and larger than Dennis, even more so compared to little Markie.

Before Dennis could react, the town kid pushed little Markie down to the ground landing him squarely on his butt. All the while the swelling crowd laughed out loud. At that moment some of the bully's friends noticed Dennis in the crowd and began to cajole him into fighting the bigger kid. The quiet Dennis didn't want anything to do with a fight but he was beginning to feel backed into a corner. Leaning over, Dennis grabbed his little brother by his coat sleeves and lifted him to his feet.

"Are you OK?" Dennis asked Markie as the crowd continued to egg on the bullies to carry on the fight.

Before Markie could answer, the town kid shoved both Dennis and Markie backwards. Now there really was no other way out. Dennis knew he had to fight back. Closing his eyes, Dennis reared back with his fist closed and threw the hardest roundhouse haymaker punch he could muster. Contact! By some miracle of chance, the punch had landed squarely on the bully's jaw, dropping him like a sack of potatoes. Dennis opened up his eyes and saw the other town boys help their groggy fallen comrade up and disappear into the dispersing crowd. Just as quickly as it had started, the fight was now over.

"Nice punch," Markie said, quite surprised by the actions of his big brother.

"*Ja*, I only wish I would have seen it," Dennis said rubbing his bruised knuckles. "I had my eyes closed the whole time."

Unobtrusively, the two quietly made their way back to class.

SCHOOL GIRL

"Let's get that hair settled," Florence said as she fussed over little Joni's fidgeting head early on a September morning.

Joni was about to attend her first day of school, at St. Mary's in Westphalia. She was excited to begin school. She particularly looked forward to playing all the games on the playground that Eddie had told her about.

At the kitchen table, Eddie crammed the last piece of toasted homemade bread, slathered in wild black raspberry jam, into his mouth and hollered out a muffled, "They're here."

Eddie grabbed the dinner pail and headed out the door and Florence followed right behind him shuffling Joni along.

Outside, the Knoops, the neighbors across the road to the north, were waiting with their car. Eddie and Joni carpooled with five neighboring families, each one assigned a specific day of the week to do the driving. With five families involved, the car was packed to the gills, and at one point in time, carried eighteen riders plus the driver: four from the Knoop's; another four from the Trierweiler's; five from the Platte's; and, another two from the Pohl's. The Wieber's turn to drive was on Tuesdays. Raymond always drove as Florence was not comfortable driving with that many riders crammed into the car. The fact that all the cars back then had manual, stick shift transmissions, didn't make it any easier on the driver, or the riders, for that matter.

"What is your name?" the nun clothed in a black dress and veil, Sister Antonio, asked Joni.

"I'm Joni," she replied with a smile.

"Joni, how would you like to be our water carrier this week?" Sister asked.

Although the school did have new flush toilets, there was only a single automated water fountain, which the Sisters dubiously called a "bubbler," in the entire school. Therefore, one of the classroom jobs was to fill the water bucket, which came equipped with three ladles in it that were shared by all. In addition to the classroom water bucket, a similar bucket with 2 ladles was made available on the playground at recess.

"Yes, Sister, I give the chickens water at home all the time," Joni thrust out her chest and proudly answered.

"Very good, Joni," the nun replied as she patted Joni on the head.

***

"It's here, it's here!" Joni yelled, running full speed from the chicken coop to the garden where Florence was weeding a row of snap beans while Janice played with a handful of pebbles at the garden gate.

"What child, what's here?" Florence asked, looking up from her weeding task.

"The new tractor, Mom," Joni, sputtered while gasping for breath, as she quickly turned and headed to the tool shed where her dad and brother had been repairing a broken wooden slate on the hay loader gathering chain. However, the sound of the truck delivering the new John Deere, model B, tractor had already alerted the two and they were walking between the toolshed and granary when the excited Joni met up with them.

Over the top of the truck cab they could see the shiny green paint and clean black rubber tires of the new machine. The new rubber tires looked especially strange to Joni. She was used to the old John Deere D, which had old-fashion steel lugs. Agriculture, and indeed the whole world, was going through rapid changes in 1941.

"Isn't she a thing of beauty," young Ron Spitzley said as he jumped out of the truck cab. Ron was the local John Deere dealer, Anthony Spitzley's son, who was just eighteen years old and already working in the family business.

Raymond had to admire the engineering wonder that was being added to his arsenal of equipment. The tractor would be used for some of the lighter duty work other than plowing, which would still be the purview of the old steel-wheeled model D, at least for the near future. The new lighter model B would take on some of the soil fitting operations that were currently being handled by the draught horses.

Raymond would still need the horses, to be sure, but, it was clear that their role on the farm was diminishing. Although Raymond was certainly a progressive farmer, Eddie noted that he never fully adapted to tractor power. In fact, Eddie noticed that whenever a tractor had to be stopped quickly, such as when seeing a rock in a windrow of seed clover being threshed, his father would instinctively holler "Whoa now boy," and pull back on the steering wheel with all his might, forgetting for the moment to instead use his foot on the tractor's brake pedal.

Eddie would watch helplessly as the rock then made its way up the conveyor into the throat of the A12 combine resulting in a two-hour repair job to dislodge the rock and hammer out the bent metal of the threshing mechanism.

"I'll back the tractor off the truck for you," young Ron offered, and said "where do you want me to park her?"

Unfortunately, mechanization on the farm was not the only transformation being brought to bear by the winds of change in the early 1940's. The radio and print media was now dominated by the civil unrest being experienced in Europe as Hitler had begun heavy bombing raids over England and Ireland.

All of that aggression and war mongering seemed light years away as Raymond and the young Ron Spitzley shared a glass of cider and talked about the local St. Mary's baseball team, the price of corn, and the variability of the last rain event. Little did the two realize that sunny care-free day, that the overseas unrest thousands of miles away, would soon claim the life of the young tractor delivery man, Ron, in a matter of only a few short years.

A CHANCE MEETING

"Keep the windows closed, or we'll all get sick." Vessie Hengesbach would insist when he drove the carpool to school.

On face value, it doesn't seem much of an inconvenience, keeping the windows shut for the five and a half mile ride to and from school. However, as soon as all of the twelve to sixteen children had piled into the car, and the doors and windows were shut tight, Vessie would methodically and systematically light the tobacco in his pipe before restarting the engine. And, maximum speed for Vessie, was about thirty miles per hour. Furthermore, with the Thelen, Schrauben, Joe Pung, Hengesbach, Frank Pung, and Platte children packed two or three deep on the passenger side of the front seat and the entire rear seat, there was very little room left in the confined car space for breathable air. It didn't take long until the remaining headspace in the car was chock full of thick, choking tobacco smoke.

Like Vessie Hengesbach, Joe Pung also smoked a pipe when driving the school carpool. However, Joe would always crack open his window, much to the relief of the young riders, to provide an exit vent for the tobacco smoke.

The widow Regina Schrauben, who was very petite and short in stature, would have to sit on a large pillow when it was her turn to drive the carpool. And, even then she would have to peer through the steering wheel in order to see out the windshield. Further complicating matters for Regina, the Schrauben's car had seen better days. The steering wheel was full of slop, and generally had to be turned about a full revolution in either direction before eliciting a response from the wheels. There was so much side-to-side play in the steering mechanism that it felt to the children, that the car was being herded down the road as opposed to being controlled with the steering wheel!

Despite their quirks and individual oddities, carpools were a necessity and common occurrence in the childhood of Dennis and Joni in the 1930's and 1940's. Without school buses, the carpool was the only transportation option for rural kids to get to school. In addition to school carpools, families also often carpooled to the weekly Sunday Mass. Norman and Mary carpooled with their neighbors, the Platte's, for the 8:00 am and 10:00 am Mass every Sunday morning.

To be sure, Sunday was considered a day of rest, and families refrained from all but the most essential work. However, even the basic essential chores out in the barn, and in the house for preparation of the Sunday dinner, required morning labor that spanned across the two Mass times. Therefore, Norman, Mary, and the younger children would drive to the 8:00 am Mass, picking up several of the Platte children for the ride. While they were at Mass, Dennis, Markie, and Clair would be out in the barn tending to the daily morning chores. In the house, Jane would be cleaning up the kitchen after breakfast and beginning the preparations for the customary Sunday chicken dinner. Then, when Mary and Norman returned, Mary would spell Jane in the kitchen and Norman, the boys in the barn. The morning chore kids would then hustle around and get ready for the Platte's to pick them up for 10:00 am Mass. The ride home with the Platte's would always include a stop at Ed Spitzley's to pick up bananas and for a short visit at Mrs. Platte's mother's house while the children waited patiently in the car.

* * *

Dennis tossed the empty feed bucket into the shed and he and Markie turned toward the main barn near which their dad was showing the hired man, Ves, the broken slats on the corn crib that needed repair. Finished with issuing instructions to Ves, Norman turned to the boys and said, *"Ja,* how about we go look at a sheep buck."

The three headed to the family car and piled inside. The mile and a half trip passed uneventfully and the car pulled into the Wieber's drive on Tallman Road, drove past the house and rounded the drive between the toolshed and granary. As Dennis got out from his side of the car, he noticed two small girls playing in a stack of chicken crates near the chicken coop. Joni was climbing in and out of the crates, used for transporting live chickens, while Janice followed along behind her.

"Gross," thought Dennis. "I wonder if those chicken crates have cootie lice in them," Dennis remarked to Markie.

Norman, followed along by Dennis and Markie, made his way to the barn, where inside they could see Raymond, Simmy Smith, the Wieber's hired hand, and Eddie sorting out the sheep. In a corner pen, already separated out, stood three young black-headed, Suffolk rams.

"Hello Norman," Raymond called out jovially. "I hear you're looking for a sheep buck."

"Ja," said Norman, who then followed up with the question, "Are these three in the corner for sale?"

Norman looked the trio of rams over carefully, checking out their vigor and body conformation. After a couple minutes of inspection, he finally settled on one that stood just a hair taller than the other two. Like Norman, Raymond's flock was considered a dual-purpose flock, bred for both wool and mutton. Norman liked to continually out-cross the flock with different breeding to maximize hybrid vigor. He liked the look of this particular Suffolk ram as it fit well into his outcrossing program.

The two men agreed upon a price and Eddie lead the ram over to the Thelen's car, temporarily tethering him to the fence along the driveway. As per custom, Norman and Raymond consummated the deal over a glass of cider in Raymond's cellar as Dennis, Markie and Eddie went up into the haymow to play.

Soon the horn on the car sounded and Dennis and Markie, headed back towards the house where Norman had already loaded the ram into the trunk of the car. Walking past the chicken coop, Dennis stole one more quick look back, hoping to catch sight of the little girl playing in the chicken crates.

WAR AND APPREHENSION

"Raymond, we need to go to Ma's right away," Florence said as she hung up the ear piece to the wall phone, adding a German "*Schnell*," to add emphasis to the urgency.

Raymond didn't question why. Things were happening fast all around the world. The unthinkable had happened at the end of 1941. The United States had been attacked by the Japanese at Pearl Harbor, instantly turning the world upside down for everyone. Even older established farmers, like Raymond and Norman, had received notices to register for conscription, known by some as "the draft." However, at 35, and 32, years of age, respectively, and both being owner operators of farms, which were much needed for national security, they both received official deferments.

Florence's three bachelor brothers however, had not received deferments yet, and their widowed mother, Eleanor, worried incessantly about their future. None of it made sense to Joni, who had just turned six years old. She remembered the scary December days when President Roosevelt's famous "We have nothing to fear but fear itself" speech was played over and over on the radio in the days following the December 7, attack on Pearl Harbor. She saw the concern on her parent's faces as they discussed things like the "European Theatre," and the "Pacific Rim," words and phrases that really had no meaning in her young, six-year-old vocabulary.

When Raymond slipped the transmission out of gear in Grandma Eleanor's driveway and engaged the handbrake on the car, Joni was instantly on her way up the sidewalk to Grandma's house. Florence and Janice were right behind her. Joni immediately sensed tension in the house. Her three uncles, Harold, Leon, and Art, weren't there. They were usually there to greet and good naturedly tease their nieces and nephews. When Florence walked in through the door, her mother started crying which of course, started Florence crying. Bringing up the rear, Raymond walked in and assessed the situation. He didn't really know what to say to diffuse the issue, but, not having much of a flair for the dramatic, he decided to simply state the reality of the situation.

"Ladies, for gosh sakes, they're just going in for their physicals, they're not even drafted yet!"

FAREWELL VISITS

"Dim the lantern down, Markie," Dennis scolded.

Slowly the three brothers, Dennis, Markie, and Clair, inched their way around to the east-facing side of the straw stack. Earlier that day, while graining the weaned lambs, the boys had observed where sparrows had been burrowing into the stack. Large straw stacks, comprised of the straw left behind from wheat threshing, were commonplace on the farms of the era. The stacks were roughly twenty-five feet in diameter at the base and rose to a height of about twelve feet. The stacks often took on a giant "mushroom" shape from cattle and pitchforks nibbling away at the straw from the base of the stack.

Straw stacks made an ideal nesting habitat for common sparrows which had reached a population of pestilence in much of the Midwest from the early to mid-1900's. In fact, the county would pay a bounty of two cents for every sparrow head. Additionally, bounties of fifty and ten cents were paid on other pests such as woodchucks and rats, respectively.

"Got one," Dennis said as he pulled his right hand out from the neat hole burrowed into the side of the straw stack.

With a quick rotation of his wrist, the unlucky sparrow had his head separated from his body.

"Open the bag, Clair," Markie instructed the youngest of the three hunters.

Dennis quickly dispatched the bird head into the bag. The birds tended to cluster together in the stacks and soon a second and third hole were located.

In addition to sparrow bounties, which were discontinued sometime later in the decade when War priorities consumed all municipal revenues, the boys also earned spending money by trapping muskrat, raccoon, and an occasional rare mink. Kids didn't get paid allowances for family farm work during that time period. Working on the farm was considered an obligation and familial responsibility. Kids had to find other creative means of picking up a little spending money.

When the boys had caught an even dozen birds, the darkness surrounding the barnyard was interrupted by the headlights of a car pulling into the driveway.

"Company?" Dennis uttered out loud.

The threesome headed directly for the house and watched as a lone shadowy figure emerged from the car and entered the house. Living in the 1940's rural countryside it was always a treat to get visitors. Whether it was the neighbors coming over to sit on the porch for the evening, or relatives coming over for a visit, families were always eager to oblige visitors with generous hospitality.

"I wonder who it is," Markie said as they approached the house and didn't recognize the now empty car from the dim light of the kerosene burning lantern.

Inside the house, Norman's cousin, Ernest Thelen, was seated in the living room, chatting with Norman and Mary. The three boys filed into the room and tumbled onto the sofa opposite Ernest. During the war years it was customary for young soldiers to make the rounds among relatives prior to their deployment. Although Ernest was about ten years older, Dennis, recognized him from the numerous family and social gatherings of the past. Ernest seemed much different now. He looked much older and important, sitting there in his neatly pressed, dress military uniform. Ernest was making the rounds visiting family before his deployment to Europe. Fortunately, Ernest was one of the lucky ones who would made it back home alive.

***

Mary's younger sister Rose, and her husband, Harold, were married in January of 1944, just before Harold was deployed to Europe. Harold had been commissioned a company commander for a supply chain operation unloading cargo ships. Rose took a state-side war job in a Lansing factory while her new husband was deployed overseas.

Like Raymond and Florence, Norman and Mary also received the State Journal newspaper on a daily basis. The State Journal, later to be named the Lansing State Journal, would daily list the names of mid-Michigan casualties and soldiers missing in action in bold letters on the front page, which the families would read with nervous trepidation fearing that they might recognize a name. Fortunately, Harold too, would make it home alive.

That next Sunday afternoon, Norman, Mary and the kids stopped in at Grandpa *Dika* Joe and Grandma Theresa's house. The family was getting together to send off young Martin Rademacher, Mary's first cousin. Martin was the son of Theresa's brother William and his wife Bertha. Martin was being deployed by the U.S. Air Force to join the Allies fighting in Italy.

It was a beautiful spring day, and a gentle west breeze sent bright green maple samaras whirling to the ground like tiny helicopters around the family member's feet. There were lots of handshakes, hugs, and toasts made for good luck as the family saw Martin off. At just nineteen years of age and in his fine white, U.S. Air Force, dress uniform, Martin was an impressive site as he graciously accepted the well wishes from his family.

Unfortunately, just a few months later, young Martin Rademacher was killed on a bombing mission over Hungary when his plane attempted an emergency landing after taking enemy fire.

THE ULTIMATE PRICE

Stateside, everyday life changed dramatically with the onset of the Great War. Manufacturing of many goods, particularly heavy equipment like domestic cars, trucks, tractors, and many home appliances ceased as factories were retooled for the production of munitions and military equipment. Families were issued ration books that contained stamps necessary to buy staples such as coffee, sugar, whiskey, and tires. Ladies nylons were not available because the nylon was needed by the military for parachutes. One of Joni's friends with older sisters remembers them applying darkening lotion on their legs and then drawing, with an ink pen, fake seams up the back of their legs to give the impression that they had nylons on.

Much farm equipment simply wasn't made during the war because like the automobile factories, many farm equipment factories also converted over to the production of military equipment. However, some farm equipment was still available as the production of food, feed, and fiber was still considered a national priority and national security issue. One particular war time advertisement for sheep shearing equipment had the following notice posted with the newspaper advertisement: *SHEARING EQUIPMENT IS NOT RATIONED BY COUNTY BOARDS. No priorities or certificates required. Those who need it simply order from their dealer. But as this equipment is limited, it is everyone's patriotic duty to do his shearing with his old machine if at all possible. Adequate supplies of repair parts available.*

Procuring replacement tires for automobiles or farm equipment was nearly impossible due to severe shortages of rubber, which of course, was prioritized for use by the military. Towards the end of the war, there was probably not a single car tire in the area that didn't have at least a couple of repair patches on it.

Getting up-to-date information on the progress of the war was challenging. Raymond perused the daily newspaper and listened to daily radio news reports on the war. Additionally, local movie theaters such as the ones in Fowler, Grand Ledge, and Ionia had informational war news trailers that followed movies. However, due to security reasons, the news was often filtered and very general in the level of detail. Families struggled to learn the whereabouts and fate of their loved ones, often going for weeks on end without knowing their fate. As many of the survivors from that period will tell you, "the not knowing was the hardest part."

The small town of Westphalia sent a significant number of men into action during the Second World War. The Westphalia Historical Society lists 96 young men from the area that served in the US Armed Forces during the war. This is an impressive number given that the entire Westphalia Township population in 1940 is listed at 1297. Three of these young men paid the ultimate price, each earning the Purple Heart.

Sgt. Martin J. Rademacher, serving with the 454-455 Bomber Squadron was killed November 20, 1944 on a bombing mission over Hungary. His plane, disabled from enemy fire, was attempting an emergency landing when it reportedly hit a landmine. He was Mary's first cousin, the son of her Uncle William and Aunt Bertha. He was 19 years of age.

Private First Class Theodore Schafer, served with Company E, 36th Infantry, 3rd Armored Division. Theodore was killed in action in France on June 29, 1944. He was the son of Nicholas and Oliva Schafer.

Corporal Ronald W. Spitzley, served with an anti-tank company in General George Patton's Army. Cpl. Spitzley fought in battles from North Africa and into France. He was awarded his first Purple Heart after having been wounded in April of 1944. Ronald was the young man who delivered the new John Deere B tractor to Raymond on that sunny spring day in 1941. He was killed in action on December 31, 1944 during the hard fought Battle of the Bulge.

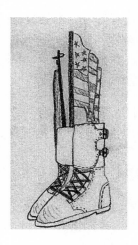

POW'S ON THE FARM

The high stake-rack truck rumbled into the driveway about the time morning chores were getting finished up.

"They're here!" Dennis called out to Markie and Clair who had just finished collecting and cleaning the eggs.

The boys were fascinated by the German prisoners of war that came to the farm to work in the sugar beets. Early in the spring of the war years the POW's showed up to block the beets, which is the term used to describe thinning out the beet stand to the desired population. Sugar beets are planted early in the growing season, and because the small-seeded plants lack early season vigor, stands are over-planted to ensure adequate emergence and final plant populations in case the early spring weather, which is often the case in Michigan, was less than ideal. Then, periodically throughout the summer, the POW's would return to the farm to hoe weeds in the beets.

The boys ran to the fence on the south side of the cow yard to watch as the prisoners one by one jumped off the bed of the truck. The prisoners originated from a POW camp at Fort Custer, near Battle Creek, Michigan, about an hour's drive to the southwest. Dressed in uniform work clothes and baseball caps, the prisoners would grab a hoe and immediately head out to the field after disembarking from the truck. One solitary young military guard, armed with a rifle, oversaw the complete work detail of about 25 to 30 prisoners. Dennis, Markie and Clair were struck by the wide age span of the prisoners. There were young men of eighteen years all the way up to older men who appeared to be well into their fifties. When the POW's had all made their way to the field, the very young-looking armed guard took up his usual spot under the shade tree in the headland of the field near the south facing cow yard fence.

The boys were fluent in the local "Americanized" German linguistics, which after four generations in Michigan had become a somewhat bastardized version of the proper German language. Nonetheless, the local vernacular was still sufficiently German enough that Dennis and his brothers could easily communicate with the prisoners.

For obvious reasons, the boys were encouraged to keep their distance while the men were working. However, on rainy days, and during their lunch hour, the prisoners would mill around the tool shed, idling away the time until lunch ended or the weather was fit to return to the field. These rainy days and lunch hours provided the greatest opportunity for Dennis to interact with the prisoners.

"Baum aste? Hohle auf himmel aus das regen," a prisoner asked Dennis one day, pointing to the sky while sitting on an overturned pail in the toolshed, waiting for the rain to stop.

Translated, "Do you have a big stick? To stick in the hole in the sky to stop the rain."

Dennis just smiled and nodded as he sat the pail of cool well water down in front of the guard. Another day, the boys recalled an older prisoner telling them how he missed his own boys back home in Germany, sons he hadn't seen nor heard from in several years.

In general, the disposition of the POW's suggested that they were content to be on U.S. soil and in good health. They seemed to have a realization that working sugar beets was far better than the obvious alternative of still being in harm's way out on the battle lines.

At lunch time, the prisoners would pull a wooden crate from the truck that contained loaves of bread and jars of peanut butter. Although certainly rudimentary in selection, the prisoners had all they wanted to eat. Norman would supply the drinking water, from the farm well. At the end of the day, the guard would sound the orders and the prisoners would file back onto the bed of the truck and head back to the POW camp in Battle Creek or sometimes to bivouac at a more local temporary campsite.

Although the war in the European theatre was over during the fall harvest season of 1945, prisoner exchange protocols had yet to be finalized. German POW's detained in the U.S. were still incarcerated, but work details were voluntary and prisoners were paid for participating. Late that fall, a couple of weeks after the last POW work detail occurred at Norman and Mary's farm, tragically, a truck load of German POW's returning from a day's work in a sugar beet field near Blissfield, Michigan, was struck by a Michigan Central Train. According to the *Battle Creek Enquirer and News*, sixteen of the twenty-four prisoners riding on the back of the stake rack truck, along with the lone military guard, were killed.

The deceased prisoners ranged in age from eighteen to thirty-five. One of the killed POW's, Hans Becker, had seven children back in Germany. The deceased American military guard, Pfc. Edward B. Loughrin, from Cadillac, Michigan, was only twenty years old. The prisoner's bodies were returned to Fort Custer for military funerals and burial, which included an honor guard of nine American soldiers. The Battle Creek newspaper reported at the time that the bodies might later be exhumed and returned to Germany. However, the exhumation and return to their homeland never happened. A German memorial with the gravestones and bodies of the German POW's still exists at Fort Custer National Cemetery, near Battle Creek, Michigan. Norman and Mary never found out if the military guard or any of the POW's who had spent time working on their farm were among the sixteen dead that tragic late fall afternoon.

MAKING HAY

"Keep 'em steady, Joni," Raymond shouted over the clackety clack of the hay loader's gathering chain.

On the farm, the hard work continued, often short-handed, due to the overseas military service of most of the young men in the area. The Wieber's hired man, Simmy Smith was no exception and he too, had left for service in World War II.

Joni tightened her grip on the thick leather reins and in the sternest voice she could muster she called out, "Psshhaaww now Prince, psshhaaww now Freddie."

The horses knew enough to straddle the windrow of clover and timothy grass hay that was being mechanically fed up into the flatbed wagon by the ground-driven hay loader attached to the rear of the wagon. Nevertheless, Joni's job of driving the team was hard work. She routinely had to stop or slow the team down to keep pace with her father Raymond, who with a pitchfork, was leveling the hay on the wagon bed as the loader dumped it onto the rear of the wagon. Additionally, when the wagon was half full, she had to stop the team while Raymond spread the second rope sling across the top of the freshly leveled hay before another layer of hay was placed atop of it. The first rope sling was laid evenly across the wooden bed of the wagon when they started the loading process.

The clover hay had been cut earlier that week by Eddie using a ground-driven sickle bar mower pulled by the draught horse team of Prince and Freddie. One of the challenges of mowing clover hay was in dealing with all the bees, bees who were not particularly enamored by having their pollen harvest interrupted. The purple and white clover blossoms were prime habitat for bees. Eddie often had to drape a burlap feedbag across his body as armor in defense of the stinging bees.

At the barn, the hay-filled slings, one at a time, would be attached to the heavy manila barn-rope of the trolley and rail system. With the help of Paint and Lady, the Wieber's second team of horses who were harnessed to the other end of the heavy trolley rope, the sling of hay would be lifted to the very peak of the barn roof. Once fully raised, the load could be directed to either end of the barn by pulling the trolley, to which the sling was attached, along a steel rail that ran the length of the big barn. The sling was released by pulling on a rope tag line that dumped the contents of hay in the proper loft.

Joni's brother Eddie, and later on, sister Janice, usually had the hot, difficult job of "mowing" the loose hay in the hay mow. This meant forking it towards the eaves of the barn and leveling it in place. Making hay was done in the heat of the afternoon when the hay was sufficiently dried to ensure that it would keep without spoiling over the coming year. Tamping down, leveling, and forking the loose, chaffy hay in the humid often 100-degree hay loft was hard work and was often done by children and sometimes even women in the family. Furthermore, work in the hay mow meant wearing a long-sleeved shirt and long pants despite the unbearable heat to protect one's hide from the scratchy stems of the hay. Haying time often meant "all hands on deck," as everyone was counted on to help pitch in with the work.

"*Ja*, that's good, Joni," Raymond pronounced with a sigh. "The wagon's full."

Joni pulled back on the reins with everything she had, saying, "Whoa now, ladies," (recall that Prince and Freddie despite their masculine names, were actually mares).

Raymond jumped off the wagon and a steady stream of sweat dripped off the tip of his nose as he bent over and pulled out the linch pin to unhook the hay loader from the back of the wagon. The green chaff from the dry hay, and black dust, common with clover hay, stuck to the sweat-drenched shirt under Raymond's bib overalls.

Climbing back on the wagon, Raymond sighed, "Pass me that water jug, Joni, and let's get this load of hay home."

Raymond sat down next to Joni on the buckboard of the wagon and leaned back into the hay as he chugged down the remaining contents of the water jug.

"Eddie should be about ready for us by now," he said catching his breath. With a satisfied smile, Raymond handed the empty jug back to Joni.

Joni slapped the reins across Prince and Freddie's rumps and the team instinctively headed back towards the barn. The mid-afternoon sun enhanced the sweet smell of the clover hay as the horses clomped their way across the stubble on the head land of the field. Just a few puffy white clouds dotted the deep blue sky of the late June afternoon. As he lay back in the soft hay, Raymond closed his eyes and let the half-gallon of cool water he had just chugged slowly rejuvenate his energy.

"Tell me the story again about grandpa making hay on the 4th of July, Pa," Joni pleaded.

There was no opportunity for conversation while the hay was being loaded, but the ride back to the barn was a brief respite from the physical labor and it afforded Joni and her father a chance to chat.

"Oh that story, again," Raymond responded. "Well, Joni as you know, the first cutting of hay should always be in the barn by the 4th of July, and Grandpa Wieber was a real stickler for making sure his hay was in the barn before the church picnic on the Fourth of July," he began.

"However, that particular year, spring came late, and all the field work was a couple of weeks behind schedule. When the Fourth of July arrived, the field just north of the house, the last field to harvest, was still not in the barn."

"Now, normally, Grandpa did not work on July 4th, but, the hay was dry in the windrow, ready to be harvested, and the shifting wind earlier that morning made Grandpa fear that rain might be on the way. Grandpa had cut the field three days earlier and had turned it twice so it was fit and ready to harvest. There was only one problem. Grandpa was scheduled to work a shift at the church picnic that afternoon, the exact time the hay would be ready to harvest. Grandpa took his church responsibilities serious, and, it was probably the one and only thing in the whole world that could keep him out of the field when the hay was down in the windrow and ready to harvest."

"Right about lunch time, as usual, your uncle Clarence showed up as he was then courting your aunt, Milberg. After hearing Grandpa's conundrum about the hay needing to be harvested, Clarence saw a great opportunity to impress his future father-in-law. "Mr. Wieber, I can get that hay baled this afternoon while you're working your shift at the church picnic," Clarence proudly offered to Grandpa. "I can even get my friend to help."

"Grandpa eyed Clarence up and down carefully, and, after giving it some thought, he replied, "Well, there are probably only about five loads left out there, so, I guess it'll be all right."

"Great, enjoy yourselves at the picnic Mr. and Mrs. Wieber and we'll take care of the hay," Clarence assured Grandpa. "Milberg and I can go down to the picnic this evening after you guys get back," he added, with a sly wink in Milberg's direction."

Joni turned the team pulling the full load of hay, onto the lane to continue their trip back to the barn, as Raymond resumed his story.

"So, Grandpa hooked up the team to the wagon and then hooked the hay loader to the back of the wagon. He lined the team up on the outside windrow heading north away from the barns. Then, he turned the reins over to Clarence and he quickly headed back to the house to clean up and head into town for the July 4th picnic in Westphalia. By the time the family had loaded up the car and headed north down Tallman Road, Clarence had made it to the end of the field and was already making his way back south down the windrow adjacent to the road. Clarence and I, um I mean Clarence and his friend, waved to Grandpa and the family as they drove by on their way to the parish picnic."

"When they arrived in town, Grandpa found a parking spot along Main Street and the family piled out of the car and headed for the picnic grounds. Grandpa kept looking towards the western sky, hoping that the cloud bank that was forming there would not bring rain, at least for a couple of hours until Clarence could get the harvested hay safely in the barn. Grandma Rosa headed for the fancy booth to view the quilts and afghans that were to be raffled off and Grandpa headed to the beer garden to work his shift, taking a break every half hour or so to scan the darkening sky for signs of rain."

"As luck would have it, the rain appeared to be holding off, and as his shift end was approaching, Grandpa was confident that young Clarence would have had sufficient time to finish the haying. When his shift was finished at 4:00 o'clock, Grandma was waiting for him at the beer garden exit. "We might as well get a bite to eat before we head home, Rosa," he said, adding, "I'm sure Clarence had plenty of time to get the hay up and in the barn." So, Grandpa and Grandma enjoyed a home-style roast beef dinner in the church hall and as they loaded up into the car to head home it began to sprinkle. "Sure was nice of Clarence to take care of the hay for us," Grandma reassured Grandpa. "Yes, he seems to be a fine young man," Grandpa replied."

"When grandpa turned the car down Tallman Road the intensity of the rain increased from a sprinkle to a steady rain. When they climbed the hill just before the farm property line, Grandpa could see the hay windrows still lying in the field. "What, !@#$%^&*," Grandpa sputtered a torrent of German swear words with enough decibels for Grandma Rosa to blush. Soon they could see the team, standing in harness, munching on wet hay, with about half a load of rain-soaked hay on the wagon, parked just across from the neighbor's, Ferdie Knoop's house. Clarence and "his friend" hadn't even completed a full round of the field. "I hope no one was hurt," Grandma said in a worried tone. Grandpa didn't answer. He knew very well what had happened. Whenever he would work the field across from the Knoops house, Ferdie would always do the neighborly thing and wave him in for a glass of cider. The way the team was parked with the half load, the location where the team was stopped, this incident had cider written all over it."

"Grandpa swung the car into Ferdie's driveway and as Grandma waited in the car, he entered the basement through the root cellar doors that led directly to where Ferdie kept his cider barrel. After about one minute, Grandpa emerged upright with Clarence and his "friend" barely able to manage a four-legged crawl out of the cellar. They had taken Ferdie up on his offer for "one quick glass of cider," but, cider has a way of creeping up on you and before you know it, one glass turns into three, which turns into five, and the next thing you know you can't even see straight. Your uncle Clarence had every intention of just having one quick glass and then returning to get the work done. However, unfortunately, the young Clarence and his "friend," were still too inexperienced to know what they were getting themselves into."

"Grandpa loaded Clarence and his friend into the back seat of the car. *"Sturzbesoffen!"* Grandpa muttered to Grandma, indicating that the boys were drunk as a skunk. Clarence commenced mumbling an incoherent form of an apology to Grandpa, as Grandpa drove back to the house. He stopped the car at the woodshed and sat Clarence and his friend under the rain, which now flowed heavily off the eave of the woodshed roof, in an effort to sober them up while he headed out to the field to retrieve the soggy team. The quality of the hay was diminished from being out in the rain, and in the next few days, Grandpa would have to tether it out of the windrow to dry and then rake it once more into a windrow before harvesting."

"Needless to say, your Grandpa was not very happy that evening with his future son-in-law, and his "friend." Poor Uncle Clarence, soaking wet, was still mumbling apologies under the eave of the woodshed roof when Grandpa returned after unhitching, wiping down, stabling, and graining the team. Milberg too, was madder than a wet hen. She had planned to go down to the picnic dance that evening with Clarence, who of course, wasn't in any shape to go anywhere but home to bed. Grandpa had to drive him back home and carry him into his parent's house."

"Daddy, where were you when all this was going on, and who was Clarence's "friend," that partnered with him to put up the hay?" Joni asked quizzically as she stopped the team on the barn hill.

"Well now," ahhhem, ahhhem, Raymond cleared his throat. "That's a story for a different day," Raymond said, recovering and winking at his little daughter. "Let's get these two slings unloaded now before Eddie and Janice run out of work to do up there in the hayloft," he said finishing the conversation with a hearty laugh.

A SENSE OF DIRECTION

"What if Jane sees us up here?" Markie asked with a hint of concern in his voice.

Dennis ignored the question. At nine years of age now, and the oldest in the family, Dennis wasn't about to let his five-year-old sister dictate what he could or couldn't do. Markie, however, already seemed to have a sensibility and awareness about him that belied his young eight years.

"Darn it, Clair's climbing up from the barn floor now," Markie observed, with more than a hint of concern in his voice.

Dennis bit his lip and honed his concentration straight ahead, focusing on the cross formed by the third rough-cut board, nailed perpendicular to the vertical support beam twenty feet ahead of him. Carefully, and deliberately, Dennis placed his left foot in front of his right and stepped along the narrow precarious path the horizontal oaken beam placed before him, inching towards his destination.

Through the thin, worn sole of his leather shoes he could feel the texture of the rough-hewn axe scars on the eight-inch-wide oaken beam, suspended high in the air like a circus high wire. Already twenty-five feet above the main barn floor, the vertical beam ahead and the five, 1x 4 x 18 inch horizontal ladder rungs nailed across the vertical beam, would take him even higher to the upper "hip" or pitch break of the hip-roof barn, thirty-two feet above the main barn floor.

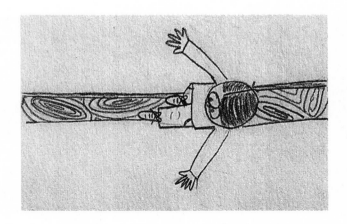

Clair was six years old, and although he considered himself a contemporary of his two older brothers, Dennis and Markie knew they'd get a spanking if Mom found out they had taken Clair out on the barn beams.

Dennis was smart enough not to look down. It was early March and that meant that hay inventory in the barn was approaching the seasonal low level having been fed out to the cattle over the long Michigan winter. To break his concentration on anything other than the cross formed by the third rung step on the vertical beam straight ahead would risk a twenty-five foot fall to his left all the way down to the main barn floor, or, a somewhat better option, an eighteen foot fall to his right down to the north hayloft floor.

"Hey, what're you doing up there?" Clair called as he scaled the round rungs of oak-hewn ladder that lead twenty feet upward from the main barn floor to the cross-loft where Markie was perched.

With only five feet remaining now, Dennis raised his arms, quickly stepped off the last few feet of his oaken beam high wire act, and safely clutched the ladder step nailed to the vertical beam. Exhaling, he turned around and allowed himself a quick glance down to the main barn floor.

"Your turn," Dennis said to his brother Markie.

"*Ja*, sure," Markie replied, quickly enough, he hoped, to disguise the nervous fear that was now settling into the pit of his stomach.

"Why don't you go over to the straw loft side," Dennis suggested," sensing Markie's trepidation.

The straw loft was on the south side of the main barn floor, on the opposite side of the hayloft which was positioned on the north side of the main barn floor. The interior beam above the south straw loft side was the right-isomer of the beam that Dennis had just traversed on the north hayloft side. It offered the same twenty-five foot fall, to the right, down to the main barn floor. However, due to the granary below the straw loft, the straw loft floor was only a six foot fall to the left. Therefore, if you felt yourself losing control on your high-wire beam walk, you could, hopefully, bail out to your left. This would of course leave you to deal with the ridicule of your brothers, but, on the upside, you'd still have your skeletal structure intact. Without responding back, Markie quickly stepped across the loosely laid deck boards of the cross-loft and hefted himself up on the straw loft side beam.

At that very moment the main barn door cracked open and the boys' sister, Jane, with younger brother David in tow, squeezed through the opening that seemed too narrow for even a sparrow to fit. Finally, the new pup, named Patsy by little three-year-old David, squeezed his chubby body through the door. The children's uncle Henry had given the dog to the family and little David had taken an immediate liking to the dog. David and Patsy seemed to be inseparably bonded.

Dennis froze in place, futilely hoping that Janie wouldn't see the boys up on the beams. However, Clair, who was rather large for his age, was caught totally exposed, in full view of Jane, halfway up the ladder leading to the cross loft.

"You boys get down right now!" Jane cried.

"Right now," David echoed his sister's words with an emphasis that caused Dennis to chuckle under his breath.

Sensing the urgency of the situation, Patsy immediately chimed in with some nervous puppy barking.

Markie exhaled, and immediately jumped back off the straw loft beam. Landing safely on the cross loft, he quickly wiped the barn beam dust that adhered to his sweaty palms onto the knee patches of his trousers. Disguising the shakiness in his voice, he blurted out, "We better get down now, Clair."

"Huh?" Clair grunted, looking up with his hands clinging to the round oaken ladder rung.

"Get yourself down, so I can get down the ladder," Markie answered back.

"I'm not even "up" the ladder yet," Clair shrugged.

Markie didn't bother to answer back and started down the ladder to force the issue. By now Janie had advanced to the center of the barn floor and although she couldn't see Dennis, who was perched twenty-five feet above and slightly behind her, he could tell she was crying from a legitimate fear that one her brothers was sure to fall.

Jane seemed to evince a mother's worth of worry over the safety of her four brothers and younger sister Rosie. To Dennis, it seemed that his little sister Jane had an almost saintly countenance and maturity about her. Norman and Mary trusted her completely and Markie and Dennis both knew they'd be in for a spanking if Ma or Pa found out they were out walking the barn beams.

The only way down for Dennis was to retrace his steps all the way back across the hayloft beam and back to the main barn floor ladder that now held his two descending brothers. Holding his index finger up to his mouth, he signaled to Markie not to give away his position atop the beam. Markie nodded a silent affirmative acknowledgement back to Dennis and with Clair right below him, they finished their descent down the ladder, jumping the final five feet, landing in a pile of loose hay on the main barn floor right in front of Jane.

"Don't tell Ma or Pa," Markie said, picking himself up and helping Clair to his feet all in one motion.

"Where's Dennis?" Jane demanded.

Spitting pieces of loose hay from his mouth and raising his pudgy hand upward, Clair started to say, "He's right up…"

"Ooomppph," before Clair could finish speaking, Markie effectively cut off the conversation with a quick kick to the back of Clair's knee which sent him tumbling backward, right back into the pile of loose hay.

In an instant, Dennis saw his opportunity. Markie, Clair, and subsequently Patsy continued to wrestle in the hay pile, successfully occupying Jane's attention. With a considerably faster pace, and just enough concentration to avoid falling, Dennis scampered back across the beam directly above the commotion below, scurried down the main barn floor ladder, and suddenly appeared as if out of nowhere, standing next to the tussling Markie and Clair.

"What are you guys doing?" Dennis said, faking inquisitiveness.

Rolling off of Clair, and with loose hay covering his smiling face, Markie exchanged a brother's glance with Dennis. Satisfied that all was well, Jane turned back towards the barn door.

Just before the kids reached the door, the slender opening between the two sliding doors was abruptly forced open, revealing the silhouette of a rather official looking man holding a clip board. The man, just as surprised at seeing the children as they were at seeing him, stepped back momentarily and the five children and Patsy scampered out the door and into the sunlight. Behind the man, an official looking car with the county seal on the door, was parked on the barn hill.

"Hello kids," the man said in mock friendliness. "What's the name of your little dog?"

"Paaaaats" little David had begun to say, with great pride, before Jane suddenly forced her cupped hand over his mouth. Norman didn't have a license for the dog. And by now the older kids had figured out that this official looking man was none other than the county dog catcher.

"Oh kaayyy now," the man uttered as he flipped through the top couple of pages on his clip board, in an ostensibly professional manner.

"I don't see here where a license has been applied for on this dog," the man said looking up from his clipboard in the general direction of the kids.

The kids anxiously shuffled their feet around and Patsy, unaware that she was the center of discussion, scampered over to the corn crib to scatter a flock of pigeons that were making a meal out of a handful of corn that had been spilled out on the ground.

"Why don't one of you go and catch that dog for me so I can have a closer look at him," the man said flatly.

Dennis, Markie and Clair exchanged glances at each other not sure quite what to do.

Out of nowhere, their saintly little sister Jane, indignantly puffed out her chest and demanded, "*Dummkopf*, go catch him yourself—you're supposed to be the dog catcher."

RACCOON HUNTING

Carefully, Eddie topped off the lantern reservoir with kerosene. "Call for Nick," he said to Joni. "And you probably better get a warmer jacket," he added as he turned the lantern fuel reservoir cap clockwise to tighten it down.

Joni headed right to the cellar for her chore coat. She knew that Nick, the family's farm dog, a collie by sheep-dog cross, would be jumping up and down with excitement as soon as he saw Eddie exit the woodshed with the lantern. It didn't make any sense to "go get him," Joni thought. Nick already knew that a lit lantern on a fall evening meant raccoon hunting.

Joni hustled up the concrete steps from the cellar, exited through the east door and crossed the sidewalk to enter the woodshed just as Eddie lit the lantern.

"Did you tell Mom we're leaving?" Eddie asked.

"*Ja*," Joni replied. "The warm rain this afternoon should bring the racoons out," Joni suggested, drawing upon her youth-limited experience.

"Sure," Eddie replied as the two left the woodshed.

As Joni predicted, Nick met the twosome outside the door, jumping up and down with excitement. The threesome, headed east down the driveway, past the granary, between the toolshed and the large hip-roofed barn, and down the lane towards the oak-plank bridge that crossed the creek known officially as the Morris Drain. Joni and Eddie paused on the bridge momentarily to see if Nick would pick up a trail along the creek bed. Nick trotted over the worn earthen path that led down the west creek bank, nose down, weaving back and forth. Failing to detect the scent he was after, Nick splashed across the creek and repeated the same pattern up the east side bank. Again failing to pick up a trail, Nick took off in a northeasterly direction through the standing corn towards the woods.

Nick, despite his multi-colored lineage, was pretty much solid black in color. He was a silent trailer, meaning he didn't bark, or sound off, while following the scent of his prey but rather waited to bay until he had won the battle and cornered or treed the adversarial raccoon. And, despite his lineage as a sheep-herding dog, which was indeed his vocation, his avocation was raccoon hunting and for a farm dog, he was amazingly good at it.

"How's your neck?" Joni asked with just a hint of sarcasm as she and Eddie continued down the lane towards the woods.

Reaching up to grab his Adam's apple, Eddie responded gingerly, "Oh, it's all right, just a little sore I guess."

That morning before school, Joni and Eddie were headed out to check a raccoon trap that they had set the previous day in a culvert where the Morris Drain crossed their north property line. Joni had gotten a head start on Eddie and in the early morning darkness she was already up to the sunken driveway just west of the big barns when Eddie rounded the woodshed. Seeing the lantern light in Joni's hands, Eddie took off in a sprint to catch up. However, in his haste, he had forgotten about the wash line hanging between the woodshed and the chicken coop. Although only ten, Eddie was already quite a lanky lad, and, unfortunately, too tall to fit beneath his mother's clothes line. Before poor Eddie knew what happened, he was sling-shot backwards by the taut wash line. The force of which upended his legs landing him flat on his back, watching the morning stars mingle with those that were swirling around his head.

Arriving at the edge of the woods, Eddie sat the lantern down on a tree stump and he and Joni parked themselves on a fallen maple log. Thus began the waiting. Now, the two would simply wait for Nick to notify them, by a steady stream of barks that he had treed a raccoon.

"What are you going to do when you get to high school?" Joni asked.

As the wispy shadows from the flickering lantern resounded across his face, Eddie traced imaginary words in the loose earth with a broken length of a stick he had picked up after positioning the lantern. "Why would I think of something like that," Eddie thought to himself.

Before he could come up with a response, Joni continued, "I'm going to play basketball."

Eddie didn't doubt it. Although only in the third grade, Joni was already quite the tomboy in terms of helping out with the chickens and farm work, hunting and trapping, and, in playing sports. It seemed a natural progression that she would likely excel in the single sport available at St. Mary's, High School, basketball. Before Eddie could formulate a response, the cooling, quiet fall air was interrupted with an intense series of barks.

"He's got one!" Eddie said jumping to his feet, adding, "Let's get the gun."

Because of their relatively young age, Florence did not want the kids carrying a gun with them in the dark fall nights while they were out on their raccoon hunts. Both Eddie and Joni had protested, trying to convince their mother that they were perfectly capable of safely handling a firearm.

Raymond, who was much less inclined to worrying, overheard the debate and offered a Solomonesque solution. "How about the kids come back to the house for the gun after they have a racoon treed?," he asked Florence turning his head slightly to sneak in a wink of his eye towards Joni and Eddie.

"*Ach ja,*" Florence sighed, shaking her head while she put the final crease in the pillowcase she was folding.

Eddie and Joni quickly exchanged anxious glances.

"Oh, I suppose so," Florence relented, sensing a futility in continuing the argument.

Eddie and Joni smiled, but suddenly realized the inordinate amount of running back and forth to the woods the agreement entailed. It was a strange feeling. They were elated at being able to use the gun but perplexed at having to return all the way back home to get the gun once they had a raccoon treed in the woods. Sensing the confounded looks on his young children, Raymond could no longer contain his amusement and let out one of his hearty belly laughs, crossing his arms over his midsection as he bent over in laughter.

Joni and Eddie immediately took off on the half-mile foot race back to the cellar to retrieve the .22 caliber rifle. They trusted that Nick would keep the raccoon at bay, but, in the woods anything could happen. They knew they'd better not dilly-dally but rather hurry back with the gun. Despite nearly doubling the amount of strides, Joni managed to keep up with Eddie as they crossed the oak-plank bridge over the Morris Drain. With a fair amount of moonlight illuminating the way, Eddie paused at the bridge and set the lantern down on one of the middle oak planks where they could retrieve it on their way back with the gun.

"You won't beat me now," he shouted at Joni.

Joni bore down hard and leaned into her stride but Eddie's relief from carrying the lantern afforded him the extra advantage he needed. By the time the two reached the large hip roofed barns, Eddie had a seemingly insurmountable lead.

Sensing defeat, Joni hollered out, "Watch out for the washline!"

Eddie immediately started laughing and it was just the edge that the diminutive, but speedy Joni needed.

"I win," she said gasping and heaving for breath as she sprinted past Eddie and smacked her palms against the house door.

"Grab the shells, and I'll get the gun," Eddie countered, in a manner communicating clearly that there'd be no time for Joni to celebrate her cleverly won victory. They had to get back to the task at hand. Nick was dutifully holding a raccoon at bay, impatiently waiting for Eddie to return and seal the deal. Joni grabbed the lantern as the two briskly walked back across the creek bridge.

"Sounds like he's in the southeast corner," Eddie said looking ahead through the darkness toward the origin of the frantic barking.

Unable to restrain their excitement, the two broke stride from their brisk walk and transitioned into a gaited run. They ran along the outside edge of the woods until they reached a point where the barking appeared to be tangentially closest to them. Extending his arm with the lantern in hand, Eddie carefully entered the woods. Running through the woods at night was foolhardy and both Joni and Eddie were well aware of that. Even when walking you'd occasionally get switched upside the head from a thin, leafless branch, too insignificant to see in the darkness but significant enough to bring a burning stinging sensation across your face and in some cases even leave a mark. Worse yet, when following someone, which is often necessitated when you only have one lantern, you can easily get whipsawed by a branch deflected off the lead person.

The cadence and volume of Nick's barking quickened and intensified as the bobbing lantern made its way closer to the tree.

"I see him," Joni said with excitement, catching a glimpse of Nick's agitated dance around an older maple tree up ahead.

"*Ja*," Eddie responded, "I see him too." "That tree is hollow," Eddie calculated. "I hope the 'coon stayed on the outside where we can get a shot at him."

Nick was jumping up against the side of the tree, all the while maintaining the frantic barking. "What have you got here, boy," Eddie said in a reassuring tone to Nick.

"Hold the lantern up higher," Joni said impatiently, hoping to be the first one to sight the treed quarry. After circling the tree twice, Joni finally caught a glimpse of light reflected from the retina of the raccoon's eyes. "There he is," she pointed, "Right in the fork of that main limb, about twenty feet up."

Switching his gaze to where his sister pointed, Eddie replied, "OK, I see 'em now." "Here, hold the lantern so I can get a shot," he added, handing over the lantern to Joni.

Steadying the rifle against a nearby tree, Eddie positioned the sights in the base of the fork in the tree where they had seen the raccoon. Joni stepped behind Eddie, holding the lantern up as high as she could. Patiently, Eddie waited for the tell-tale reflection to reappear.

"Crack!" the .22 fired. Joni waited for the expectant "bump, bump, thud," of the raccoon falling out of the tree. Instead, there was sudden and complete silence. Nick stopped barking for a few seconds, expecting the same outcome.

"Did you miss him?" Joni asked incredulously. Eddie and Joni both practiced shooting the .22 caliber rifle regularly and both were excellent marksmen, able to shoot a catsup bottle cap off of a fence post from fifty yards. It seemed unlikely that Eddie would miss a set shot like the one the raccoon had just offered.

"Here, give me the lantern," Eddie said exchanging the rifle for the light. The two circled the tree again with Eddie holding the lantern at multiple angles trying to throw a little light into the upper reaches of the tree.

"He must be caught up there in the fork where we last saw him," Eddie finally surmised. Today's raccoon hunters have powerful flashlights, upwards of two million candle power, that could pretty much light up the whole side of the woods. However, back in the mid 1940's, all Eddie and Joni had available to them was a kerosene lantern, with the kerosene rationed by the County War Board, no less.

"I'm going to have to climb up there," Eddie relented. "Here, hold the light as best you can," and he handed the lantern back over to Joni.

After what seemed like ten minutes of struggle, Eddie finally reached the forked limb. "Yup, here he is, I didn't think I missed him" Eddie said reassuringly as he reached for the tail of the now dead raccoon to dislodge him from where he was stuck in the fork of the tree. Joni and Nick then heard the previously expected, "bump, bump, thud," as the dead raccoon bounced out of the tree and hit the ground. Nick immediately pounced on the prey while Joni struggled to wrestle it away from him. Finally, Joni won the battle and dumped the raccoon into the burlap feedbag, which served nicely as a poor man's game bag.

Just then a nasty, guttural snarl penetrated the brief moment of silence. Instantaneously, Joni, with the hair standing up on her neck, jumped up dropping the feed bag. Nick broke out into a torrent of hysterical barking, leaping unrestrained at the tree. The commotion on the ground was immediately punctuated by the crashing sound of breaking limbs as the startled Eddie lost his grip plummeting through the lower branches of the old maple tree.

Eddie lay flat on his back on the forest floor exactly as he had done earlier that same morning under the wash line. He again watched as the stars circled his head and mingled with those in the sky. Meanwhile, Nick continued his frantic barking and leaping up the side of the tree, jumping all over

Eddie in the process. Joni, caught up momentarily in the chaos busting loose around her, froze holding the lantern.

"Are you all right?" she finally muttered.

Eddie just groaned.

Finally, Eddie pushed Nick off of him and pulled himself up to a sitting position. Once again, defying serious injury, Eddie stood himself upright, although he was unable to suppress a cuss word, generated from the re-agitation of the bump on the back of his head.

"Did you hear that growling?" Joni asked, her eyes as wide as saucers.

"*Ja*, there must be another 'coon up there," Eddie said now rubbing the back of his head. "Probably up inside the hollow of the tree."

Feeling sorry for her banged up and bruised brother, Joni volunteered to look up into the opening at the base of the hollow tree. She hesitated a moment after sticking the lantern into the tree's cavity, wanting to make sure that the critter behind the nasty snarl wasn't lurking right at the base of the tree. Satisfied, Joni dropped down on her hands and knees and slowly pushed her head through the hole. She had to squint at first; the lantern engulfed the tubular cavity of the hollow tree and flooded it with light. Quickly, she made out the movement of a second raccoon, hissing and prancing around on an interior ledge about fifteen feet up inside the trunk. At the sight of the hissing fangs Joni hastily withdrew her head from the tree hole.

"It's huge!" was all she could muster.

"Let me take a look," Eddie said and groaned from his sore back as he dropped down to see for himself. "Wow! It is huge," Eddie confirmed.

"How are we going to get him out of there," Joni asked. "He looks like he's as big as Nick!" she added.

Eddie pondered the situation. He knew this second raccoon was bigger than any he and Joni had ever encountered before.

Rubbing the bruise on his right hip, he thought for a minute that maybe the two should just head home, satisfied with the one raccoon already in the burlap bag.

Sensing a slight equivocation in Eddie's fortitude, Joni quickly chimed in, "We've got to get 'em, he's huge." "We can't let this one get away."

Eddie groaned again as he shifted his weight to his sore right knee. "Well, we could try shooting up the trunk," Eddie reasoned. "It's probably worth a try."

Eddie loaded a shell into the chamber of the single-shot .22 and confronted the hole at the base of the tree. Dropping down to his knees, he snaked the gun, business end first, into the hollow cavity. It would have to be a blind shot. Eddie was a smart enough boy not to have his head in the hollow with the gun and a snarling raccoon when the gun was fired. With his body outside the hole, he clasped the forestock of the rifle with his left hand, positioning the barrel against the interior wall of the tree where he had last seen the raccoon. He placed his right hand around the stock near the trigger, moving his right thumb through the trigger guard.

"Here goes nothing," he said, and with his right thumb, he engaged the trigger.

"Crack," the rifle shot echoed up the trunk of the hollow maple. Instinctively, Eddie pulled the gun back out through the entrance hole. "Whhuummpphh," the raccoon crashed to the base of the tree. Before the raccoon even hit the ground, it seemed, a growling Nick had reached in through the tree hole, trying to pull the critter out.

After the flurry of excitement subsided, Joni admiringly admitted, "Nice shot."

Eddie shrugged, and with a legitimate look of surprise still on his face, he replied humbly, "Mostly luck, I guess."

While Joni held Nick back, Eddie tried to pull the raccoon through the tree hole. "Wow, this thing is huge!" "I can barely get it out through the hole."

The two admired the catch. It was indeed, by far, the biggest raccoon the two had ever seen. "Let's take it back and show, Pa," Eddie said concluding a very successful hunt.

Back home, Raymond placed the huge boar raccoon on the Fairbanks platform scale he used for weighing grain. Little Janice poked at the carcass with a broken stick, all the while keeping a safe distance from the needle sharp white incisors exposed on the side of the dead raccoon's mouth. Raymond moved the cast iron sliding weight across the steel weigh-bar marked in one-pound increments until the counter weight was balanced.

"Thirty two pounds," Raymond said. Eddie and Joni looked at each other unable to suppress the huge smiles that overwhelmed their faces.

MARKIE

"Hurry up and finish mucking Jake's stall," Dennis urged Markie, adding, "Pete and Mary Louise are coming over this morning with some skates to give us."

Markie picked up the pace, pitching the horse manure with even more fervor on that particularly ordinary cold and dreary Saturday morning in January. Jim, "Pete" Pung, Dennis' neighbor and good friend, was an extremely large boy for his age, and he quickly outgrew his clothes, shoes, and in this case, ice skates. The Thelen's profited handsomely from Pete's rapid growth, procuring many of his hand-me-downs as he was the youngest in the Pung family.

As the boys were finishing up their morning chores, Pete and his sister showed up on the main barn floor.

"Did you bring the skates?" Markie asked, peering at Jim and Mary Louise's feet through the manger access door from his position in the lower level horse stalls.

"Oh, there you are Markie," Mary Louise laughed. Bending over to peer through the floor level opening, she added, "And, yes, we brought the skates."

Just then Dennis entered the main barn floor from the dairy stanchions on the opposite side of the horse stalls.

"Here, try these on," Pete said and tossed his older brown skates over to Dennis. "Markie can wear these," he added with a giggle, holding up an old pair of Mary Louise's white skates. Markie didn't care about having to wear girl skates. He was just anxious to get out on the ice.

The poorly drained northeast corner of the farm was usually partially ponded during the winter months and the kids figured it would be a good location to try out their new, used skates. The sky started to spit out a damp cold snow shower during the twenty-minute walk down the lane and the northeasterly wind began to swirl in gusts when the Thelen and Pung kids plopped down in the snow to lace up their skates. However, being practically raised outdoors, they were oblivious to the cold damp air. The foursome laughed and joked at each other's lack of skating prowess as they sprawled out on the ice upsetting each other in the process. Eventually they began to rediscover their balance and skating aptitude, even managing to get in a few rounds of "crack the whip."

That evening after his Saturday bath, Markie mentioned to his mother that he didn't feel well. Reflexively, Mary cupped her right hand over Markie's forehead. He was burning up.

"I have a sore throat," Markie added, trying to the best of an eight-year-old's ability to sound grown up, and not appear like a whiny child.

In the dim light of the backroom, Mary held her second born child in her arms wrapped inside a towel. A split second of panic flashed through her mind. A mother intrinsically holds a deeply protective maternal instinct, to abate at all cost even the tiniest threat whatsoever against her children. Mary, like the mothers of her generation, knew all too well the potential threat winter ailments posed on children. Even a common cold, which would today be considered a mere nuisance, could potentially have deadly consequences in the 1940's. Common bacterial ailments, easily treated with antibiotics today, were still potentially life threatening back then. Although penicillin was discovered in 1928, it was not purified and readily available to most of the general public until the end of World War II.

By Monday morning, Markie's condition had not improved and he wasn't able to attend school. Norman decided to take Markie into town to see Dr. Cook. The good doctor examined Markie and explained to Norman that the sore throat and fever could be any of a number of common ailments. However, he cautioned that if Markie's symptoms did not improve in a couple of days to bring him back in for another visit. In the meantime, they were to keep him as comfortable as possible and in bed so he could rest and hopefully his body would fight off whatever appeared to be ailing him.

After several days, there was no observable improvement; in fact, the symptoms seemed to have worsened. Norman and Markie returned to see Dr. Cook. This time the doctor's demeanor was more serious. The sore throat had visibly digressed. Dr. Cook feared the worst and suggested that Norman take Markie to see a physician practicing in the town of Wacousta, near Lansing. The Wacousta physician had recorded some success in treating patients with rheumatic fever. Norman was stunned. He and Mary's worst fears were beginning to materialize.

Rheumatic fever is an infectious disease caused by streptococcus bacteria, the same pathogen that causes the common malady known today as strep throat. When not treated with antibiotics, the pathogen can potentially progress from the throat to the heart where it causes damage to the heart muscle, particularly to heart valves. In modern times, the incidence of rheumatic fever is greatly reduced due to timely treatment of strep throat with efficacious antibiotics. Prior to the availability of antibiotics like penicillin, rheumatic fever was most common in five to fifteen year-old children, though it could also develop in younger children and adults.

Norman and Markie returned to the Thelen home in a silent car. Inside the house, Norman steadied himself against the back of a kitchen chair and told Mary of Dr. Cook's recommendation to see the doctor in Wacousta, who specialized in treating rheumatic fever. Carefully he emphasized that this doctor had had some success in pulling patients through the disease.

To Mary, the news was suffocating. The instant of panic which had crept up on Mary that Saturday night in the dim light near the back washroom again rushed over her, smothering it seemed, her very breath. Shaking herself free from the terror filled grip of her own thoughts, Mary exhaled, and in a deliberate but hushed tone, replied, "I'll make the appointment right away."

The family set up a small bed for Markie in the first-floor parlor so Mary could more easily tend to him during the long winter nights. The Wacousta doctor had prescribed bed rest and Mary was resolute in following the recommendations, even to the smallest detail. Norman's sister Dora once again moved in with the family to help with the household chores so Mary could devote more time to caring for Markie.

The children were fond of Dora and looked forward to her visits, particularly the extended visits when she helped Mary after each childbirth. She had been widowed at a young age without children of her own and she bonded affectionately with the Thelen children. She had nicknames for each of the kids and they enjoyed playing little pranks on her to illicit her usual response of *"Du bis ein hunse wicht"* (You are my clown). She was dating a widower from the area who, like Dora, enjoyed teasing the children. When he would arrive at the house to visit Dora, he would playfully humor the children, formally introducing himself by saying, "Hello, I am Henry Ford, what is your name?"

Father Joseph Byrne, a priest at St. Mary Church in Westphalia came out to the farm on a regular basis to bring Holy Communion to Markie who was now unable to leave the house. Dennis and all the children were instructed to kneel in the doorway of the parlor and to pray, very still and quiet, while Father Byrne was in the house. One time while Father was praying with Markie, and the children were in their usual silent repose, baby Rosie who was then two years old, from her kneeling position with the other children, blurted out loud, *"Mama Hanshin, du bis mitch hans worsch"* *Mama Hanshin* was the term of endearment Rosie had for Dora, and, translated, little Rosie had called out loud to Dora, "I'm your little sausage," which was what Dora often called baby Rosie.

The other children bit their lip to keep from laughing out loud, but needless to say, Mary kept a close watch over little Rosie during future visits from Father Byrne.

Winter progressed into spring and Markie's condition saw no improvement. Norman set up a little chair next to Markie's bed from which Dennis could keep his brother company. Dennis noted how when he sat with Markie, the bed would actually shake from Markie's labored breathing. The strep infection had taken hold of Markie's heart.

At the age of eight, most boys already long for some sense of independence, some assurance that they're progressing from a stage requiring a mother's constant care, to a more mature stage of being able to contribute and help like an older boy. Markie was no different. Mary had instructed him to use the chamber pot kept in the parlor for his sake and to call her if he needed it emptied, even if it was in the middle of the night. However, on several occasions, Markie had willed himself out of bed at night to take care of the chore himself. Once, Mary caught him in the act and gently reprimanded him for not following the doctor's orders. Norman bit his lip. He was beginning to sense the terminal nature of the contagion that mercilessly gripped young Markie's body. He could not bring himself to issue even a quiet reprimand to his ailing son.

Early that summer Norman hired a local carpenter, Louie Droste, to screen in the front porch so Markie's bed could be carried outdoors to catch the shaded breeze facilitated by the large silver maples on the south side of the house. Throughout their young lives, the boys had always spent most of their waking hours outdoors in the summer months and the ability to move the little bed out to the porch, if even for just a few hours a day, had an immediate positive effect on Markie's attitude. However, the improvement in attitude was tempered by the relentless progression of the rheumatic fever on Markie's weakening body. During the warm summer evenings, Dennis noticed how the bed shook even worse as Markie's breathing became increasingly more labored.

By August, Markie could no longer sit up. Throughout the heat of the warmest month of summer, Dennis would sit by Markie's bedside, feeling his heavy breathing and watching the bed tremble with each labored breath.

One never prepares sufficiently to withstand the loss of a child. At 4:00 AM on Saturday morning, August 21, 1943, two weeks shy of his ninth birthday, Markie's young life slipped away. Norman and Mary were at Markie's side at the time of his death and when he had passed, Norman went upstairs to awaken Dennis. He brought Dennis into the parlor and sat him down on the chair which Dennis had used over the past six months, solicitously tending to his brother.

Dennis' eyes squinted in an effort to adjust to the dim light of the parlor's single incandescent bulb, which cast a somber shadow on the south wall as Norman knelt down beside the chair.

"Markie died," Norman told his ten-year-old, eldest son.

Dennis looked upon his brother. He noticed right away that Markie and the bed no longer shook. There were no more labored breaths, and somehow Markie looked relieved and peaceful. Dennis didn't know what to say or do. Markie was gone.

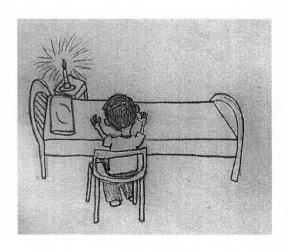

The next morning Clair and Jane rose as usual and went into the kitchen for breakfast. Their mom wasn't in the kitchen so they went to the parlor where she could usually be found since Markie had taken ill. Mary was there, taking Markie's bed apart.

"Where is Markie?" Jane asked. Sitting down, Mary informed Jane and Clair that Markie had died earlier that morning.

That afternoon, Herm Geller, the local undertaker, brought folding chairs over to the house for the wake. Markie's casket was set up in the parlor and folding chairs filled the parlor, dining room, and living room area. Chairs were also set up out on the front porch. During the wakes, a rosary was prayed for Markie, and Dennis remembers that people were even standing out on the lawn as the available seating in the house filled up.

Uncle Raymie, Mary's youngest brother, brought several of the nuns who had taught Markie in school, out from town to attend one of the wakes. Before taking the nuns back to St. Mary's, he asked Dennis, Clair and Jane to ride along. On the way home he stopped in Westphalia and bought the kids an ice cream cone.

The last wake was held at the house on Tuesday morning, just prior to taking Markie into Westphalia for his funeral Mass and burial at St. Mary's Cemetery.

***

"Dennis, Grandpa *Dika* Joe is going fishing today and he wants to take you along," Mary said that late August morning when Dennis was finishing up his oatmeal.

Dennis swallowed hard and looked up at his mother.

Mary wiped her hands on her apron, "He'll be here to pick you up after morning chores," she added, turning around to dab an accumulation of oatmeal off of little Rosie's cheeks.

Grandpa *Dika* Joe liked to fish and he enjoyed taking one or more of his grandchildren along with him, as well as his regular fishing partner, his brother, George. Dennis enjoyed the fishing and the time with his Grandpa, and, Grandpa *Dika* Joe seemed to enjoy Dennis' company too.

The usual destination was the aptly named Fish Creek, just north of Hubbardston. *Dika* Joe knew a farmer whose land bordered the creek. Grandpa would pull the car into a gated pasture just north of the bridge on Hubbardston Road. From there, the fishermen would hike across the pasture, all the while keeping a wary eye on the resident bull, and set up for the day at Grandpa's favorite fishing hole.

At about eight o'clock that morning Dennis came in from his morning chores and washed his hands and face in the backroom sink.

"I'll call Grandpa and let him know you're ready to go," Mary said, turning her attention away from the blueberries she was cleaning in a large tub on the kitchen counter.

As any mother would, Mary continually had the best interest of her children at heart, and she was as anxious for Dennis to get away from things for a day as Dennis himself was. Tough times seem to have a way of pulling families closer together. Grandpa *Dika* Joe and Grandma Theresa who had always been close to their daughter Mary, also had the family's interest at heart, particularly that summer as the family grieved the loss of their beloved Markie.

The old Ford bumbled along the bumpy graveled roads reaching peak speeds of about thirty-five miles per hour. Dennis, sat patiently in the back seat listening to *Dika* Joe and George talk shop. Finally, after about a thirty-minute trip, they pulled into the pasture drive and parked alongside the gate. They didn't dare drive into the pasture. Cattle have an uncontrollable impulse to lick and slobber over any type of machinery they come into contact with and Grandpa wasn't about to subject the Ford to the slobbering tongues of his friend's Holsteins. So, they grabbed their gear, a jug of Grandpa's cider, a few sandwiches that Grandma Theresa had packed, and headed out on foot for the fishing hole.

Back then, fishing poles were not very common in the rural areas. Rather, a fishing line, quite heavy and coarse compared to today's modern braided or monofilament lines, was used without benefit of a pole. A few short pieces of line, called leaders, were attached to this mainline. A cork, used as a bobber, was attached to the top of each leader and a common fish hook, usually baited with an earthworm, was tied to the bottom of the leader, along with a lead weight "sinker." The fishing depth was controlled by how far up the leader the bobber was tied relative to the position where the sinker was tied.

Soon the happy threesome of fishermen were settled down at the fishing hole with three lines in the water. Grandpa *Dika* Joe, assumed his usual spot, sitting on the creek bank with his back resting comfortably against the trunk of a large shade tree and the cider jug strategically placed an arm's length away.

"Dennis, did I ever tell you the story of when ol' George here tried using live frogs for bait?" Grandpa *Dika* Joe asked.

Before Dennis could answer affirmatively, *Dika* Joe began, "Well, you know George isn't much of a fisherman to begin with," *Dika* Joe said as he cracked a wry smile at George. Dennis enjoyed the brotherly banter between his Grandpa and George. He swatted away a pasture fly buzzing harmlessly around his forehead as *Dika* Joe continued with the story. "Well, George had read somewhere in the newspaper that frogs were the bait to use if you really wanted to catch a lot of fish. So, George here shows up at our house one morning with a small bucket full of live frogs he managed to catch down at his pond, and asks me if I want to go fishing. Well, of course I did, so we came right out here to this very same spot. We each tied three leaders to our lines, mine baited with worms, and ol' George's baited with a single frog on each leader."

"After about an hour, I had already caught a half dozen keepers. So, I wandered over to where George was fishing and was surprised to see that he hadn't caught anything yet. "What's going on George?" I asked, "Why aren't you catching any fish with that fancy new bait of yours?" "George just shrugged his shoulders and didn't answer. So, I went back to my spot and later that afternoon caught another half dozen fish."

"Well, by now, it was time to head home so I went back over to where George was fishing. "Time to go now," I said, adding. "Did you catch any yet?" "No," he replied. "Well, pull your line in its time to go," I repeated. George pulled his line in and as the first bobber came into site, I could see that it had a frog sitting comfortably on top of it. Soon, the second bobber appeared and it too had a little frog sitting on top of it. Finally, the last bobber appeared, and, of course, it had a frog sitting on top of it, too."

Dika Joe roared with laughter at the conclusion of his story. George, who had endured the joke numerous times before, simply ignored his brother. At that moment, Dennis' bobber jiggled and quickly submerged beneath the water.

"Here let me help you with that," *Dika* Joe said, and with his arm around Dennis, the two pulled in a keeper from the cool, life-sustaining water of the little country stream.

VE DAY

"Don't forget your jacket, and make sure that Janice wears hers," Florence called out to Joni as she rushed out the door. It was Tuesday, May 8, 1945. Being a Tuesday, it was the Wieber's turn to drive the neighborhood school carpool and with time running short, Raymond had already backed the car out of the woodshed garage. Eddie and Janice were seated inside waiting along with their Dad.

"If you wouldn't spend so much of your chore time playing with your chickens you'd have a lot more time to get ready for school, Joni," Raymond half-heartedly admonished his tardy daughter.

Despite it being the start of the very busy planting season, there was an unusual lightness, and an air of great expectation that permeated the countryside. It had everything to do with a war weary nation beginning to see a great light at the end of a long dark tunnel. Joni jumped in the rear seat with Janice, and Raymond headed the car over to the Knoop Farm across the road for his first pickup of the morning run into schoool. Raymond enjoyed taking the kids into school, and, in later years when the school district had switched over to providing bussing for rural families, Raymond became one of the areas early school bus drivers after retiring from faming.

Throughout the spring of 1945, the news from the European front was overwhelmingly positive. In early March, the Allies, with the US contingent led by General Omar Bradley, crossed the Rhine River and quickly overran West Germany. In late

April, the Allied troops who had attacked from the west, and the Russian Armies, attacking from the east, joined forces to secure the capture of Germany proper. Then, on April 30th, while the battle of Berlin raged above him, Adolf Hitler, hiding in the confines of his security bunker with no viable escape in site, committed suicide, effectively putting an end to the Nazi Party.

At 2:41 A.M., May 7, at the Allied Expeditionary Force Supreme Headquarter's offices in Reims, France, representatives from the victorious Allied nations met with German officials to sign the official surrender documents. It was agreed by leaders in the United States, Soviet Union and United Kingdom, to delay the release of the news of the historic signing for 24 hours and announce it simultaneously on May 8th.

Raymond pulled the car up to St. Mary's School on Westphalia Street, and like a water balloon bursting at the seams, the Platte, Trierweiler, Pohl, Knoop, and Wieber children all spilled out of the car.

"Let's go see the goldfish," Duane Platte suggested, adding, "We've got time before the first bell.

It felt good to be upright and walking again after the cramped ride into town. Even though the entire carpool trip was only about five miles, riding three deep in a 1936, Ford was still a claustrophobic experience. Joni was glad to stretch her legs and along with the other kids, she ran behind the school to where the old school outhouses had once stood before the indoor bathroom was constructed. Father Gutha had the old concrete latrine pits cleaned out and left in place after the razing of the two old outhouse buildings, which previously stood directly over the pits. Now that spring had arrived, the pit was filled with water and goldfish were added, a poor man's forerunner to modern Koi fish ponds. Father Gutha was truly a man ahead of his time.

Joni reached into her lunch pail and fumbled for her peanut butter sandwich. Carefully she trimmed back the top crust from both slices of bread and dropped the pieces into the water. Immediately, a swarm of the bright orange fish coalesced around the floating bits of bread and within a manner of seconds, the bread and the goldfish had dispersed and vanished.

In time the bell sounded and the children, much like the goldfish, quickly disbanded, heading off to their respective classrooms. Joni, as usual, made her way to Sister Marguerite's fourth grade class. The school day began quite routinely, when abruptly word of the historic treaty signing reached the school. Even at the young age of nine, Joni and her classmates knew the historical significance of VE Day. For the past few years the war had permeated their home life, their prayer life, the discussions at school, even what their parents could and couldn't buy at the store.

In addition to bringing an end to the war on the European Front, the victory brought a tremendous surge in momentum to troops still fighting in the Pacific. So much so that the renewed energy and hope had even trickled down to American servicemen held prisoner in Japan. Historical accounts of American Pacific-based POWs recounted how word of the Allied victory in the European Theatre had provided hope for their eventual liberation, helping them to hang on and survive the extremely horrid prison camp conditions and cruel treatment from their captors.

As word of the victory in Europe spread from classroom to classroom at St. Mary's school, an excited buzz filled the hallways. At first the good Sisters weren't quite sure how to react to the overwhelmingly good news that was the answer to so many of their prayers. After some initial confusion on what to do next, the nuns took the school children over to church, where many in the small community were beginning to gather. Joni remembered seeing her parents there who had come out from the farm after hearing the news on the radio. The simple fact that her father, Raymond, would be in church on a Tuesday morning during the busy planting season really brought home the significance of the moment. The image of her parents prayerfully giving thanks for this important milestone marking the beginning of the end of the Great War stuck with Joni throughout her lifetime.

BITTERSWEET

Over at the Thelen farm, it seemed, things began happening fast again in 1945. Norman and Mary started the year by having their seventh child, a boy, Tommy, in January and ended the year having their eighth, a girl, Virginia, in December. On a global scale, the Allies continued mopping up from village to village in Western Europe following VE Day, and during the summer of 1945, were, with only minimal resistance, conducting reconnaissance flights over mainland Japan. Nationally, the mood was cautiously optimistic that Japan might soon surrender putting an end to the terrible war. Locally the emerging optimism was very real but somewhat tempered, and not universally embraced, as the heavy war casualties suffered in the previous few years, particularly in the defining moments of 1944, left a dark ribbon of grief still hanging over many families. Nevertheless, the increasingly positive news reports were generating an eager hope that the horrible war would soon be over.

"Sorry but you won't be able to drive through." "The street is closed off for the marching band to get through," the man apologized to Norman through the lowered car window. Dennis peered out the side window from his position in the back seat of the car. Outside, the townspeople were gathering for a planned celebration to commemorate VE Day, which had just occurred the previous week. Unfortunately, the mood inside the car was one of grief and not of celebration. The family was returning from a very sad wake. Looking away from the window, Dennis fumbled with the rosary in his trouser pocket and thought again about his fishing excursions with Grandpa *Dika* Joe.

A few days following the announcement of VE day, Mary and Norman, and the children, were jolted by the news of a tragic car accident. Mary's parents, *Dika* Joe and Theresa, were on their way to a wedding reception in nearby Fowler, Michigan, when a heavy oil truck with failed brakes ran through the town's only stoplight striking Grandpa *Dika* Joe's car broadside.

Norman and Mary were having supper with their family when the telephone rang the requisite number of times to signal that the call was for them. Mary answered the phone, but upon the news, was overcome with grief, dropped the receiver, and slumped into her chair. Norman picked up the dangling ear piece to continue the call while the children tended to their grief-stricken mother.

Grandma Theresa was thrown from the vehicle but *Dika* Joe, along with Mary's youngest brother, Raymie, and his then girlfriend, and eventual wife, Joan Trierweiler, had been trapped in the wreckage. The force from the collision had rammed the car through a utility pole and rescuers had to wait until the live electric line draped across the car could safely be removed before accessing the wrecked car's three remaining occupants. *Dika* Joe, it appeared, had died upon impact and Grandma Theresa died several minutes after, where passers-by had propped her up against the red-brick bank building at the four corners of the town's main intersection. Fortunately, young Raymie survived the crash with non-severe injuries and Joan survived after a several months long, hospitalized convalescence.

The next day the State Journal newspaper reported: "*...the driver of the oil truck is being held, pending an investigation of the accident being conducted by the Clinton County Sheriff's Department and Coroner Oliver Smith of Ovid. Smith said he* *would not decide on conducting an inquest until investigation of the accident had been completed."*

***

"Run the heifer with the blaze face over to Pung's this morning," Norman told Dennis after the two had loaded the Ford car with three, two hundred pound bags of wheat. Norman had removed the back seat earlier that morning to accommodate the large load which was headed into town to be sold at the Westphalia Mill. The family car served double duty as the primary means of transportation and also to haul grain into and supplies back from town. New farm equipment and automobiles were still not readily available, although the European phase of the Great War had just ended.

"You better take Clair and David with you," Norman added, slamming the back door shut. Dennis bit his lower lip. He knew all too well that he would indeed need his brothers' help. The heifer he was referring to, ol' Blaze, was a handful to handle on a normal day. However, today she was in estrus, or in heat, which was the more common way the condition was referred to on the farm, and needed to be herded down the road to rendezvous with the neighbor's bull.

Joe Pung owned a fetchingly handsome Milking Shorthorn bull that he made available to neighbors who were willing to run a cow or heifer over for servicing. Since the two farms were only a half-mile apart, Norman made good use of Joe's bovine stud service, relying on Dennis, Clair and David to herd the physiologically amorous female partner up and down the road. It generally wasn't too difficult to get the heifer or cow down the road to the bull. They usually would wander back and forth between the roadside fences, bellowing out hormonally charged "mmmooos" along the way, but, they generally moved steadily in an eastward direction towards the bull. Once there, the boys would introduce the cow or heifer to the bull and then run off and play with Pete for the hour or so it took for the bovine pair to get romantically acquainted. For obvious reasons, the hard part of the whole operation was getting the forlorn cow or heifer headed down the road back home.

When Norman returned from town that afternoon the boys, after much effort, had just turned a happy and satisfied Blaze back into the cattle lot.

"I wonder if Pa was able to get the galvanized pipe?" David asked.

Norman and Mary had planned on building a new bathroom, with indoor plumbing, on the east side of the house after the Great Depression had ended and were about set to do so when the Great War broke out. The rationing of most building supplies effectively put the indoor bathroom building project on hold.

Fortunately, Norman had installed an electric water pump in a sump on the northeast corner of the house before the war rationing began. The pump transported water from the well, located beneath the windmill, to the sink in the backroom of the house. This setup replaced the hand-pump in the backroom sink that used to pump the roof-collected rainwater from the underground cistern, used for nondrinking purposes. Now, they had clean well water available at the turn of a faucet and no longer used the cistern water. Dennis, liked the arrangement as he no longer had to carry buckets of well water in from the outdoor well for drinking or cooking. But, indoor bathroom facilities were put on hold and would have to wait until after the war.

Shortly after VE day, May 8, 1945, Norman was able to procure the necessary County Board approvals to begin work on the indoor bathroom. The building project was again progressing. Norman and the boys had hacked and dug away at the hard packed clay soil that surrounded the foundation of the house with shovels and a pick ax. Norman's brother-in-law, Oscar Schafer came to help pour the footings for the walls of the new addition. Each step in the construction process took another foray into the wheat granary and subsequent trip into town to fund the next purchase of building or plumbing supplies. The bathtub, which required a separate permit from the County War Rationing Board, was purchased just before the construction began and was now stowed away in the machine shed, awaiting its turn in the construction process. If Norman was able to procure the galvanized drainage pipe, the final plumbing phase of the project could proceed.

"Pa stopped the car at the foundation hole," Dennis noted out loud.

"Must be he got the pipe," David said as the three boys hurried over to the ten by ten foot hole on the side of the house, beside which Norman had just parked the car.

Dennis and Clair began pulling the two-inch diameter pipe out of the back of the car as Norman inspected the recently poured footings and sidewalls.

"You boys can go ahead and backfill the foundation now," Norman observed, adding, "I'll call Uncle Arnold to come out and start plumbing the drains tomorrow." Uncle Arnold Wieland had married Norman's older sister Matilda and he dabbled in the relatively new but rapidly expanding trade of household plumbing.

"I'll get the shovels," David volunteered, and sped off to the machine shed to retrieve them.

At twelve, nine, and six years of age, Dennis, Clair, and David were already a tremendous help for Norman. Much the same way, Jane, now eight years old was already a huge help to Mary, particularly in helping with Rosie, age four, and the new baby Tommy. Dennis didn't think about child labor or about what he might be missing while he shoveled the heavy soil against the new foundation. Daily work, hard work, was a simple fact of life. It was as much a part of a typical day as breathing.

Work wasn't viewed as hardship or something to be tolerated. It was simply a necessary part of living. And the pace was such that, enjoyment, fun, and even contentment were found in the work associated with everyday tasks such as caring for livestock, planting, tending, and harvesting crops. In addition to the constant thread of twice daily chores, there was also a seasonal aspect to farm work. The cyclical characteristic of the farm work was determined by the natural rhythms of time. The early spring was lambing season. The ewes would lamb on warm straw beds in the barn during the transitional month of March, timed so that the fresh abundant pastures of May would be available when the young lambs were about ready to be weaned and would most efficiently use the available pulse in pasture grasses.

Following lambing, the spring manure hauling would begin whereby the straw manure packs that had accumulated over the winter, were hand-pitched into the manure spreader and hauled out to the fields as a fertilizer source for the soon-to-be-planted crops. When the barns were cleaned out, the spring planting work would commence, beginning with oats which were planted as soon as the winter soil moisture had subsided to the point where the earth was tillable. The oats were generally planted as a nurse crop along with perennial clover which would eventually take over the stand.

Sugar beet planting followed the oats. Next in line was the corn planting. After planting season, which was usually complete by the first week of June, the labor switched to first-cut haying. Cultivating the row crops for weed control was next. Wheat was generally ready for threshing about mid-July followed immediately by oat threshing and a second cutting of hay.

The dog days of August would bring a brief respite from the field work giving time to mend fences or perhaps work on a building project. During September, clover seed harvest would begin followed by planting the next year's winter wheat crop. After the wheat was planted, the corn and sugar beet row crops were ready for harvest which was usually completed by the end of November. Winter months were busied with repair projects and by cutting firewood for heating and cooking.

The pace of work would ebb and flow with the season, but most every job, no matter how physically demanding, had opportunities for gaining contentment intrinsic to the task. The long hours in the fields provided a front row seat from which to observe the Divine touch of nature. Working with the farm animals was a daily touchstone with the natural cycles of life, death, and rebirth.

The three boys worked efficiently and rapidly backfilled the foundation on the outside walls of the new bathroom building project. Next, they leveled the soil on the inside of the walls to form the floor for the crawlspace in which Uncle Arnold would fit pipe for the new tub, toilet, and sink. Leonard Smith and Freddie Feldpausch, local carpenters, were hired to frame and tie the new bathroom addition to the existing house. And, by the end of the summer, the simple addition of an indoor flush toilet and a plumbed bathtub revolutionized daily life in the Thelen household and in many similar households across the rural U.S.

VJ DAY

It was unseasonably cool on August 14, 1945 in mid-Michigan with the daily high reaching only 68 degrees. It was the beginning of the lull period sometimes referred to as the "dog days" of August, when the calendar provides a brief respite from dawn to dusk field work. Generally, by this time, the spring planted crops of corn and sugar beets were laid by, meaning all the cultivating, fertilizing, and weed control efforts were completed and it was up to Mother Nature to do the rest of the work in maturing the crop.

Raymond Wieber had completed harvest of the winter wheat and spring-planted crop of oats, and the spring-accumulated barn manure had been applied to these fields following harvest of the residual wheat and oat straw. The dog days of August provided Raymond and other farmers a much needed ten-day breather from long workdays, with the exception of course of morning and evening chores. Other than the cool weather on this particular mid-Michigan mid-August day, something else remarkable, though much anticipated, was about to emerge from the current chaos on the world stage.

"How would you kids like to go to a movie today?" Florence asked at the post-morning chores breakfast table.

In unison, Eddie, Joni, and Janice all responded with an enthusiastic and affirmative, "Yes!"

Television sets were very rare in the rural Westphalia community until after the war. Movies were still the only real option for moving picture entertainment and were considered a real treat. The three kids were thrilled.

"The Song of Bernadette is playing in Portland," Florence continued. "We'll plan to leave right after supper and catch the 7:00 pm showing."

The movie which was originally released in 1943, featured Jennifer Jones in the lead role for which she won the best lead actress Oscar. Unlike today, when movies typically are released on video within months after their cinematic release, movies back then often stayed in theaters for years after their release, showing first in the large coastal cities, and eventually making their way across the country to the Midwest's smaller towns.

As the children chattered excitedly about the Bernadette movie, Raymond slipped away from the breakfast table to tune in the family radio hoping to catch the latest emerging news from Japan.

The previous week, the world was stunned by the complete obliteration of Hiroshima on August 6th, and Nagasaki on August 9th. Until that time, "atomic bomb" was not even in the world's vocabulary. Now, in a matter of a week, it dominated discussions around the globe. Never before in the history of mankind, had such utter and complete destruction been wrought by a single weapon. The earthly devastation and colossal loss of life brought to bear by these two singular events shocked humanity in all corners of the world. Viewed through the analytical lens of history, the decision to deploy nuclear technology appears to have hastened the end of the war in the Pacific Rim, and as such, may have actually saved lives in the long run. Nonetheless, at the time, the horrific desolation wrought by the bombs on the people of Hiroshima and Nagasaki affirmed the fear and ribbon of darkness that had gripped the heart and soul of the world since the onset of the Great War.

Raymond fidgeted with the radio dial and through the static-laden air, he heard the long awaited broadcast announcing that Japan had finally surrendered, unconditionally, to the Allies effectively ending World War II. Since then, both August 14, and August 15, have been known as "Victory over Japan Day," or simply "V-J Day." The term has also been used to commemorate September 2, 1945, when Japan's formal surrender took place aboard the U.S.S. Missouri, anchored in Tokyo Bay.

That afternoon, as Raymond drove the family car into Portland, heading for the theater, crowds of people were already gathering at the corner of Bridge and Kent Streets, celebrating the War's end. Similarly, all across the U.S. extemporaneous celebrations erupted everywhere. The Detroit News headline read, "US Fleet Radios: JAPS QUIT." The Chicago Herald headline read, "Victory! Japan Surrenders." In New York City's Times Square, photographer Alfred Eisenstaedt, on that same afternoon of August 14, 1945, snapped one of the most famous photos ever taken, "The Kiss," of a sailor embracing a nurse in a spontaneous kiss that came to symbolize the euphoric atmosphere across the nation.

By the time the Wieber family exited the movie theater, the crowd in Portland had spilled over into the streets and a large bonfire was lit at the Bridge Street and Kent Street intersection. Joni watched through the car windows as jubilant people danced around the fire.

"I think we'll drive through Westphalia on the way home and see what's going on there," Raymond said as he turned the Ford left onto Divine Highway.

In the little village of Westphalia, an impromptu crowd had constructed a bonfire at the local assembling area on the northeast corner of the main intersection between the old grocery store-hardware and the telephone office. With their noses against the window glass, the three Wieber kids watched the celebration from the slowly passing car.

The Great War was finally over.

THANKSGIVING

The victorious summer of 1945 eventually gave way to fall and the turn of the season pulled the farm families back into the fields for harvest.

"Why don't you and Clair hook the grain wagons up this morning," Norman told Dennis as he propped up the last of the three cleaned and sanitized stainless steel milk buckets upside down onto the milk house drying shelf.

For a brief period in early October, the farm was enveloped in hues of orange and yellow, centered in a brilliant panorama, with the farm's colorful woods directly to the north, and, to the south, the Gutha farm's equally colorful woods. Dennis took in the vivid color as he and his father exited the milk house and descended down the barn hill and around towards the cow lot corner post.

The drying brown leaves from the large burr oak that stood stately outside the southwest corner of the farmstead rustled overhead as Norman and Dennis climbed over the wooden plank gate leading into the cow lot. In the distance, Dennis could make out the distinctive honking from a low-flying flock of Canadian Geese, just visible in the blue air on the northern horizon. The unmistakable bellwether sound of fall drew the father and son's attention to the sky. For a moment they paused, watching and listening as the honking din of the approaching flock grew louder and louder reaching an almost deafening crescendo as the flock passed over the angle formed where the two large hip-roofed barns converged, directly overhead from where the father and son now stood at attention. The message from the geese was clear; the growing season was over. It was time to bring the corn in from the fields.

Corn harvest was fundamentally different in the mid 1940's. Modern day corn is husked and shelled in place, right in the field, by huge machines called combines which strip the ear from the rest of the corn plant, whisk the husk from the ear, and glean the kernels of corn grain off of the cob. Conversely, Norman and the farmers of his generation, used a machine called a corn binder to cut the stalks and tie them in bundles of roughly twenty-five plants each, called shocks. The shocks were often left in the field until the grain dried down sufficiently to avoid spoilage during storage.

Once sufficiently field dried, the shocks were loaded onto wagons and brought up to the farmstead. At the farm, the corn plants were fed into a machine called a corn husker, which separated the ears of corn from the rest of the plant, called the fodder, or stover. The ears were then stored in open air corn cribs and the fodder was stored in the barn and fed to livestock as a winter forage. As grain was needed throughout the year, ears were dispensed from the crib and either fed as whole ear corn, or, if desired, the ears were shelled to remove the corn grain kernels from the cob.

Additionally, some farmers would feed corn silage. Silage is the fermented end product of the whole-plant of corn, basically the fodder plus the ears, all chopped up together. Today, most corn silage is stored in huge piles on concrete slabs, known as bunker silos. In Norman and Dennis' day, most silage was stored in upright silos. Similar to corn harvested for grain, Norman would first cut the corn with the corn binder and tie it into shocks. Corn harvested for silage would be cut several weeks earlier than corn harvested for grain to ensure sufficient moisture to promote the ensiling process. The shocks would then be transported to the farmstead right after binding and deposited next to the silo. At the silo, the shocks would be fed into a machine appropriately called a silo filler, which would chop the corn plants into pieces a couple of inches in length and blow the chopped material up over the top and into the silo. In the upright silo, the weight of the accumulating plant material would squeeze out the oxygen facilitating a yeast-based, anaerobic fermentation, analogous to the sauerkraut produced in Mary's basement. The end product, silage, would then be preserved and ready to feed out over the course of the coming year.

Loading the dried shocks of corn onto the wagons was hard work. But, fall in Michigan can be one of the best places, weather-wise, to be on the planet. Deep blue October sky formed the backdrop as the hauling crew moved the corn shocks up to the farmstead. About half of the harvest was deposited outside the hog house where it would be run through the corn husker and stored in the in-barn corn crib. Extra ear corn was also stored in the loft on the south side of the hog house above the hog pens. The other half of the corn shock harvest was deposited outside the corn crib, which was a long, narrow, stand-alone structure, about six feet wide, twenty feet long, and twelve feet high that stood in the center of the farmstead between the house and main hip roof barn. After being husked and loaded into the crib, this corn was subsequently fed to the dairy herd. The fodder, which was the rest of the plant remaining after the ear corn had been removed, was carried to the big barn where it was stockpiled and throughout the winter mixed into cattle rations with hay and grain.

Fall also meant Halloween, and, in Catholic communities, All Souls' Day, which falls on November 1st. On All Souls' Day, Mary would take the children to Mass to pray for the repose of the souls of all those recently deceased. Nowadays known as All Saints Day, it was believed that indulgences could be gained for the poor souls in purgatory by saying sets of prayers on All Souls' Day. One of the stipulations was that after praying one set of prayers comprised of six Our Fathers;

six Hail Marys; and six Glory Be's, you had to leave the Church and then return to pray yet another set for each individual deceased soul. Jane once remarked that as a child, every time the family finished a set of indulgence prayers and walked out of the church, she would say an extra prayer that this would be the last one and that they could finally go home. But, much to the chagrin of the children, invariably, Mary would march the family back in again to offer up prayers for yet another recently deceased individual from the local community.

The busy harvest of the farm fields and garden would continue through November and the closeness to the land kept the family in a seasonal resonance with the earth. Generally, by the time Thanksgiving rolled around, the crops would all be safely stored in the corn cribs, granaries, and barns on the farm. The celebration was a heartfelt recognition of gratitude for the recently completed harvest. Thanksgiving, like other holidays for the Thelens, was usually shared with the Armbrustmachers. When the families celebrated at the Thelen's, Thanksgiving Dinner would be served in the dining room, using the good dishes, and the parlor doors were opened up to accommodate the two large families. Norman would butcher several chickens and Mary would keep one whole for stuffing. Additionally, either mashed or riced potatoes would be served. Mary would make a delicious salad with lettuce, once-a-year-rare pineapple chunks and marshmallows. Thanksgiving also meant fresh cranberry and pumpkin pie—all made from scratch.

At the Armbrustmacher's music was a big part of every celebration. Pauline's husband Clem played the fiddle, Pauline played the banjo. Their two eldest children Jim and Mary Ann played piano. Everyone would sing. Clem and Pauline also owned the first television set in the extended family, purchased from Huggett's Hardware, the local John Deere dealer in nearby Fowler. The screen was small and round and produced a snowy image. Nonetheless, the novelty of television was compelling and the first few months Clem and Pauline owned the television, they would invite Norman, Mary and their family over as often as twice a week. Boxing matches and cowboy westerns were the usual shows to watch.

CHRISTMAS

"The thermometer read only six degrees, this morning," Raymond said referring to the thermometer mounted on the side of the woodshed, read by lantern light while Raymond replenished the firewood in the wee hours of the morning.

It was early Saturday, December 22, 1945 as Joni sleepily spooned the last bit of oatmeal from the bottom of her ceramic breakfast bowl. Instinctively she looked out the east window, right next to the kitchen table. Frost obscured her view of the woodshed, sending as definitive a message as Raymond's temperature pronouncement that it was cold outside. Joni thought how docile and basically immobile the cold-blooded chickens would be in a few minutes when she would head out into the cold to feed them. She also thought about what a hassle it was going to be to have to chip the ice out of their waterers.

"Do you kids remember what you and Pa are doing today?" Florence asked teasingly.

Joni labored to pull her still sleepy brain away from chickens in an effort to focus on her mother's question. Before she could clear her thoughts away from the last chicken, her little sister Janice shouted out, "Christmas tree!"

Immediately Joni began to perk up. After chores, she, Janice and Eddie would be riding into town with Raymond to buy a Christmas tree. The tree would be put up in the parlor and adorned with fancy ornaments. And, providing extra excitement this year, the tree was going to be lit up with their newly purchased electric Christmas lights.

On the third kick from Joni's boot, the frozen-stuck chicken coop door finally burst open. As Joni suspected, the hens, inert and hapless with cold, scarcely reacted to her presence. It was early enough in the winter that many of the hens were still not in molt yet, so, Joni had to stick a mittened hand under each indignant hen to check for the presence of an egg. In the end, she was able to gather an even ten eggs. Not bad, considering the cold, she thought to herself. After a quick trip to the granary to retrieve a bucket of corn-based chicken feed, Joni flipped open the protective wire access grid of the chicken feeder, and dumped in the feed bucket's contents. Between Joni's prodding under their bellies and the clamor of the feeder being filled, the chickens were beginning to move around and a few of them began pecking at the corn grain in their freshly filled feeder.

Back in the house, Joni warmed her hands up against the basement woodstove and hung her barn coat and mittens along the wall to dry. She lingered a little bit longer than usual in the furnace room, long enough to bake away the morning chill she had absorbed outdoors. Satisfied, she sprang up the initial few steps to the exit door landing, turned left, and bounded up the final three steps to the dark-stained wooden kitchen door. Florence was at the kitchen counter elbow deep in Christmas cookie dough, with Janice pitching in as her helper.

"I got a call from Grandma, while you were out doing chores," Florence said without turning her attention away from the cookie dough. "Uncle Leon, is on his way over to deliver your Christmas gift," she said, now turning around to witness the anticipated excitement envelop her daughter.

Joni squealed, and without realizing it, began to jump up and down around the kitchen. Janice looked up from the spatula she had been licking and soon the infectious excitement of Christmas had overtaken her, too, and she joined Joni's jumping up and down.

Uncle Leon was Joni's godfather, and ever since her awkward emergency baptism almost ten years earlier, ol' bachelor Leon had developed quite a soft spot for his little tomboy goddaughter.

"Calm down now," Florence said, adding, "Sit down at the table; here's a couple of warm cookies to settle you down."

Joni and Janice sat at the table, as Florence pulled a pitcher of whole milk from the ice box and poured out two large glasses, sufficient to wash down the Christmas cookies.

"What do you think you'll get," Janice asked. Like most little girls her age, Janice preferred playing with dolls and didn't share Joni's affinity for all things outdoors.

"Don't know," Joni responded back, picking at her plate to wipe up the last few soft crumbs of her lebkuchen cookie.

Suddenly, Joni heard the outside basement door bang against the frame as it swung shut, and almost simultaneously the kitchen door swung open. There on the basement landing was Uncle Leon, holding a chubby, large-pawed, little brown puppy. The pup had a red Christmas bow neatly tied around his neck.

Baffled by this living, breathing, gift, Joni's jaw dropped and initially she couldn't move or come up with any words. She had expected a more girlie type of gift, like a doll or something. This was great! After a short suspended silence, a "Wowwwww," finally emerged from Joni. Just then, Raymond and Eddie entered through the basement door, crowding up with Uncle Leon on the entrance landing.

"Whatcha got there, Joni?" Raymond laughed heartily.

***

"Joni, you better get down here right now," Janice demanded.

"Not until I see Santa," Joni retorted indignantly.

The Wieber household had a longstanding custom for passing the time on Christmas Eve while waiting for Santa to show up. The family would gather in the basement furnace room. There, they would shuck and eat salted-in-the-shell peanuts in the cozy warmth of the wood burner's heat. At about twenty minute intervals, one of the children would be sent upstairs to check until, lo and behold, Santa would somehow have magically completed his annual duty of delivering a Christmas gift for Eddie, Joni, and Janice.

However, this year, Joni had other plans. She was determined to meet Santa face to face.

"She better get down here or Santa's not going to come," Jancie pouted to Florence.

"Don't worry, I bet she'll lose her nerve and be down here with us in no time," Florence reassured her.

After another anxious half hour of peanuts and eggnog, Janice could no longer restrain herself, "Joni's going to ruin Christmas," she blurted out.

Florence nodded at Raymond impatiently and brushing an accumulation of peanut husks off of his pin-striped bib overalls, he pulled his large frame up from the wooden stool. "I'll go talk to her," he said.

Reluctant to be too stern on Christmas Eve, Raymond first tried coaching Joni down the stairs.

"No, Pa, I want to stay up here so I can see Santa," was her adamant reply.

"Well, Santa might be reluctant to come at all if he sees you up here trying to spy on him," Raymond countered.

"Oh, I'll be real quiet," Joni replied, slowly raising her pointer finger to her pursed lips, and adding a faint, "ssshhhhh," for emphasis. It was all the good-natured Raymond could do to keep from laughing out loud. Still confident that his little girl's fortitude would soon buckle, he returned to the basement.

"Where's Joni?" Janice demanded upon noticing that her father had returned empty handed.

Florence gave Raymond a puzzled look as he reached for his cider glass and tapped the barrel for a second round. Settling back into his comfortable, barrel-side wooden dowel chair with the wicker seat, Raymond was thinking how the slightly acidic cider really cut through the salt of the peanuts and refreshed his palate, when all of a sudden he realized that his three co-occupants were all staring impatiently at him. "What?" he asked with feigned inquisitiveness. "She'll be down here in a few minutes," he chuckled.

"Eddie, why don't you sweep up those peanut husks by Pa's chair and throw them into the furnace," Florence said impatiently as Raymond finished off the last of his fourth handful of peanuts.

Looking down into his now empty cider glass, Raymond sighed, "Well, I guess I better go up and get Joni." "Looks like she's bound and determined to wait this one out."

A few minutes later, Raymond returned to the cozy furnace room, with his large, thick hand leading the tiny, petite hand of a hugely indignant Joni.

"I know I would have seen him," she pouted to no one in particular.

"How soon before he comes now?" Janice asked jumping up into Florence's lap.

"Oh, let's give ol' Santa at least a few minutes, now," Raymond responded, clearly enjoying the impatient drama unfolding in the warmth of the cut stone house's little basement furnace room, drama which only he seemed able to appreciate.

"Hummpphh," Joni sputtered and tramped over to the corner of the room to emphasize her displeasure of having her plan thwarted.

After a couple of minutes, Raymond winked at Florence. "OK, kids, let's go take a peek and see if Santa made it over."

In unison, the three kids rushed up the stairs, ran through the kitchen and over to the parlor. Sure enough, Santa had somehow magically appeared in the few minutes Joni had relinquished her post standing guard behind the kitchen doorway. Her bewilderment was instantly washed away in the excitement of Eddie and Janice tearing into their presents.

The remaining gift was in a square shaped package wrapped in red tissue paper with Joni's name on it. Wide-eyed, she carefully tore back the paper and opened the box to reveal a black, toy metal bull with rubber horns. On the bull's underside a finger size wind-up handle protruded, which when wound up, would cause the bull's tail to switch at a small yellow bumble bee sitting on the bull's back. In her heightened excitement, Joni was initially afraid of the bull's horns, after all like most farm kids, Joni had a parentally instilled healthy respect for the farm bull. After some earnest assurance from Eleanor that the toy bull's horns were only rubber, her fear subsided and sitting cross-legged on the floor, she began playing with the bull.

With each of the children now preoccupied with their new Christmas toy, Eleanor sighed and plopped down on the davenport next to Raymond. Putting his arm around his wife's shoulder, Raymond chuckled to himself thinking how appropriate a gift the little toy bull was for his strong-willed daughter.

EIGHTH GRADE GRADUATION

In the fall of 1946, Dennis began the 8th grade at St. Mary's School. Grade eight was a transitional year for boys in rural Michigan during the time period of the mid-1940's. Many of the young farm boys opted out of school after eighth grade, choosing to commence their farming vocations early rather than finishing out the last four years of schooling.

The quiet Dennis wasn't quite sure what he wanted to do. He liked reading, and learning new things, but, he was quite sure that he wanted to be a farmer. Norman and Mary were also undecided about what path would be best to take. Norman liked the idea of having Dennis around on a full-time basis to help with the farm work. He could certainly use the help. However, the world, including the business of farming, seemed to be changing fast, particularly with the end of the Great War.

Always a progressive farmer himself (Norman was the first on the milk route to switch from cans to bulk milk, and would eventually build one of the first milking parlors in the area), Norman also wanted Dennis to take full advantage of the educational opportunities to which he himself was not afforded. Nevertheless, an important decision for Dennis' future would have to be made by the end of the '46-47, academic year.

The precocious nature of the times, with many of the boys fully cognizant that grade eight was their final year, exacerbated the normal chaos associated with the awkward hormone-filled years of middle school. Although, disobedience within the strictly run classrooms of the nuns was almost unheard of, the boys, particularly those on their final school-year, tended to be a little more rambunctious on the playground and during after school get-togethers. Concomitantly, girls began to look more interesting to the boys and vice versa. Combined, this milieu of awkwardness, hormones and transition, laid the groundwork for an exciting year.

And so it began. That fall, school started with excitement, change, and new responsibility. Dennis who was now 13 years of age, was allowed to drive Norman's car over to the Pung's on the days when it was the Thelen's turn to drive for the school carpool. Pete Pung, who was now a sophomore in high school, had been driving the carpool since he was in ninth grade. Once at the Pung's house, Dennis would turn the wheel over to Pete who would then drive the Thelen's car into town. In addition to Jim's sister Mary Louise, and Dennis's siblings Clair, Jane, and David, the remaining carpool members were Frank Pung's daughter and Vessie Hengesbach's two boys. On the way home, after the Hengesbach boys and Helen Pung had been dropped off at their homes, Pete and Mary Louise would exit the car at their house, and then, finally, Dennis drove the ½ mile back home with Clair, Jane, and David.

One particular afternoon, giddy with the heady wine of eighth grade bliss, Dennis, driving the short ½ mile back from Pete and Mary Louise's, came in for the home landing a little too fast. Dennis did not apply the brakes soon enough and failed to negotiate the 90 degree turn into the driveway. He overshot his mark, plowed into the ditch and wedged the bumper of the '36 Ford into the fence line corner post. There the car sat, in full view of the living room window of the house, and, in plain view of any of the neighbors who might happen by.

"What are you doing!" Jane scolded her brother.

"Pa's not going to like this," the usually stoic Clair deadpanned.

Quickly, Dennis shifted the car into reverse. The engine revved but the car didn't budge. The front end of the car was irretrievably hung up on the fence post. David giggled as he, Clair and Jane ran for the house.

Dennis knew he was in big trouble. In frustration, he banged his head down on the top of the steering wheel. Just then he heard a tap on the window. Pulling his forehead off the wheel, he turned and saw the large, work-worn hand of their neighbor, Frank Pung, rapping against the window. Frank was Pete and Mary Louise's uncle who lived just down the road, east of them. His youngest child, Helen was a classmate of Dennis', and of course, rode in the neighborhood carpool. Sheepishly, Dennis rolled down the window.

"Hello Dennis," the stern Frank said matter-of-factly. "I've been meaning to ask you if you'd be willing to drive the carpool in the future for us on the days it's our turn," he said pausing long enough to step back and survey the situation.

"It seems with Pete graduating soon, you're the likely successor to be our neighborhood school carpool driver?" Frank added in a tone severely lacking in confidence.

"Yessss, sure, I guess so," Dennis responded, embarrassed to be seen in the full glory of his driving inadequacy and equally puzzled by the absurdity of the timing of his neighbor's request.

"Good, then," Frank responded, and turned around, got back into his car, and drove off.

***

That fall, the Thelen's had to absorb another family loss. Mary's best friend and sister, Pauline Armbrustmacher and her husband Clem lost their daughter. Mary Ann Armbrustmacher, was just several weeks younger than Dennis. She seemed somewhat delicate and maybe a little bit frail, but she was always able to keep up with the other cousins. In the simple limitations of the era's medical acumen, the family was told that Mary Ann had kidney trouble. None-the-less, she was able to keep up her schooling, was a very talented piano player, and being Pauline's oldest daughter, she was a big help with the household chores.

Mary Ann was attending the eighth grade at a small country school north of Fowler when she suddenly, but without apparent suffering, just slipped away. She passed on Halloween day, 1946. Dennis and the Thelen family were planning to attend a Halloween party that the Armbrustmachers were hosting that evening. The Armbrustmachers did not own a phone, but somehow they were able to get word out to the other family members that Mary Ann had unexpectedly passed away that day. The Halloween party was now, of course, off, and the family would instead be holding a wake in their home for Mary Ann.

Unfortunately, another family from the St. John's area did not get the message. That evening, while the Thelens and Armbrustmachers were in the house mourning at the wake, they suddenly heard a ruckus outside. Dennis and Clair had to rush outdoors and break the news to the stunned, and embarrassed family who were parading around the house in their Halloween costumes. Everyone felt bad about the incident, none more so than the poor, uninformed, family from St. Johns.

The loss was tough for the family and friends of the Armbrustmachers. Mary and Pauline had just lost their parents, *Dika* Joe and Theresa, in a tragic car accident the previous year. Mary Ann was a precious, delicate, young girl, just beginning to grow into a beautiful young adult. Her presence would be greatly missed by the family, but especially so at family gatherings when they would assemble in the living room for singing and music. Gone now was the harmonious accompaniment of Mary Ann's talented piano and especially, her gentle, sweet voice.

***

The eighth grade graduation at St. Mary's School in the mid 1940's was a big deal. Almost as big a deal as high school graduation. And, probably rightly so, as for many of the boys, it was the end of their formal education. A special Eighth Grade Graduation Mass was held on Sunday morning in the church, officiated by Father Gutha. It was a formal affair, with the class sitting together in the front of the church. Dennis and the rest of the boys sported their Sunday-best clothes and the girls were decked out in their finest Sunday dresses.

Following the Eighth Grade Graduation Mass, the class reconvened in town to take a special, eighth grade class field trip. This year the trip was scheduled for Fitzgerald Park, in nearby Grand Ledge, where the class would enjoy a picnic lunch featuring hot dogs grilled over a charcoal fire. After lunch, the excited teens explored the trails carved into the layered geological formations of deposited sedimentary rock, exposed on the steep cliffs cut by the erosive forces of the Grand River. The network of narrow trails winding along between the vertical cliff banks on one side, and the wide, slowly flowing river on the other side, created a perfect atmosphere for forced conversation and chatty discourse between shy farm boys and pretty school girls. Dennis enjoyed the park.

After the park excursion, the class took in a movie at the Grand Ledge, Sun Theater, located on the southwest side of town near the end of Bridge Street. Since there were no school buses in Westphalia during the spring of 1947, the class had to find someone with a stake-rack farm truck willing to haul the class out to Grand Ledge. This wasn't an easy task as large trucks were still somewhat rare on local farms with the end of the war having arrived just a little over a year and a half earlier. Fortunately, for the St. Mary's eighth grade class of 1947, the school was able to talk Leon Keilen, who was several years older than Dennis, into hauling the class on the back of his family's farm truck. After the movie concluded, a light, May shower was falling in the warm spring evening air. Fortunately, Leon had been prepared and had brought along a heavy truck canvas to lash to the side racks on the back of the truck. This created a cozy cargo bed in the back of the truck, sufficient to shelter the kids from the warm spring rain.

Over the course of the summer, Norman and Mary, had reached a consensus, although a bit shy of a full conviction, to try and persuade Dennis, their oldest child, to stay in school and return to St. Mary's that fall for the ninth grade. Only five boys from St. Mary's enrolled in the ninth grade the fall of 1947: Hillary Feldpausch, Roger Fox, Joe Pohl, Dan Spitzley, and Dennis. Of these five, only two would still be around to graduate with the St. Mary's senior class of 1951.

WHEAT THRESHING

From mid-July on through to the sweltering heat of August, small grain harvest, primarily wheat, for flour production, and oats, for livestock feed, constituted the predominant farming activity in mid-Michigan. Prior to 1946, when Raymond purchased his own combine, a John Deere, model 12A, the grain threshing was done by his brother-in-law Clarence Freund, who owned a stationary threshing machine and ran a threshing crew which included himself as the thresher operator, and a crew of "bundle pitchers." Small grain harvest was extremely labor intensive, and, as such, was usually a task accomplished as a group effort involving neighbors and extended family.

"The Knoops pulled in!" Joni exclaimed with excitement as her neighbor Ferdie Knoop guided his team of horses and flat-bed wagon into the wheat field immediately south of the Wieber farmstead.

Raymond met Ferdie at the field gate. The last vestige of the early morning humidity, emanating from the overnight deposit of a heavy dew, was quickly evaporating into the bluebird sky. Despite the early hour, Raymond already had beads of sweat forming on his forehead just below the brim of his straw hat. The respective roles of the neighbors, bundle pitchers, equipment operators, and, even the farm wife, were well understood among the group now assembling at Raymond and Florence's farm. And, well they should, as the same personnel had already successfully completed the wheat harvest at the Knoops' and Millers' down the road. And, after

Raymond's wheat was harvested, the crew would repeat the process, in reverse order, by harvesting the oat crop on each of the neighbors' farms.

The Wieber's wheat was shocked two weeks earlier by Raymond, Joni, and Eddie, along with help from Leon Wohlfert, whom since the end of the War, Raymond now periodically hired on an as needed basis. Shocking wheat involved the use of a binding machine which, with a ground-driven sickle bar knife severs the stalk of the plant from its crown, approximately six inches from the ground. The detached wheat plant, consisting of the head, wherein the wheat grains reside, and the remaining stem, which eventually becomes straw bedding, were fed to the binding mechanism of the shocking machine. The binding mechanism accumulated the wheat into approximately thirty-five pound bundles which would then be neatly tied into a tight shock. When five individual shocks were aggregated, they were dropped off the binder, and stacked by hand into pyramid-shaped stacks, designed to shed rain and moisture while the grain fully matured and dried.

With a squeal of delight, Joni jumped on the back of the Wieber's own flatbed wagon as her brother, Eddie, joined Ferdie in the wheat field with their team of horses and wagon. To begin the day's work, the wagons headed down to the southernmost border of the field, furthest from the farmstead, near the hickory trees along Pratt Road. The role of the neighbors during the threshing operation was to gather up the shocks from the field, usually using their own team and wagon, and transport them to the threshing machine, which would be set up near the cattle barns in the owner's farmstead.

When the wagon was filled with dry wheat shocks, the team made its way back to the farmstead. Arriving at the threshing machine, the wagon would be met by the bundle pitchers, two or more young men who were sometimes employed by the threshing machine owner, to quickly unload the shocks of wheat. Clarence's primary bundle pitchers were a pair of local brothers, Eddie and Cliff Bengal. On this particular day however, Raymond and Leon Wohlfert were ably filling in the role of bundle pitchers.

After unloading the wheat shocks, the wagons returned to the field to gather another load. Meanwhile, back at the thresher, Leon and Raymond untied the shocks and pitched the dry wheat plants into the threshing machine. The threshing machine was a ginormous monstrosity of sheet metal, belts, pulleys, and conveyors, all operating in unison in a giant cloud of dust and noise. The threshing machines of the time were powered by an engine mounted on the threshing machine itself, or, externally, from a belt, powered by a tractor. Clarence busied himself by greasing bearings, checking belt tensions, oiling conveyor chains, and bantering with Raymond and Leon.

As the shocks of grain were fed into the throat of the threshing machine, gear-mounted rotating paddles physically beat the wheat to separate the kernels of wheat grain from the straw. The freed grain would sift through sieves to a hopper positioned at the bottom of the machine and the straw was worked, by a series of mechanical arms called straw walkers, towards the rear of the machine. The grain collecting in the hopper was augered across additional screens for a secondary gleaning, after which it was either augered into a waiting wagon to be stored as bulk wheat, or, diverted to the threshing machine bagging unit where workers would fill the clean grain into large, two-bushel, one hundred twenty pound, canvas bags.

The straw, now mostly separated from the grain, continued to the rear of the machine by way of the mechanical straw walkers, to glean the last bits of grain, and then was elevated up a conveyer. The conveyor would then spew the straw out the back of the threshing machine where it would be packed down into a dome-shaped straw stack. Packing down the straw pile as the straw rained down upon you from above, was the dirtiest job in the threshing operation.

On Clarence's threshing crew, Johnny Lenneman would usually volunteer for the dirty job of building the straw stack. Johnny dressed in a long-sleeved shirt and trousers tied at his wrists and ankles with string to minimize the incursion of chaff and dust up his sleeves and pant legs. He tied a hanky around his neck, which he pulled up over his mouth and tucked under the goggles he wore around his eyes. His head was topped off with a wide-brimmed straw hat which he wore tugged down snugly around his head, as far as he could pull it down. Once the straw pile rose to a height of about twelve to fifteen feet, as high as the thresher conveyer could reach, the threshing machine was moved to another location on the farmstead depending upon where the owner wanted the next straw stack located.

The environment around the threshing operation, like many farming activities was fraught with inherent danger. Certainly, the constant dust endured by the threshing machine operator, the bundle pitchers, and the straw stacker, would radically exceed modern day worker protection standards. Additionally, the array of unguarded whirling belts and spinning pulleys presented a constant danger to life and limb. Furthermore, the dry, ever-present, extremely flammable dust, created a constant fire hazard. Years previous, old Joe Platte, did custom threshing with his steam powered thresher. Joni's grandparents, Eleanor and Edward Fedewa hired old Joe for their threshing work. On one particularly busy threshing day, Joe had to maneuver the heavy steam-powered threshing machine between two freshly completed straw stacks in order to make a new, third stack. Unfortunately, ol' Joe managed to set both existing straw stacks on fire with stray sparks from his coal-fired steam engine before finally navigating the thresher to its new site of operation.

When it was meal-time, Janice helped her mother Florence fill a large galvanized steel washtub with warm soapy water. The water was heated by the side water heater attached to the kitchen wood stove. Janice and Florence carried the washtub out to the small cut-stone smoke house and milk house where Raymond stored ten-gallon milk cans filled with cream, prior to pick-up from the Westphalia Creamery. At noon, the entire crew made their way up from the threshing activities near the big barns, slowly and tiredly ambling towards the house, they paused by the milk house, one-by-one, to clean up in the washtub of water. Johnny Lenneman, because he was the dustiest, and dirtiest, of the crew, patiently waited to wash up last. By the time Joni was summoned to dump the water, it was black as coal dust from the smutty, sooty, dust imparted on the workers from the wheat straw. Yellow wheat chaff, floated and bobbed on the surface of the black water.

And what a meal it was. Florence, with help from the neighbor ladies, worked all morning and afternoon in the kitchen at an energy level equivalent to that of the field workers. As usual, meat and potatoes, was the staple of the meal, which of course, was washed down with generous quaffs of cool cider fetched from Raymond's cellar. The large dinner was served at mid-day, and, at around five in the afternoon, Clarence called the threshing to a halt, and the ladies served up supper. After supper, the tired but happy neighbors and threshing crew all returned home to their own farms where evening chores awaited them. Come morning, weather permitting, the entire process would repeat itself over again until all the wheat, oats, and sometimes barley, were harvested at each of the three neighboring farms.

***

White wheat, as opposed to red wheat, was exclusive to the mid-Michigan area during Raymond's farming tenure. White wheat is used in the production of bread and pastry flour for human consumption. Raymond, like most farmers of his time and geography, would generally bin store his wheat and market it throughout the following winter as prices were favorable. Raymond marketed his small grains through the Fowler Co-op Elevator, who would load the wheat onto Co-op owned trucks, on-farm, from Raymond's granary. Occasionally, when prices did not reach a level required for profit, Raymond would elect to feed the wheat to his livestock.

After the war ended in 1945, American manufacturing returned again to the production of consumer goods including farm equipment. New tractors, and particularly combines, which were still very much new to mid-Michigan agriculture, slowly began to appear on local farms. Combines greatly simplified, and reduced the manual labor requirement of small grains harvest.

In 1947, Raymond purchased a John Deere, model 12A combine, which had a six foot cutting width and a twenty-five bushel grain bin. The model had a crank-start, built-in frame mounted engine for powering the threshing mechanism. The engines mounted on the 12A combines were notorious for being extremely difficult to start. Because the 12A combine was self-powered with its own engine, Raymond's relatively small John Deere B, tractor, purchased just prior to the war, had sufficient power to operate the combine in the field. Thus, Raymond no longer needed a threshing crew. With the family labor and hired man currently available on the farm, Raymond could now complete small grain harvest in-house without help from the neighbors. Though certainly more efficient from a labor standpoint, the new combines, perhaps somewhat sadly, marked the end of the memorable era of neighborhood threshing events.

Pulled along by the post-war prosperity enveloping the nation, Raymond added a third tractor to his fleet, a John Deere model A, later in the 1940's. The acquisition of the new larger tractor, on rubber, not on steel wheels like the old model D, provided Raymond with the necessary horsepower to power one of the new model, John Deere 25A, combines which were powered by the tractor's power take-off shaft. The opportunity to be rid of the hard starting engine on the 12A combine was motivation enough, and Raymond purchased a new 25A combine and sold the 12A to a neighbor. The new 25A, in addition to the tractor-powered drive, featured a seven foot cutting width. Additionally, Raymond had Leon Wohlfert build a specialized, gravity-box wagon for transporting grain in bulk from the field to the granary.

GROWING UP

Sunday morning, June 20, 1948 the dew was heavy on the pasture when Dennis brought the cows in for the morning milking. The clear, starry sky reflected zero heat back downward to the chilly air below, and, consequently, the night time temperature had spiked downward like an ice pick in what had been an otherwise balmy springtime to date. In the predawn moonlight, the temperature had dipped to 40 degrees. Dennis caught sight of his breath, sending a quick shiver up his spine. He shook off the chill, recalling that Pete and his dad, Joe Pung, would be picking him up that afternoon to watch Pete play baseball in nearby Fowler. And Dennis, like any farm boy, knew the cool, crystal clear, predawn sky was a reliable harbinger of a sunny clear day ahead.

***

Pete Pung was developing into an outstanding young baseball player. Although soft-spoken and easy going like his father Joe, Pete was also gregarious and fun loving. And, at six-feet-five-inches, in height, and with a strength and athleticism that exceeded his giant frame, he was gaining a reputation as one of the better baseball players in the mid-Michigan area. Pete played a surprisingly nimble first base for his size, and the monster homeruns he hit attracted the attention of professional scouts. In the late 1940's Pete played minor league ball for the Wilson, North Carolina Tobs (Tobs is short for tobacconists) in the Coastal Plains League. According to the Sporting News, Baseball Guide and Record Book of 1950, published by Charles C. Spink & Son, Pete was one of two first basemen in the Coastal Plain League credited with a triple play during the 1949 season. However, drawn by a sense of familial obligation, Pete soon returned home to help his father Joe on the farm, abruptly ending his professional baseball career.

Pete was always large. Birth weight records weren't kept at the time, but his was the subject of much speculation. Even at a young age, it was clear that Pete would be a giant among his contemporaries. In height, he quickly surpassed his father Joe, and everyone else in town. When pitching manure on the farm, Joe would use a regular four-tine manure pitchfork like everyone else. However, young Pete would use a silage fork, about twice the width and capacity of a regular manure pitchfork, in order to more efficiently utilize his abnormal strength. When Pete turned twelve, his father Joe gave him a double barrel, twelve-gauge shotgun. Despite his young age, Joe figured anyone that large ought to have his own hunting gun already.

As a teenager helping Joe plant wheat, Pete would carry two, one hundred twenty pound, bulky sacks of seed wheat, one tucked under each arm, to load the grain drill. In addition, Pete had an appetite to match his great size. When working together at threshing or putting up hay, the neighbors would marvel at the amount of food the young Pete could put away. Later on in life, when attending Detroit Tiger baseball games, Pete would routinely down a hotdog and beer—each inning, even if the game went into extra innings!

As his friend and neighbor, Dennis always looked forward to riding along with Pete and his father Joe to watch Pete compete in the local baseball games, which were often the only live entertainment available in the small towns of the area. It was a real treat to get off the farm on Sunday afternoons and enjoy the competition and social aspects of the games.

***

With his left knee, Dennis pushed the wooden gate, which separated the concrete cow-lot from the grass pasture, up and over the ledge of the cement and into the closed position. Reluctantly, he pulled his still warm hands from his pockets, and secured the cold steel chain in place to lock the gate. Ahead, in the dim light of the stanchion barn, he could hear the clanging of the metal stanchions as his father Norman, and brother Clair, began locking in the first group of nine cows for the morning milking.

The routine was the same every morning and evening, and the three worked seamlessly and in concert without the need to speak. Clair stepped across to the front of the stanchions and measured out a scoop of grain for each cow as Norman and Dennis washed and prepped the udders of the three cows occupying the three western-most stanchions.

Each mechanical milking unit was comprised of four teat cups, which of course, corresponded to the cow's anatomical structure. The four teat cups were directly plumbed into the lid of a flat, round block-of-cheese shaped, stainless steel bucket which, when in use, was suspended from a leather strap laid across the cow's back. The stainless steel bucket was coupled to a rubber hose that was plumbed into a vacuum line, powered by an electric vacuum pump. A pulsator mechanically oscillated the vacuum to each teat cup on and off to mimic a sucking sensation. The milk collected in the stainless steel bucket as the cow was milked out.

While the first three cows in the line of stanchions were attached to the milking machines, Dennis and Norman washed and prepped the three cows occupying the next three stanchions. About the time the next three cows were washed and ready, the first three were just about milked out. When the cow was milked dry, the steel bucket and its contents were uncoupled from the vacuum line, and carried out of the stanchion barn, into the adjacent milk house, where the milk was emptied into ten-gallon, metal milk cans. In the 1940's, the milk was still cooled by well water pumped up from the underground well and hand carried over to the milk house.

While Dennis and Norman switched the milker units over to the next three cows, Clair, with help from younger brother David, would release the first three cows from the locking stanchions, shoo them out of the barn, and bring in and lock up the next three cows. And so the routine would repeat itself until the entire herd was milked, twice daily, seven days a week, 365 days per year.

Being Sunday, Norman had to leave the barn at about 7:15 to get ready for the 8:00 am Mass. Without the need for spoken words, Clair assumed Norman's role in the routine and David, who had just re-entered the stanchion barn after having fed the young calves, took over Clair's usual role in the milking process.

"Where's the game at today," David asked Dennis, while Dennis was applying a slight downward pressure on the slow-milking right rear quarter of the last cow in the barn.

"Over in Fowler," Dennis replied, as he removed the right rear teat cup, detached the vacuum hose, and lifted the now full milk bucket off the black leather strap suspended over the cow's back.

Straightening himself up, with the heavy milk pail in his right hand and the pulsator, vacuum line, and teat cups in his left, Dennis stepped over the manure gutter behind the stanchioned cows and turned towards the door separating the stanchions from the milk house to dump his load of milk.

As David let the last cow out of the barn, Clair and Dennis rushed through cleanup of the milking equipment in the milk house. David then cleaned up the stanchion barn by first scraping all the manure into the eight-inch-deep, sixteen-inch-wide, barn gutter, which ran the length of the barn behind the stanchions.

"Hurry up out there," Dennis chided David as he pushed the manure down the gutter and out the east door. "You're going to make us late for church!"

***

The old car rumbled south down Tallman Road, and the driver, Joe Pung, dumped the ashen remnants of tobacco out of the bowl of his smoking pipe, banging the stem of the pipe methodically on the open driver side window.

"You'll have to stop in for a glass of cider," Linus Thelen told Dennis, Pete, and Joe Pung after stepping out of the car. Linus was an occasional pitcher for the Westphalia baseball team, and when needed, Joe Pung would usually give him a ride since he lived with his folks nearby on Tallman Road.

"I guess we've got time before chores," Joe, who never seemed to be in a hurry anyway, replied.

Dennis and Pete knew it was a foregone conclusion that they'd end up in somebody's cider cellar at some point after the game on that fine Sunday summer afternoon. The cider cellar was the default venue for socializing in the rural communities of the area. Being a Sunday afternoon, after a ballgame, and with time to spare before chores, it was going to happen.

The four entered the house and descended down the stairs to the musty smelling cellar. There the group immediately assembled around the two wooden kegs. The kegs were made in Kentucky, and were originally used as whiskey barrels. Now, the kegs held hard apple cider squeezed from apples grown on Linus' parents' farm.

"*Das gute*," Pete sighed in affirmation, imitating the German approval for good cider that he'd heard his Dad Joe and other elders say many times before.

When prohibition ended in 1933, the state of Michigan imposed a 21-year old, minimum age requirement to legally purchase alcoholic beverages. However, cider drinking was so entrenched into the social fabric of rural mid-Michigan that no one thought twice about young men in their later teens partaking in a glass or two for social celebration.

Dennis drank in the festive mood around him as he sipped the cool cider. The June afternoon weather outside was perfect. The clear atmosphere that had brought about the cool morning air now just as eagerly allowed the sun to warm the day. The cloudless, June sky held with it the tantalizing promise that summer was really only just beginning.

There is a certain joy inherent in a June Sunday. The first tangible measure of summer becomes real before our eyes and can be felt by the warmth of the sun on our face and witnessed by the explosion of green everywhere around us. A century earlier, the poet James Russel Lowell, penned his *What is so Rare as a Day in June* poem, an ode to the precious nature of the early summer season, that perfectly fit this enjoyable summer day.

The talk in the cellar centered initially on the activities of the day. The Westphalia team had played well and had won a relatively easy victory. An abnormally large crowd of spectators had gathered to watch the game, probably due mostly to the near perfect June weather. The crowd was drawn from the two adjacent small towns, where for the most part, everyone knew everyone else, and, despite the underlying competitive nature of sport, the ambiance within the crowd was comfortably sociable. Soon, the basement conversation meandered to the upcoming 4th of July celebration in Westphalia, which was for most of the town's residents, the most festive social celebration of the year.

"Don't you boys know what happened today?" Linus' mother Margaret said in a voice that seemed to come out of nowhere, shattering the serenity of the Sunday afternoon.

Without waiting for a response from the now silenced group in the basement, Margaret continued her affront down the cellar steps, "The Pohl boy, Joe, drowned in the pond over near Hinman Road earlier this afternoon.

"Herman's boy?" Joe Pung responded reflexively.

"Ja," was the response from the stairs and with that, the door was firmly closed.

Dennis was stunned. He struggled to process the news but it wouldn't reconcile with the June day. Joe Pohl was his friend, one of five male classmates, including Dennis, who had just finished the 9th grade at St. Mary's. In silence, the cider glasses were emptied. With a heavy sigh, Joe Pung rose from his stool and instinctively the boys followed his lead.

Dennis forced one foot in front of the other to climb the basement stairs and the bright sun blinded the threesome's eyes as they stepped through the cellar door and back into the stark revealing daylight of the June afternoon.

***

"Are you sure you're not just making things up?" the well-meaning but poorly informed nun scolded Dennis.

Dennis was incredulous. He couldn't believe his teacher's response. It was the beginning of 10th grade, and, hoping to gain some useful knowledge he could apply to his goal of becoming a farmer, he had asked his teacher if he could study the new farming technology of herbicide use that was just then being introduced to Midwest agriculture. Unfortunately, Dennis' teacher had no idea what he was asking. Somehow, the audacious concept of simply spraying some magic potion over the top of a crop to remove the weeds seemed like fantasy to the St. Mary's school teacher. Weeds, in the good Sister's reality, were analogous to their many biblical references. They must be hoed, winnowed, pulled, burned, and physically toiled against. Dennis was frustrated for having been turned away, but, worse than that, he had been dismissed as "making the whole thing up!"

Dennis was frustrated. The semester had just started, but already he was weary of St. Mary's School. Most of his boyhood classmates had left school after the eighth grade, and, with Joe Pohl's untimely drowning death just a couple of months previous, there were now only four boys left in his class. He wanted out. That evening during chores, Dennis told Norman he was ready to quit school. They had had a similar conversation after Dennis finished the eighth grade. At that time, Norman and Mary had convinced Dennis to stay. However, this time Norman sensed the resolve in his son's request.

Norman, and to an even greater extent, Mary, had hoped their oldest son Dennis would finish high school. However, on the other hand, Norman could use Dennis' help on the farm. The ongoing drainage work in the northwest fields was burdensome to Norman who had a hard enough time just keeping up with the regular farm work on the expanding farm. Norman knew that Dennis could be fully employed with work on the farm, particularly with the drainage project.

The county drain board had commissioned work on the drain that transected the western most border of the farm. Norman had toiled for years to drain that section of the farm, and a new open drain would greatly help matters. Portions of the drain were being rerouted and a section of the drain that was previously underground tile, was being excavated and converted into open ditch consistent with the rest of the drain.

The next morning, Norman accompanied Dennis to St. Mary's to formalize his leaving school. Dennis was elated. He felt as if a burden had immediately and completely been lifted, and, at the same time, a new door had been opened.

It was a clear, spectacular, harvest day in October, of 1948 when Dennis and Norman returned from town. To those who work outdoors, particularly farmers, there is a special appeal to October. It is a season of harvest. The long sun-filled days of summer leave the fields bursting with grain and the months spent on lush, verdant green pasture leave the livestock sleek, clean and fattened. Furthermore, the shortening day lengths advance the promise of the upcoming relaxed work pace of winter when field work ceases and the daily barn chores mark the extent of a day's work.

However, in addition to all its abundance and perhaps divinely limited to only those who dare to feel slightly more deeply, an almost imperceptible, but just as real, undercurrent of sadness is ushered in by October. It can be sensed as a sudden chill, felt towards evening when walking through a slight valley or dip in the road where the cold influx of fall air has settled in place for the night. It comes with the browning of the landscape where day by day the verve green color of the surrounding fields is slowly drained away. And, it advances steadily with the ever darkening slant of the dimming autumn sunlight.

BUTCHERING

"Raymond, wake up already," Florence groaned, shaking the big man's shoulders in an effort to get him up and out of bed. "The alarm is going off."

The ringing, wind-up alarm clock read 4:00 am and the one-hour earlier arousal time was proving difficult for Raymond to process. However, the snooze button had not been invented yet, and, fortunately, Florence's act of blindly grabbing the noisy clock and setting it on Raymond's chest, was sufficient to clear the last vestiges of cobwebs remaining in Raymond's head. Pushing the patchwork quilt aside, Raymond swung his legs out of bed.

Outside the air was crisp. Raymond gathered an armful of wood from the woodshed and made his way towards the hog barn. Once inside, Raymond, fumbling around in the dark, struck a match and lit the kerosene lantern. Immediately, a flickering orange light flooded the end of the hog barn surrounding Raymond. Within the corner of the barn, outside the hog pen, sat a bricked-in cauldron. The entire fixture stood about waist high to Raymond. On the front face, a steel door opened up exposing the underside of the suspended cast iron cauldron kettle, which was essentially a large fifty-gallon, open topped cooking pot.

Raymond shoved the firewood through the open door of the cauldron and carefully positioned the logs around the base of the cauldron kettle. Using the open flame of the lantern, Raymond lit a corner of the wadded up newspaper he had carried over in the back pocket of his bib overalls and transferred the flame over to the kindling he had nested within the firewood. While the flames built up inside the brick walls of the cauldron, Raymond began filling the cast iron cauldron kettle with water he carried over in buckets from the cistern.

Today was butchering day at the Wieber farm, and, much like threshing, it was a group effort. Joni's bachelor uncles, Art, Leon, and Harold Fedewa, and Grandma Eleanor would be arriving shortly, right after morning chores were complete. Leon Wohlfert was also coming over with a hog of his own to butcher. Additionally, friends of Raymond and Florence would be stopping over throughout the next two days to visit and pitch in with the busy work of butchering.

While the water slowly heated up in the cauldron, Raymond began the morning chores. Soon he was joined in the big barn, by a sleepy Joni and Eddie. Inside the house, Florence and Janice had already begun the preparation for the multitude of butchering day tasks that would take place inside the house, mostly in the cellar. And, as always, there would be a large crowd to feed.

At around eight o'clock, the Fedewa's pulled into the drive, with their two fat hogs in tow in the single-axle trailer pulled behind the car. Right behind them, Leon Wohlfert pulled in with his pig. The hogs were unloaded into the holding pen adjacent to the cauldron inside the hog barn, in which three of Raymond's own hogs were already waiting. The hog carcasses would require time to hang and cool for a while before the meat could be cut, so the crew got right to work with the butchering.

Each finished hog weighed about 280 pounds, slightly larger than the finished weight of commercial hogs today. Conservatively estimating, each pig probably had the strength of two equally sized grown men. Some men, Raymond included, preferred not to shoot the pigs first as they thought the bullet wound and subsequent bleeding somehow adversely affected the taste of the meat. Therefore, the hogs had to be caught, restrained, and then "stuck" with a well-positioned knife stab in the jugular vein to quickly and cleanly let the carcass bleed out.

As you might imagine, catching and subduing, a screaming, fighting-for-his-life, 280-pound muscle and sinew bound beast, while your buddy tries to surgically place an awl shaped knife in the neck area just below the beast's squealing mouth, is not easy. Rather, it was a task equal in strength and finesse to any athletic feat witnessed in the professional sports world of today's society. Or, as was usually the case, equal in comic value to any Three Stooges comedy of errors in the contemporary entertainment industry.

After assorted bruises, scrapes, minor cuts, many laughs, and occasional swear words uttered in German, Uncles Art and Harold managed to apprehended the first hog while Raymond adroitly placed the knife. While the hog bled out, Raymond collected the steady bloodstream in a bucket to be used later in making blood sausage. Uncle Leon and Leon Wohlfert then hoisted the dispatched hog onto a makeshift table comprised of saw horses and oak planks, which Joni and Eddie had set up next to the cauldron. At the end of the table, a used cider barrel, with one end removed, was set up and filled with boiling hot water from the cauldron. Uncle Harold held the barrel in place at a 30-degree angle, while the Leons sloshed the 280-pound hog carcass in and out of the boiling water to scald the skin and remove the hair. Then, using special, round, cup-shaped, sharpened scrapers, all the men teamed up to aggressively scrape the still hot carcass, removing the outer layer of skin. About this time, Johnny Geller showed up.

Johnny Geller was an elderly man who never married and lived alone in a dilapidated old shack northeast of the church in Westphalia. Raymond had taken it upon himself to look after Johnny, and in addition to hiring him to do simple chores around the farmstead and garden, Raymond and Florence also kept a room upstairs in the house reserved for him to stay overnight, an accommodation which he frequently accepted.

Johnny Geller was pretty much an adjunct family member of the Wieber's.

***

It would probably be an understatement to say that Johnny's house in town was the most decrepit, rundown building in Westphalia. Because the shack was within eyesight of the church and school, it had gained somewhat of a reputation among the children in the area as being a bit spooky. The fact that none of the children had actually been inside of it, only added to the mystery and stigma of the place. One day, Raymond had suggested to Florence and the kids that one of the kids should probably go and clean the place up for ol' Johnny.

"Who wants to ride into town with me and go do some house cleaning for Johnny?" Raymond asked one evening after chores were finished and the family was gathered up in the living room for a relaxing evening.

Joni and Eddie quickly begged off and before little Janice knew what happened. She had been volunteered by her older siblings to do the job.

"What!" Janice exclaimed incredulously, but to no avail. "That place is scary!" she pleaded again.

"Oh, nonsense," Florence retorted.

"Good, let's go then," Raymond chimed in with a smile, effectively putting an end to the discussion.

Florence handed Janice a bucket and scrub brush as Janice and Raymond headed out the door. Joni shuddered a little, thinking how close she had come to being the one who had go over to Johnny's. "Poor Janice," she thought to herself and turned her attention back to the homework she was working on.

The car ride into town was silent, and Janice bit her lip as she thought about the task before her.

"I'll drop you off at the house," Raymond said before adding, "Then I'll go over to the tavern to look for Johnny— that's where we'll probably find him."

Janice swallowed hard. Dusk was just settling into night when Raymond pulled the car into Johnny's driveway. In the beams of the headlight, Janice could see the weathered grey sideboards of the shack. Raymond pulled the stick shift into the neutral position and engaged the parking brake.

"Go on now," he said encouragingly, "Do a good job cleaning that place up."

Trepid, and nearly paralyzed by her wildly running imagination, Janice forced herself out of the car.

"But there aren't any lights on," Janice protested through the open car door.

"That's because Johnny is probably in town," Raymond reminded her, "Just tap on the door and then go on in and turn the lights on."

Evening shadows danced wildly about her as Janice reluctantly made her way through the light from the car headlight beams towards the front door, bucket and brush in hand. At the door, she paused briefly, looking over her shoulder back in the direction towards the car.

"Go on now," Raymond encouraged his youngest daughter.

With her knees and shoulders shaking in fear, Janice weakly tapped on the door. Before she finished the last tap, the door suddenly sprang wildly open. CLACKETY CRASH BANG! Instantly, the night violently erupted into the ear-smashing clash and clamor of a cascade of falling pots and pans. Dropping her own wash bucket and brush, Janice flung herself back towards the car and within an instant, sat gasping for breath, in the front seat, next to Raymond.

Roaring with laughter, Raymond reached over and gave his little daughter a big bear hug. The two pranksters, Raymond and Johnny, had cooked the whole thing up as a ruse.

***

Back at the hog barn, old Johnny helped himself to a couple of draws from the crock jug of cider Raymond had placed in the corner right next to the entrance door, and took up his usual place atop the wooden stool next to the cauldron, where he would periodically open the cauldron hatch, and, with a sense of deliberate importance, stoke the fire beneath the cauldron kettle.

"This one look like it's skinned clean and ready to go, Johnny?" Raymond asked, glancing in Johnny's direction.

"*Ja*," Johnny said, nodding his head affirmatively in response.

Satisfied that the carcass was adequately scraped, Raymond rinsed it once more with hot water. All three of the uncles then hoisted the heavy carcass under an oaken beam Raymond had temporarily strung across the work area, supported on the one side by the corn crib that made up the west wall of the hog barn, and on the other side by the loft that formed a ceiling over the hog pen. As the men lifted the heavy carcass under the beam, Raymond secured each rear hock with a meat hook suspended by a length of log chain which was strung across the beam. Now that the pig carcass was successfully hanging, the uncles went to capture the next hog to be processed, while Raymond summarily gutted the hanging pig, carefully setting aside the small intestines in a clean wash tub.

Once the intestines were removed and placed into the wash tub, Eddie and Joni each grabbed one of the tub handles and carried it to the house and down into the cellar. There, Eleanor, Florence, Joni, and Janice began the arduous task of cleaning and scraping the small intestines, for use later as sausage casings. Once cleaned free of fat, Florence soaked them in a tub of salt water. Eddie, hustled back outside to clean the large wash tub and return it to the hog barn for the next pig. There, the process repeated itself until the last hog was securely hung from the suspended beam, right next to the previous five.

When the butchering was complete, the men turned their attention to the severed hog heads. Pretty much the entire hog was used productively, including the heads. Very little waste remained to be tossed aside for the farm cats. Even the excess fat was saved and later trans-esterified with lye, retained from wood ash gleaned from the wood stove, to make soap. The head meat, rich in collagen was used to make a dish known as head cheese. Lungs, heart, and liver tissue were saved for the liverwurst. The blood, collected earlier during the butchering, was used to make the blood sausage. Brains were rolled in flour, and fried in butter to make a delicacy known as sweetbread. The five men made quick work skinning and removing the meat from the six hog heads.

"This head look clean enough?" Raymond asked Johnny who was still occupying the stool next to the warmth of the cauldron.

"*Ja*," Johnny again nodded in reply.

After clean up, Raymond once again passed the cider jug around. When the jug returned empty to Raymond, he smiled and said, "*Ja*, let's go eat then."

Raymond pulled the sliding door shut behind the men as they exited the hog barn, being extra sure the door was secured sufficient to prevent a stray cat from squeezing its way in.

Back inside the house, the women had completed cleaning the intestines and had set out a dinner of meat and potatoes. The happy crew ate heartily, joked, and basked in the satisfaction of completing a good morning's work. After the meal, the group disbanded, returning to their homes for a quick nap, followed by an afternoon of work on their own farms.

As the crew left through the door, Raymond dismissed them with thanks and a hearty, "We'll see you tomorrow."

That afternoon, Raymond and Eddie readied the basement for cutting meat the next morning. Two tables were set up in the north room. The hand cranked sausage stuffer was set up on the end of the second table. The sausage stuffer had a rack and pinion gear that pushed a plunger through a cylindrical container which held the ground bulk sausage. The pinion gear was attached to a manually operated handle that when turned, would advance the plunger, which was attached to the rack gear, through the cylinder forcing the sausage out a cone-shaped exit hole over which the sausage casings were placed. As the crank was turned, the sausage was forced out through the cone, filling the gut casings plump full with sausage. While Raymond and Eddie continued to ready the basement by setting out the sharpening steels and knives, Joni, Janice and Florence gave the intestines, harvested earlier that morning, one final rinsing, and set them out in the woodshed to cool overnight in salt water.

The next morning, Raymond slept to his usual 5:00 am wake up time. And, just like the day before, Joni watched as the uncles and her grandma, Eleanor, as well as Leon Wohlfert, pulled in the driveway after morning chores. The men went immediately to the hog house where the hanging carcasses, which had thoroughly cooled over the winter night, were quartered, with a heavy, hand operated, meat saw. The men took turns working the saw back and forth, and as a quarter was cut free, one of them would carry it down to the cellar. When Uncle Art had cut the last hind-quarter free, Leon Wohlfert hefted it up on his shoulder. Uncle Leon grabbed the cider jug, and collectively the group marched off to the cellar.

"Come on down," Raymond invited Johnny Geller, who pulled in as the men were heading down the basement.

In the cellar, the uncles assembled around the tables to cut up the quarters. The trimmings and neck meat were cubed into one to two inch pieces which were tossed into a tub to be ground up into sausage. The hams were removed from the rear quarters, and along with the belly-cut bacon meat, were placed into large crocks filled with brine. Here, they would soak for a few weeks, after which time, Raymond would hang them in the smokehouse beneath a hickory fueled smoldering fire, where they would cure to a delicious smoky, salty, taste.

"Getting pretty thirsty over here," Uncle Harold said aloud.

In the cellar, the men worked with a glass of cider next to them, unlike the barn where they would all drink from the same crock jug. Over by the cider barrel, old Johnny Geller, in his usual spot on the three-legged stool jumped up to refill Harold's glass. Continuing around the table, Johnny, with a tin pitcher, topped off the busy workers' glasses. After an hour or so of cutting, enough sausage meat was accumulated in the wash tub to begin making sausage. Leon Wohlfert and Raymond broke off from the cutting work to begin grinding the sausage meat. Florence had premixed a concoction of seasoning spices which Raymond now sprinkled over the tub of cubed meat. Leon rolled up his sleeves and submerged his arms, elbow deep, in the cubed meat to thoroughly stir in the spice mix.

The meat grinding was done in the woodshed. Raymond had purchased a new cast iron meat grinder, but he didn't have an electric motor for it yet. Rather, he had mounted a large flat pulley on the drive shaft, which configured to the drive belt of the John Deere B. However, since butchering was always done during the cold of the winter months, when it was difficult to start the engine of the B, Raymond had mounted the drive belt to the rear tire of the family car, the axle of which he had jacked up on blocks. With the car engine idling and the meat grinder ready to go, Raymond sat waiting for Leon to show up with the tub of seasoned meat cubes. After a few more minutes of waiting, an impatient Raymond returned to the cellar to see what was keeping Leon.

"I know it's got to be in there somewhere," a desperate Leon murmured as he, Florence, and Eleanor pawed through the wash tub full of freshly seasoned, cubed meat.

Puzzled, Raymond leaned over the trio, who were all elbow deep in the meat, and asked, "What's going on?"

Turning her head from the tub, Florence spoke up, "Poor Leon has lost his wedding ring."

Uncles Art, Leon, and Harold, who were all bachelors, gathered around the wash tub crew. The commotion, much to the chagrin of Raymond, had effectively stalled the meat cutting operation to a complete halt.

Leon Wohlfert, who had just recently married, was now even more desperately searching through the slimy meat mixture.

"If you'd never gotten married, you wouldn't be having this problem," Uncle Art chuckled.

A stern glance from Eleanor put a quick and efficient end to the chuckling from her three grown but not married sons.

"*Ja,*" the old bachelor Johnny Geller chimed in with a grin from his stool near the cider barrel, to no one in particular.

Finally, after a few more minutes of panicked searching, Leon located the ring, which coated in slimy fatty swine meat, had blended in perfectly with its surroundings.

After the tub of meat had been ground up in the woodshed, Leon, with his wedding ring now cleanly washed and safely stashed in his front pocket, carried the tub back into the cellar and placed it on the floor at the end of the table where the sausage stuffer was securely mounted with two heavy "G" clamps. Joni enjoyed the sausage stuffing aspect of the whole butchering operation. Collectively, she, Eddie and Janice would operate the sausage stuffer. Eddie loaded the cylinder with freshly ground meat from the tub Leon had just carried in. He then set the cylinder into the frame of the stuffer, and with a short, half-turn of the handle, he had the plunger firmly set in the rear of the cylinder.

Joni locked the six-inch cone onto the other end of the cylinder and pulled a length of clean intestine that was soaking in brine in the tin pot Florence had placed on the table. Carefully, so as not to tear the somewhat fragile gut casings, Joni using both hands, manipulated the five-foot length of empty intestine until it was all bunched over onto the six-inch cone.

"Ready," she said, keeping her attention on the small, one-inch diameter opening on the end of the cone.

Eddie then slowly began turning the handle which forced the plunger into the cylinder pushing the sausage meat through the cone and into the casings. Joni deftly let the emerging meat, under the pressure of the plunger, fill the casings, and, as it did so, slowly pull the remaining empty casing, little by little, off the cone. It was important for Eddie to turn the hand crank slow and steady, without pause, and it was important for Joni to apply just a slight amount of back pressure, to prevent air pockets from forming in the cased sausage.

Making the cased sausage was the most time consuming activity of the meat processing part of butchering, and the three kids took turns with the hand cranking and casing filling roles. Bratwurst, liverwurst, blood sausage, and other types of sausage would be made, all depending upon the particular seasoning and cuts of meat used. The uncles had finished up the meat cutting, and Leon and Raymond had finished grinding the sausage meat well before the kids had the last of the sausage casings filled. While the men cleaned up the cellar, equipment, and themselves, the women returned upstairs to prepare dinner. This time, the dinner included fresh sausage, sweet bread and potatoes in pork gravy.

The kids continued to work as the men, now themselves cleaned up, gathered around Johnny and the cider barrel for several games of euchre on a makeshift card table. Finally, about the time the last casing was full and the last tub of seasoned, ground, meat was plunged through the cylinder, Florence called down from upstairs, "Dinner is ready."

DAVID

Early October of 1949, was a particularly trying time for the Thelen family. On October 7, Pauline and Clemens' son, Elmer Armbrustmacher, who was only nine years old, the same age as David, passed away from complications of a brain tumor. Just three years before, his sister Mary Ann, had passed away unexpectedly on Halloween, at the delicate age of thirteen. Elmer had undergone surgery a couple of months prior and seemed on the road to a full recovery. With a sense of pride, he would show David, Dennis, and Clair the scar on his head from the surgery. However, the tumor came back. The doctors informed Pauline and Clemens that a second surgery would be futile.

That evening, the Thelen family piled into the car to console their closest family friends. They stopped to pick up Mary's brother Henry, and his son, Ron, who was close in age to David, and Elmer Armbrustmacher. It was a difficult and sorrowful visit. The Armbrustmacher's were understandably shaken at the loss of young Elmer, especially given that they had lost their daughter, on a similar October day just three years prior. Also understandable, was the grief the loss imparted on David, having been the same age and a close friend to Elmer. Mary hurt deeply for her sister and the outpouring of grief rekindled the pain she had felt six years previous at the loss of her own eight-year-old son, Markie.

The very next morning, a Saturday, a grief stricken Norman, Dennis, Clair, and David toiled through the morning chores and made plans for the day's work on the drainage project in the northwest corner of the farm. Norman and Dennis had been making steady progress in draining the low spots in this area by installing underground tile lines that vented to the open creek drain that was being dug on the west border of the farm. This particular fall they had turned their attention to the chronically wet area along the west property line. The border of the field was in the shape of a backwards "L." The low area was located at the top member of the "L" and to reach the creek without crossing through the neighbor's property, required a deep cut through a clay hill in the northwest corner of the field.

That fall of 1949, a crane operator had been contracted by the County Drain Commission to dig the trenches for the underground component of the County Drain system traversing the Thelen farm. The drainage tile were made of baked red clay, fired at a factory in nearby Grand Ledge. Each tile was a cylindrical tube, ranging in size from a four inch inside diameter for the smaller lateral lines all the way up to a foot or more in diameter for the main lines into which the lateral lines would drain. You could order a variety of lengths of the cylindrical clay tiles with most being in the one to three-foot range.

The individual tile were laid end to end in the bottom of the trench, with a slight fall in the direction towards the open stretch of the County Drain. Water would percolate into the clay tile drains through the small cracks occurring between the individual clay tile pieces and flow in the downward direction in which the tile were laid towards the open creek.

As expected, the crane operator pulled into the farm yard right after morning chores were completed, as he had been doing for the past week. At the farmstead, before heading out to the field, the crane operator and Norman discussed the intended tasks for the day, including extending the length of the trench they had begun the day before. The clay tile had already been delivered and several pallets of tile were placed in the field along the intended route. As the crane operator dug the trench, Norman, Dennis, Clair, and Mary's brother Henry made up the trench crew, laying down the tile at the bottom of the trench.

Much care had to be taken to ensure that the trench was cut straight and that the bottom of the trench had the proper slope, or "fall" to drain the water in the intended direction. Dennis and Clair would periodically pound a stake on either side of the cut trench. A piece of baling twine was then suspended across the trench, tied to the stakes the boys had driven into the soil. Another piece of string, with a weight suspended from it, was tied to the center of the twine to make an effective plumb bob by which to determine whether the trench was cut at a true right angle to the surface, and to site along to ensure that the tile were laid in a straight line within the trench. As the tile line advanced, the crew would move the poor man's plumb bob to a new location further down the trench. A wooden-handled carpenter's hammer was used to drive the wooden stakes into the ground and also doubled as the weight suspended through the loop on the end of the plumb bob string.

October 8, 1949 was unseasonably warm, with historical weather records showing the daily high reaching a sticky 84° F. In the heat of the afternoon, the tile laying trench crew had reached the deep cut of the trench on the hillside in the northwest corner of the field. With his sons and brother-in-law drenched in sweat, Norman declared that it was time for a break. The hot and tired crew climbed the wooden extension ladder out of the fifteen-foot-deep trench and headed for the cool shade of the hickory trees growing on the property boarder fence immediately on the west side of the drainage creek.

**

"David, Rosie, come and take the water and cider out to the men," Mary called out from the back door of the farm house.

The two had been making leaf houses from the abundant, autumn drop of maple leaves on the front and west side lawn.

"Uh, oh," Rosie confided to David, "I haven't finished my chores yet."

The two clamored out from beneath a crunchy pile of red, yellow, and brown leaves.

"You'd better stay here and finish your chores," David instructed his sister, "I can run the water and cider out to the field by myself."

David accepted the water and cider from Mary and hustled the quarter mile or so north down the lane to the top of the farm's central hill, about half way down the lane. From there, he could see the crane laboring away and could make out the distant shapes of Clair, Dennis, Uncle Henry, and Pa emerging from the freshly dug trench. David cut across the field, and within several minutes, joined the crew under the shade of one of the hickory trees. The parched crew quenched their thirst with water and cider. As they relaxed under the tree, they began to crush, with hand-held rocks, hickory nuts collected on the ground beneath their feet.

"The hammer down in the trench would work better for this," one of the guys thought, but spoke out loud.

David, who like any nine-year-old boy would, jumped at the chance to climb down into the recently dug trench and quickly chimed in, "I'll go get it."

The crane operator, working eastward from the drainage creek to the target low area to be drained, continued his digging and the drone of the crane engine filled the hot afternoon air with a steady hum as the trench crew continued to catch their rest in the shade.

Dennis took a long draw from the water pail and watched as a lone leaf from the very apex of the hickory tree crisscrossed its way down to the ground. At once, a dull, shuddering, horrendous "whooommmph" thundered through the warm October air, eclipsing the background droning of the crane engine. In the same instant, a violent tremor shook the ground beneath Norman, Dennis, Clair and Uncle Henry's feet.

"David!" Norman moaned with a guttural, fearful, panic stricken voice.

Springing to their feet, the four ran numbly back across the creek, forcing their steps the twenty-five or so yards to the trench. The twelve-foot-deep cut had caved in completely. In the paralyzing vacuum of the moment, they fearfully hoped for a miracle. Already in shock, the father, brothers, and uncle clawed away at the heavy soil with all their might, terrified of what the next few moments would reveal.

The ground had collapsed in the trench around the point where the ladder was positioned. The heavy falling earth had snapped the wooden ladder and the broken splintered top of the ladder extended from the caved-in trench. They couldn't see David, at all, or anything of the shovels and equipment they had left in the trench. Frantically, the four continued clawing at the tons of collapsed, heavy clay soil.

The crane operator, who witnessed the trench collapsing, joined the desperately struggling rescue, carrying with him a shovel he kept with him on the crane. From his vantage point on the crane seat, he had seen David climb into the trench and grab the hammer. He said David was two steps up the ladder when the sidewall of the trench collapsed.

The heavy clay layer of topsoil and ten feet or so of clay subsoil was supported beneath by an unstable layer of saturated sand. When the trench was cut, the bottom, unstable, saturated sand layer, slowly and imperceptibly began to squeeze into the space vacated by the trench cut. Eventually, the instability of the lower sand layer no longer provided sufficient support of the heavy clay soil above which then collapsed under its own weight into the trench. The weight of the falling ten feet of soil was massive. Under the circumstances, no manner of rescue, no matter how heroic could ever be successful. David was gone.

Five miles away in Westphalia, the emergency siren sounded as word spread quickly of the cave-in. Well-meaning men rushed out to the site and cars began to line up along Wright Road as the men ran the quarter mile across the field to offer their assistance. In a bitter twist of irony, just a mile and a half away, Joni and Eddie Wieber were picking up nuts for their mother in the grove of hickory trees lining Pratt Road. They heard the sirens sound in town four miles away but were oblivious to the cause for the alarm. In the rush of cars that subsequently flew past the two down Pratt Road heading for the Thelen's, Joni's dog, Trixie, was struck and killed.

An even more tragic irony was that David had just the night before, attended the wake of his cousin and best friend Elmer Armbrustmacher. Born to sisters just seven months apart, the two had perished on consecutive days in only their tenth year.

In any tragic fatal accident, perhaps even more so when the victim is a child, the grief is often compounded by second guessing the decisions made leading up to the accident; with guilt and remorse over actions taken or not taken; or, in some cases blaming others for what occurred. Could we have dug faster? Why did we leave the hammer in the trench? Why did we begin to crack open the nuts? Why did David come out to the field at the moment the trench caved-in? Should the trench have been located elsewhere? Should we have even tried to drain the field in the first place?

Conversely, had Norman waited another five minutes before calling the break, there would have been four certain, and possibly even five, casualties. The endless number of "what if scenarios" only supports the grim reality that in a world of infinite chance, accidents will always happen. Nonetheless, the four survivors of that sweltering October afternoon suffered and grieved considerably from the tragic consequences of the day. So much so, that Dennis would not even speak of the tragedy until over sixty years later.

When word of the accident reached the house, Mary was wholly overcome with grief. Her sister and best friend, Pauline Armbrustmacher, already in mourning over the loss of her son just the day before, came over to console Mary as soon as she received the terrible news. The overwhelming grief, multiplied by the double loss of the two young boys, had spun the usual security of the family home into an almost chaotic, unrecognizable place. Pauline and Mary clung to each other physically, and emotionally, as did the children.

As insurmountable as the compiled and heartrending double loss would seem, the two sisters, both endowed with a strong sense of faith, managed to draw upon a synergy dwelling between them. The sisters were able to summon a deeper strength and fortitude and push forward through the grief. The Armbrustmacher and Thelen children, though already dealing with the recent loss of Mary Ann and Markie, just three and six years previous, somehow managed to muddle through the darkness of grief and move forward.

Norman, however, seemed to be especially troubled. The loss of a second son, which as a father, he naturally, though perhaps not logically, felt responsibility for, proved to be more than he could overcome. On the outside, mechanically, and pragmatically, Norman went through the motions at David's wake and funeral. He numbly accepted the condolences of family and friends as they passed through his house in the days following the accident. Inside, he was crushed and broken by the weight of losing first Markie and now David. The heaviness and relentlessness of the grief suffocated him both emotionally and eventually physically. Overcome, he bordered on the precipice of despair. The despondency continued to the point where Norman was no longer able to even physically function, walk, or even get out of bed.

In those dark days of the late fall of 1949, despite the unwavering faith of his mother Mary, Dennis, now sixteen years old, sensed that the wellbeing of his father, and by extension, the entire family, was in jeopardy. In addition to the irreplaceable loss of Markie and David, the younger children, baby Linda just nine months old, Tommy, and Virgina, both under five years of age, were all now dealing with the onset of scarlet fever, caused by the same pathogen which progressed to the rheumatic fever that took Markie several years earlier. Although antibiotics were now available to combat the disease, they were expensive and had to be purchased without the benefit of health insurance. Clair was now thirteen, and Jane twelve, and thus were a tremendous help on the farm and in caring for the four younger siblings. However, given the labor requirements of running a farm and household of nine, Dennis knew they would not likely make it with Norman despondent and incapacitated in bed. Something had to be done. And, it couldn't wait any longer.

Amassing a courage previously unknown to him, Dennis went to Norman's bedside and confronted his father with the same blunt, steely cold, hardness that *Reicha* Joe had instilled into Norman, and that Norman had subsequently instilled into Dennis. Life at times was just plain cold and hard, and all civility aside, it sometimes required an equally harsh and brutal fortitude just to survive. There was a time to grieve, feel hurt, and even immerse oneself in sorrow. But, by God, when the sun came up the next morning, you put your feet back on the floor, austerely pushed the pain aside, and you forced yourself back into the fight. It was simply what it took to survive. It was just the way it was.

"Get up Pa," Dennis said with conviction, pointing his index finger at his father, "And put your feet on the floor."

Norman, who although not quite forty years old, appeared more like an aged, seventy-year-old man as he lay on his back in bed.

"You still have us left to care for," Dennis added with his voice, though still strong, quivering just slightly.

Dennis, maintained his eye contact, but lowered his now trembling finger.

"You need to get up now," Dennis uttered again quietly, as he turned to leave his father's room, "And put your feet on the floor."

"*Ja*," Norman wept silently to the empty space where Dennis had just stood, acquiescing to the infinite empty space the loss of Markie and David had left inside him.

Drawing a deep breath, Norman closed his eyes. Pulling his arms back he pushed against the bed with his callous hands to force himself into an upright sitting position. Then, relying on a physical strength which exceeded that remaining within himself, he swiveled around and planted his feet back on the cold, hard, wooden floor boards. With heroic determination that required every fiber of his existence, Norman willed one foot in front of the other and stepped towards the doorway.

Life would go on.

TRIP TO LANSING

As a rule, the Wiebers did most of their shopping at Snitgens Store, in Westphalia. However, several times a year, once in August for school supplies, and once in December for Christmas gifts, the family would take a shopping trip into Lansing, the nearest "big city." And, occasionally, they would do some big city shopping while visiting the families of Raymond's four sisters who were all married and living in Lansing.

It was a local custom for many of the farm families in the area to school shop on the Feast of the Assumption of Mary, a holy day of obligation that falls on August 15. It became a big shopping day since many of the farmer's abstained from work in observance of the religious holiday. To shop on any other day meant time away from work since stores were not open on Sundays back in that time period.

"Raymond, hurry up," Florence intoned in her haste. "The kids are already in the car."

Florence, like some women of her time, very seldom drove the family car. If she did, it was only the short distance to Westphalia or to visit her mother several miles away on Grange Road. The twenty-five mile trip to Lansing was a major excursion that required Raymond to drive. Raymond didn't particularly like the shopping trips but he understood that he was the only means for his family to get to downtown Lansing. As it was, he made the best of it.

With the war now over for several years, Raymond had recently purchased a new Dodge Coronet. The Coronet was Dodge's first postwar body style, and the sedan, which Raymond had purchased, could comfortably fit eight people. The extra seating capacity came in handy for the large school carpools of the day. Raymond enjoyed driving the new car and was looking forward to taking it on a long trip, at least long for the travel standards of the time.

Once in Lansing, Raymond would seldom participate in the family shopping. Rather, he would pass the time sitting in the parked car reading the State Journal newspaper. Sooner or later, Raymond would spot Herman Spitzley, who, formerly from Westphalia, was now a Lansing beat cop who patrolled the downtown Lansing area on foot. When Herman would walk by, Raymond would flag him down and the two would catch up on the news of the day.

The bi- or triannual shopping trip to Lansing had, over the years, evolved into pretty much its own routine. The family excursion would begin after morning chores were finished. The major stores of the time period, JC Penney, Walgreens, Woolworths, and the Knapps department store, were all located downtown and that's where Raymond would drive, finding a parking spot along the street or in one of the downtown city lots. After an hour or so of shopping, Florence and the kids would meet Raymond at the car and walk over to either the

Home Dairy, on Washington Avenue, or sometimes to the Woolworths lunch counter to have a bite to eat for lunch.

Since the trip only occurred a couple times a year, eating out was a big, big, deal. Joni would bask in the novelty of placing an order at the lunch counter, or perusing over the many food selections at the Home Dairy Cafeteria. Following lunch, Raymond would head back to the car for a nap and Florence and the kids would finish up the day's shopping.

***

"Hand me the polish again," Joni said to Janice.

Janice reached over to grab the tin of white shoe polish that was sitting to her left, atop the newspaper that had been spread across the kitchen floor, lest the girls should spill. It was the afternoon of Holy Saturday, and, now that the girls were approaching their teen years, they were able to have a pair of special white shoes which were worn only during special events like Easter Sunday, Christmas, or perhaps a family wedding.

Florence instinctively glanced over at the girls from her position at the wood stove, where a large kettle of eggs was happily boiling away. During that time period, the emphasis for Easter basket treats was on the eggs, although there would be a couple pieces of chocolate candy, and a few jelly beans waiting in the kids' baskets come Easter morning. Atop the kitchen table, Florence had set out a series of bowls, each containing a different colored food dye. Easter eggs were colored back then much the same way as they still are today. Florence, Joni, and Janice would color two dozen eggs for the family of five.

When Easter morning arrived, Eddie, Joni, and Janice marched over to the south facing, side door entrance to check out their baskets before heading out for chores. They couldn't eat anything. Like any other day they attended Mass, they had to abstain from food and drink until after they had partaken of Holy Communion.

"You'd better get started with your chores," Florence's voice echoed from the kitchen, adding, "Knoops are driving for the early Mass and you girls will likely need a little more time getting ready."

Like most families in the area, the Wiebers had to split up for Mass in order to get the morning barn and kitchen chores done. Florence and usually Eddie rode with the Knoops to the 7:00 am Mass, while Raymond would be doing the milking chores. Meanwhile, one or both of the girls stayed behind to either help Raymond in the barn or be excused to the kitchen to keep an eye on the Sunday dinner preparations. Conversely, Raymond would drive to the 9:30 am Mass with Joni and Janice, stopping at the Knoop's to pick up their riders. With Raymond and the girls at Mass, Eddie would finish up the morning chores while Florence continued with the Sunday dinner preparations.

Easter Sunday Mass meant that the girls would wear their special white shoes, their fanciest spring dress, and to top it all off, an Easter bonnet. Florence, too, would dress up, and, Raymond would purchase a corsage which Florence wore neatly pinned to her dress. At noon, the family would sit down together for the Easter Sunday dinner, which was somewhat like a regular Sunday dinner with the exception that it usually featured ham, carefully brined and cured from one of Raymond's own pigs. After dinner, the family would head over to Grandma Eleanor Fedewa's house where the men would play cards and the children would play with their many cousins.

Joni's uncles, Isadore, Harold, Leon, and Art Fedewa, like many in the area, loved to play cards. Uncle Harold, especially, liked to gamble and would frequently goad the others into wagering a little bit beyond their comfort level when playing in-between and high-low poker, or perhaps euchre around the dining room table.

"You don't HAVE to gamble to play cards," Florence scolded Raymond on the short, four-mile drive home.

Raymond didn't answer. He was still fuming inside over how Harold had managed to bilk him out of all the spare cash he had in his wallet. He seemed to have had no luck whatsoever, several times drawing a King on in-between.

"Oh well," he thought to himself, "My luck will surely change next time."

It didn't change quick enough, however.

"@#$%^!," the German swear words rang out and echoed across the farmstead when Raymond entered into the barnyard that evening.

"Eddie, run and get the butcher knives!" was hollered out in and among more German swear words.

Raymond had several nice gilts, young female hogs he was saving for breeding purposes, penned up in the barnyard with the cattle. The hogs had a penchant for burrowing into the several straw stacks which had been constructed in the barn yard during the previous summer's threshing. The hogs liked to snuggle up with each other in the warmth afforded by the straw stacks. Today, however, one of the large stacks had collapsed around several of the gilts that had burrowed into its center. Unfortunately, the pigs were suffocated. With quick work, Raymond managed to save the hams and better cuts of meat. Nevertheless, it wasn't a very happy or prosperous afternoon for Raymond.

***

As Joni progressed through her teen years, she acquired a proclivity for mischief at least equal to, if not in some instances, exceeding that of her peers. Perhaps, like many aspects of her tomboy nature, it had something to do with the countless hours she spent tagging along with Raymond on the farm or on his somewhat frequent social visits to his own cider cellar and to those of his many friends and neighbors.

To be sure, Raymond possessed an austere, strict, authoritative disposition, particularly when carrying out his parental duties. And, his burly outward appearance, generally packaged in a pair of large, pinstriped, bib overalls, wouldn't usually be construed as warm and fuzzy. Nonetheless, he had a twinkle in his eye that often betrayed his ostensibly stern personality with one of jovial merriment. Joni, too, had acquired the same mischievous twinkle, a peculiarity that had not gone unnoticed by her more serious mother.

One particular prank that Joni and her girlfriends would partake in was called "chicken 'cooning." The activity, as the name implies, is roughly based on the more sportsman-like activity of hunting raccoons, which Joni also did regularly. Like raccoon hunting, the activity took place at night, often with the aid of a lantern. Unlike raccoon hunting, a chicken was the intended prey, and the hunting did not take place in the woods, but rather, in someone's unsuspecting hen house. Now, lest we be too harsh on Joni, the perpetrators allegedly only conducted their raids on each other's own chicken houses. Furthermore, no chicken was wasted in the process as the highlight of the chicken raid was when the raiders dressed and cooked up their unfortunate victims and enjoyed a tasty meal together.

Another recreational mischief Joni availed herself to was hosting an occasional party, usually in cahoots with her brother, Eddie. During Joni's teen years, one of her somewhat older, considerably less mischievous cousins, Kenny Pasch, was attending seminary school at Mount St. Francis, in Indiana. Occasionally, Florence and Raymond would travel with Florence's sister Bea and her husband Marcus, down to Mount St. Francis to visit Kenny. Despite instructions to the contrary, Eddie and Joni would invite friends over, usually for some 'cooned chicken. The two would usually coerce the younger Janice into making popcorn for the guests.

Like many teens of yesterday and today, Joni would also occasionally find herself in trouble for returning home with the family car past curfew. One particular Saturday morning after a Friday night in which Joni had been out gallivanting and driving around with her friends, the family got up early to attend the 6:00 am Saturday Mass. Much to the chagrin of Raymond and Florence, they noticed that the Dodge's engine was still warm when the family sleepily piled into the car! Needless, to say, Joni was on her best, most reverent, behavior during Mass that morning.

WORKING FOR A LIVING

After the tragic October of 1949, work on the Thelen farm continued, though the joy and reward that Dennis used to feel in the daily farm tasks was somewhat dulled around the edges and, on the worst days, replaced with a slight sense of drudgery. He even began to second guess his decision to leave school. However, despite having prematurely ended his formal education, Dennis remained an avid reader. Norman subscribed to several monthly farm publications including the *Farm Journal*, and *Hoards Dairyman*. In the evenings, when Dennis' farm work was done for the day, he would read these magazines from cover to cover, soaking up with interest information on modern farming trends and methods, most of which were still very novel to the rural mid-Michigan agricultural community.

Work on the tile-drainage project on the northwest corner of the farm continued into the first few years of the early 1950's, despite the accident. The county had decided to reopen the short section of the drain that cut through the hill on the very northwest corner of the farm, the area adjacent to the hickory trees. Previously, this section of the drain consisted of buried tile, with the drain being open on both the north and south side of it. It seems that a short section of buried drain, bookended on either side by open drain didn't work too well.

Norman avoided going out to the northwest corner of the farm. He busied himself with the tasks and chores around the farmstead while Dennis, with occasional help from Clair and his uncles, shoveled, dug, and laid tile, sporadically between field work, chores, and other farm work, for the next couple of years. The thankless grind of the ditch-digging work ended when the drainage project was dubbed by the county Drain Commissioner as sufficiently complete to be walked away from.

Despite the post war economic boom during the late 1940's, agricultural mechanization was limited, and many basic tasks were still accomplished with manual labor. Equipment factories that had been pulled into service for munitions and army supplies had to retool. After four plus years of filling military orders, manufacturing lines had to be changed over to consumptive goods, and for recapitalizing industry such as agriculture. Farmers often had to wait a year or more to take delivery on an ordered piece of farm equipment. Needless to say, in the years after leaving school, Dennis had no problem being fully employed as a general farm laborer.

He was frequently in demand from his uncles on Mary's side, mostly Norman M, Henry, Walter, and Raymie, to help with their sheep shearing business and with field work. In return, the uncles often made themselves available for similar work on Norman and Mary's farm.

Dennis enjoyed working with his uncles. To be sure, they would relish the opportunity to tease their young nephew, but it was all done in good humor. Shocking wheat, and other jobs that required multiple workers, were occasions when Dennis would help his uncle Walter who had now taken over *Dika* Joe's home farm. Uncle Raymie, too, was often on hand to help at Uncle Walter's with the wheat shocking, and, he'd invariably snatch Dennis' straw hat off his head, toss it onto the canvas conveyor of the binding machine, and, before Dennis could retrieve it, his hat would be neatly bundled into the middle of a shock of grain.

In the early spring of 1949, Uncle Norman M, came to visit Norman and Mary, with an idea to further vest Dennis into the custom sheep shearing business operated by himself, and Uncles Henry and Walter. The uncles appreciated Dennis' laconic disposition, and good work ethic. Uncle Norman M, suggested that Dennis attend a short course at Michigan State University that provided instruction on a new "Australian" method of shearing sheep.

"Henry, Walter, and I might be getting too old to learn anything new," Uncle Norman M, said with a laugh. "We think Dennis should be the one to learn this new technique and maybe he can teach the rest of us a thing or two after all," he added with another chuckle.

Dennis was excited about the concept, but his shyness kept a lid on his outward enthusiasm. The arrangements were worked out and Dennis was signed up for the two-week course which took place in late February, in time for shearing the Michigan State University flock. Two other young men from the area, Bob Miller and Leon Wieland also enrolled in the short course. Classes were held three days a week, during the two-week course. There was morning class room instruction on sheep husbandry and shearing technique followed by hands-on shearing in the afternoon. The classes and shearing took place in the old Livestock Pavilion which used to be located in the center of the East Lansing campus between the east and west bound tracks of Shaw Lane Boulevard, directly across from Anthony Hall.

After completing the course, Dennis purchased his own new set of clippers. The clippers were factory-compatible with the power drive unit already owned by his uncles. No longer would he have to use his uncle's old spare set. After returning from the short course and rejoining the shearing crew with his uncles, Dennis' pride was puffed up taut to near bursting when his uncles gathered around him asking questions about the "Australian" technique and watched closely as he neatly dispatched another fleece from a bleating, ungrateful ewe.

Dennis enjoyed sheep shearing season. During morning

milking chores at home, he looked forward to heading out with his uncles to the next farm on the shearing docket. He enjoyed the constant bleating of sheep in the background from the waiting pen of plump, wool laden sheep. He liked the oily smell of the equipment, the drone of the power unit, and the clackety-clack of the individual clippers. He also enjoyed the company of his uncles and the farm families.

The farmer was expected to have on hand an individual to tend each shearer. This person would fetch a sheep from the waiting pen, drag it over to the shearing station of his assigned shearer, and then when the shearer finished with a sheep, the tender would swap the unshorn sheep for the freshly fleeced sheep and escort it back to the "finished" pen. In addition, the tender would roll up the fleece and stack it on the growing pile of freshly made woolen bundles. Often the tender would be a son, neighbor, or hired man of the farmer. Dennis felt a sort of importance at the idea of having his own sheep tender, dutifully keeping a steady supply of sheep available for him to skillfully fleece.

The shearing days were long. However, Dennis and his uncles were invited in for dinner and supper at every farm they worked. Meals were another aspect of shearing that Dennis enjoyed. It was interesting to break bread with the different families, all of which, invariably presented a great feast, based of course, on the local staples of meat and potatoes. For the most part, Dennis remained silent and enjoyed the conversation between his uncles and the farmer and farm hands. Dennis respected his place as the youngster in the group, but, nonetheless, he felt a sense of importance in being one of the shearing crew guests.

After supper and after the last sheep was shorn for the day, the work was far from over. The individual clippers had to be torn down, the blades removed and sharpened, and all the universal joints of the drive mechanism had to be lubricated and prepped for the next day. And, finally, when Dennis returned home, there was still his regular barn chores to do.

The shearing season ran from late February through April. Dennis' uncles were all married and had young families and farms of their own to tend to in addition to the custom shearing side business. By mid-April, when the shearing season began to encroach upon the planting season, the uncles would let Dennis handle the couple of smaller flocks still remaining to be sheared, by himself, thus freeing themselves up to begin field work on their own farms.

"They'll be easy to handle," Uncle Norman M, would say. "The lanolin will be runny and the fleece will practically fall off of them."

Dennis was happy to oblige, although Norman and Mary weren't overjoyed at having to do without Dennis for a couple of early season, spring field work days. None-the-less, the parents were pleased at the industry and productivity Dennis employed in going about his daily work.

One of the late-shearing flocks which Dennis would tackle on his own was owned by Simon "Simmy" Miller. Simmy's farm was on the corner of Tallman and Jason Road, just about three quarters of a mile north of Raymond Wieber's farm. Simmy, a life-long bachelor, lived with his three old maid sisters, and had a small flock of some forty-eight ewes to shear. The first time Dennis showed up alone to shear the flock, Simmy was certain that it would be after dark before they could possibly be done.

"I should be able to finish the job before dark," Dennis assertively reassured Simmy.

Dennis looked over the flock. Simmy, as usual, had done an excellent job of prepping the ewes. The sheep were exceptionally clean and the holding pen, crowd gates, and shearing setup were ideal. Furthermore, the recent warm weather, a direct result of the lateness of the season, had, as Dennis' uncles predicted, rendered the lanolin at the base of the wool near the sheep's skin, very liquid. The more liquid state of the sheep's naturally produced lanolin facilitated a relatively easier shearing job compared to the shearing conducted during the cooler early season of late February and early March when the lanolin had a thicker pastier consistency.

"Yes, the wool should practically fall off them," Dennis chuckled to himself recalling Uncle Norman M's prophecy.

Regaining his game-face, Dennis quickly went about his work. Deliberately, he set up the electric motor and power unit. With a dry rag he carefully wiped down the cutting edge of his clippers so as not to stain the day's first fleece. By the time he attached his clippers to the drive arm on the power mechanism, Simmy had the first sheep laying on its side, ready for business. At this late stage in the shearing season, Dennis had perfected the new "Australian" shearing technique and with an efficiency equal to that of a big city barber, Dennis confronted the worried, disconsolate ewe before him.

By the time dinner rolled around, Dennis already had twenty-four sheep shorn. In a similar fashion, the afternoon flew by without a hitch.

"*Ja*, you're going so fast, I'm worried my sisters won't have supper ready yet when you're done!," Simmy exclaimed as he dragged the last sheep up to Dennis.

Simmy couldn't believe the speed at which the quiet, young, Dennis, and his new "Australian" shearing method, had buzzed through his entire flock.

***

Norman and Mary's farm, like post war agriculture across the U.S., did quite well in the several year period following the war. According to USDA statistics, in the 100 some years prior to World War II, average U.S. corn grain yields hovered steadily near 25 bushels per acre. After the war, agronomic and genetic advances have kept corn grain yields on a steady incline, with the current national average now at 158 bushels per acre.

Farmers also began to receive better prices for their grain immediately after the war. In the ten-year period leading up to the war, the average price received for a bushel of corn grain was $0.81. In the ten-year period following the war, the average price jumped to $1.52. Concomitantly, the price for agricultural land experienced a steady incline in the post war years. Federal statistics show that land prices were quite steady in the 1935-45, timeframe, with a national average of around $24.70 per acre, with little year-to-year fluctuation. During the 1946-55 post war timeframe, land prices soared, increasing by 107% to a national average of $51.20 per acre, figures which seem ridiculously low relative to today's formidable land prices.

Earlier in 1949, Norman purchased a Ford 8N tractor, which considerably sped up the field work. It was the first tractor purchased since the F-14, International Harvester, which was purchased ten years prior in 1939. The 8N tractor was ideal for the lighter tillage and planting work on the farm and considerably decreased the time needed for planting and harvesting the crops. The new tractor eliminated the need for draught horses on the farm entirely and the remaining team of horses was sold off. Another major post war purchase of Norman's was a used, heavy duty, International, truck. Norman had educated himself on the benefits of adding calcium carbonate, also known as lime, to soil for the purpose of increasing the plant availability of the micronutrients already present in the soil. The purchase of the truck was motivated primarily for purposes of hauling the lime from the Lansing based, Michigan Sugar Company, to the farm. The lime was produced as a by-product of sugar processing at the refinery.

In addition to working on the home farm, Dennis continued to work for his uncles in his late adolescent years after leaving school. During the winter months, he often cut wood with Raymie and Norman M. In the spring sheep shearing season, he continued to work with Henry, Norman M, and Walter in their custom sheep shearing business. And, during the field season, he continued to help at Walter's farm, often with Raymie, all the while continuing to work with his brother Clair as the hired men at home for their father, Norman.

Sugar beets were still grown in the area and Dennis picked up work in the fall driving truck for Leo Fedewa who farmed with his family in nearby South Riley Township. Leo owned a sugar beet harvester, a couple of trucks, and had a busy custom harvest business in addition to his own farm. Dennis would haul beets from the farm to the Michigan Sugar Company, which at the time owned nine sugar refineries in the state, one of which was located on Grand River Avenue, in Lansing. The Lansing plant was in production until circa 1954.

Finally, Dennis would also custom deliver tractors for his Uncle Henry, who had recently procured a job as a tractor and farm equipment salesman at the John Deere dealership in nearby Fowler. Dennis had worked out a deal with his father Norman to use the family's recently purchased International truck to deliver the tractors which Uncle Henry sold. About thirty miles per hour was all the old truck could do when loaded down with a new tractor on the truck bed.

Occasionally, Uncle Henry took delivery of new tractors from the John Deere Company, before the official John Deere new model release date. Under these circumstances Dennis would have to clandestinely deliver these tractors to several hiding places Henry had devised until they could be officially made available to the public. One of these hideaways was an old barn on the Pratt Road Farm, just west of Grange Road, that Uncle Raymie and his new bride Aunt Joan were renting.

A particular facet of the tractor delivery job that appealed to Dennis, was that once the new tractor was delivered, he would invariably be invited down into the new owner's cider cellar for a tall, refreshing glass to commemorate the new capital purchase. Even though the making of hard apple cider was practiced ubiquitously in the rural Westphalia area, not everyone was endowed with the fermentation skills necessary to produce "good" cider.

The quality of one's cider was a matter of great pride and social stature in the community. To possess a reputation of having "bad" cider carried with it a stigma that was almost impossible to overcome. Any self-respecting citizen of the surrounding country side would avoid that reputation at all cost. In fact, the stigma was so bad that the "badness" of one's cider was not openly revealed to the unsuspecting fermenter of same. If someone served you a glass of cider in the sanctity of their cider cellar and asked you how you liked it, you would never, ever, say anything remotely negative. Rather, you would eke out some type of compliment, maybe a, "das gute," or at least an affirmative, *"Ja."* To do otherwise would constitute a breach of the sacrosanct, gentlemen farmer, cider maker's unspoken code of honor. The unintended circumstance of this benevolent reluctance to reveal "bad" cider, was that the unlucky fermenter of the "bad" cider, never knew that his cider was indeed actually "bad."

Unfortunately for Dennis, one of Uncle Henry's best customers was a notoriously, to everyone but himself at least, wickedly bad cider maker. After one such tractor purchase by the hapless cider maker, when Dennis and Henry had the new tractor securely fastened down in the back of the truck and ready for delivery, Uncle Henry confronted the young Dennis with a somber face.

"*Ja*, when you accept the glass of cider," Uncle Henry warned Dennis, "Make sure he's not looking when you dump it out."

BASKETBALL

As an eighth grader, in the late-fall of 1949, Joni was bitten by the basketball bug. Her brother Eddie, was already playing basketball at St. Mary's as a high school sophomore. That year, due to a plethora of girl players, St. Mary's had a team comprised of senior girls and a second team comprised of all junior girls. Mrs. Herman Geller coached both girl teams, and, led them both to undefeated records. The girls' and boys' games were usually all played on the same night, beginning with the girls and ending with the varsity boys. The excitement at St. Mary's in those years centered around the girls' teams and by the time the varsity boys played, the gym was pretty much empty of spectators. The dominant girls' basketball program was the pride of St. Mary's and Joni couldn't wait to be a part of it.

Unfortunately, she would have to wait another two years, until a sophomore, to be eligible to play. Nonetheless, she and Eddie would shoot baskets before and after chores, using the makeshift rim and backboard Eddie had hung up in the hayloft of the barn. Fortunately, Joni had the opportunity to learn all about basketball by being able to attend the girls' and boys' games once Eddie started playing.

Eddie, however, didn't have the luxury of ever attending a basketball game prior to his first game as a player. Eddie had grown into a tall, lean, and strong lad, and due to his precocious physical build, and a scarcity of boys remaining at St. Mary's,

Eddie was forced into a prominent varsity starting role his first year out for the sport.

In the first game of his first season, which happened to be against the nearby Carson City team, Eddie ripped down the first rebound of the second half, raced down the court going coast-to-coast on his own, and finished with a clean, uncontested, layup. Turning around, Eddie noticed that he was the only player on his side of the court. His teammates, and the Carson City squad, looked on from the far end of the court in disbelief, and suddenly it dawned on Eddie why his coach, the town undertaker, Mr. Herman Geller, was jumping up and down, pointing in the other direction. Eddie had scored one for the other team. Eddie's basketball fortunes would eventually take a turn for the better though, as a senior, Eddie led the 1952, St. Mary's boys' basketball team to the school's best season to date, capturing the school's first boys' district title.

Back then, girls' basketball was played differently than was the boys' game. Six players from each team would be on the court at a given time. Three forwards played offense and three guards played defense. Players could not cross the half-court line and only forwards were allowed to shoot the ball. Growing up a tomboy, years of shooting practice with her brother Eddie, and a competitiveness that belied her short stature, all contributed to a successful basketball career for Joni.

In her first year, as a sophomore, Joni played forward and wore number 18, on her jersey. She was coached by Estelle Geller, the undertaker's wife, in what would be Mrs. Geller's final year of a very successful coaching career at St. Mary's. When Joni was a junior, Connie Koster took over coaching duties for the St. Mary's girl basketball program. Joni, now wearing number six on her jersey, helped the St. Mary's girls' team to another undefeated season, with a record of 7-0. In winning the seven games, the girls scored a total of 237 points, giving up just 130 to their opponents. Their closest game, with only a six-point margin of victory, was to the rival Pewamo girls' team, just down the road.

In Joni's senior basketball season of 1953-54, Coach Connie Koster returned, and Joni, now wearing jersey number 12, was determined to contribute her best and hopefully make her final season another successful one. The team got off to a good start winning big November 20, on the road at Lyons, by a wide margin, 42-11. However, the second game of the season, November 27, the day after Thanksgiving, the St. Mary's team dropped a heartbreaker at rival Pewamo, losing by a score of 33-30. The sluggish St. Mary's team looked like they had eaten too much Thanksgiving turkey the previous day. Joni was disappointed despite having scored the most points of her career.

"The gym is too darn small," Joni complained of the Pewamo gymnasium to no one in particular in the car ride home.

It was the St. Mary's girl basketball program's first loss in two years. The team managed to rebound from the loss, and went on to win their next three games handily. Thus the stage was set for the big January 22, rematch with the Pewamo team. St. Mary's would have the opportunity to avenge the earlier loss, this time playing on their own St. Mary's home court.

All that week, Joni couldn't wait for Friday to finally roll around.

"Sit down and eat your breakfast," Florence said as Joni rushed around the kitchen gathering up her school things with a nervous energy.

"Why've you got a bee in your bonnet this morning," asked a bemused Raymond, knowing full well about the big game that evening.

Amid the bustle, Janice looked up from her oatmeal and realized that she'd be stuck with most of the barn chores again that night with Joni and Eddie both playing basketball.

The St. Mary's ladies played determined that evening, winning a defensive struggle by a score of 27-22. Joni felt vindicated. The team went on to win the remainder of their games that season finishing the regular season with a 7-1 record which was good enough for them to win yet another district championship.

After finishing high school, Joni went on to play basketball for a Lansing City League, women's team, a team that also included players from her old nemesis, Pewamo. The Lansing team, comprised of Westphalia and Pewamo girls coasted to the City League championship in their first year.

CONSCRIPTION

The serious looking envelope, addressed officially to "Mr. Dennis Joseph Thelen" lay on the dining room table when Dennis came in from the evening milking chores. It was early in 1953. Dennis, who had just turned twenty years old, carefully tucked his thumb under the corner of the fold-over top of the envelop and tore the paper away from the adhesive, revealing the official contents. The letter stated, which Dennis had already known from a previous notice, that he was classified "1A, Eligible for Service." The letter further informed Dennis of his conscription into the US Army and instructed him to board a bus in St. Johns, Michigan departing for an Army personnel processing facility in Detroit to receive further instruction and complete a thorough health examination.

The letter wasn't unexpected, but a rush of adrenalin pulsed through Dennis as he quickly perused the letter. In the five years since leaving St. Mary's School, Dennis had employed himself with a multitude of agricultural, mostly manual labor jobs. In fact, on his official military record, he was classified as: "Farm Hand, General; Self-Employed." In other words, he was well-travelled, but, only within the confines of the tiny, Westphalia vicinity. Despite being geographically limited, and never having travelled out-of-state, Dennis was an avid reader, and a significant part of him longed to escape from the fence lines of rural Michigan and see firsthand, at least a small sampling of the destinations he had read about.

Dennis placed the letter down on the table without thinking to return it to the envelope. Even though he wasn't really settled into any one specific job, Dennis felt a small measure of anxiety about leaving his responsibilities behind. Clair was still at home and little Tommy, although only eight years old, was certainly capable of taking on more of the routine chores. In addition, Jane, would be turning sixteen years old that summer, and, she along with Rosie, now twelve, had already expressed a willingness to help with the field work and drive tractor once Dennis' expected call to military service occurred.

Similarly, Dennis' uncles, although they greatly benefited from Dennis' sheep shearing, field work, and wood cutting, could, without significant hardship, get along without him. One of the benefits, perhaps to some extent even the design, of the bigger families in the rural areas of that time period was a large, ready, and replaceable labor force. Norman, and the Uncles had other sons and nephews in the pipeline available to help with the multitude of manual labor demands associated with the farm. Besides, there really wasn't much choice in the matter anyway. Dennis had to report, or, face the wrath and legal consequences imposed by the US Government.

"Let's get going," Norman said, encouraging Dennis to wolf down the last mouthful of his homemade toast.

Norman was driving Dennis over to St. Johns, where a bus was waiting to take him on an overnight trip to Detroit to complete his induction responsibilities with the US Army. In the weeks leading up to the trip, Dennis had learned that Jerry Pung from Westphalia, as well as Melvin Stump from nearby Pewamo, and Jerry Wieber from Fowler, would also be on the same bus.

The Unites States was about to enter into a relatively peaceful period in time, particularly relative to the Great War it had just endured. The Korean conflict, which was more or less a vestige of WWII, when the Soviet Union, China, and the US began to occupy the previously Japanese-ruled country of Korea, would soon end with the July 1953, signing of the Korean Armistice Agreement. The agreement repositioned the border between North and South Korea, and created the two and a half mile wide demilitarized buffer zone between the two countries.

The pending period of relative peace seemed to deescalate the usual sense of danger and foreboding associated with military service. The two-day trip to Detroit felt like a mini-vacation of sorts and left Dennis excited about the prospect of the uncharted waters of the two years ahead of him. Leaving behind the familiarity of his rural Michigan, busy work life for a brief stint in the army didn't seem like such a bum deal after all. The return bus trip to St. Johns was filled with lively conversation, joking, and witty banter, especially compared to the sullen quiet ambiance of the inbound trip to Detroit. The young men had gotten to know each other a bit over the two days and had begun to develop at least the nascence of an army buddy comradery. Melvin Stump invited everyone over to his place for a party later that evening in Pewamo.

Several weeks later, Dennis and Norman were putting up grass hay for the sheep flock they kept, on shares, with Frank Pung's sheep. Frank had recently retired and moved to town. Before retiring, Frank worked out a deal with Norman to have Norman move his flock over to Frank's large hip-roof barn that stood alone on the south side of Pratt Road, about three quarters of a mile east of Norman and Mary's farm. In return, Dennis and Norman tended to the flock, keeping a share of Frank's profits for their efforts. Norman had purchased a new forage chopper that summer. However, the grass hay for the sheep, was better if put up as loose dry hay. So, Norman and Dennis were toiling away the old fashioned way, slinging the loose dry hay up into the barn's haymow.

Many of the farms in the area including Dennis' other neighbors, Joe and Pete Pung, had also purchased forage choppers which greatly reduced the labor required for putting up hay. Mechanization was slowly but surely finding its way onto farms in the area. The timing was perfect, as many young men from the area, who grew up working on farms, were now taking high paying manufacturing jobs in the auto industry which was growing at exponential rates in the nearby city of Lansing.

Sweat drops dripped down Dennis' nose as he hooked the grapple hook to the clasp on the hay sling. He had backed the loaded wagon into the large west facing main doors of the Frank Pung barn. Now with the sling secured to the trolley rope, Dennis hopped off the loaded wagon and looped the other end of the rope through the clevis attached to the rear hitch of the Ford 8N. Clutching the treads of the 8N's rear wheel, he pulled himself to an upright position, and with his pocket hanky, wiped his brow. As he stuffed the handkerchief back into his pocket, he could see his sister Jane, pulling into the barn driveway with the family car, along with his mother in the passenger seat.

"Great," thought Dennis, time for the afternoon cider break.

Mary got out of the passenger seat, and handed Dennis the jug of cool cider he had been anticipating.

"*Ja*, your letter came today," she said, handing him the official looking envelope the family had been expecting from Uncle Sam.

Wiping his hands on his trousers, Dennis opened the letter. His orders were to report to Detroit on August 25, 1953 to commence his active service in the US Army. A bus would again be available for transportation to the Detroit Base, departing from St. Johns on Monday, the 24th of August.

That following Sunday afternoon, friends, including Pete Pung, Jim Mckeone, and Alfred Hengesbach, stopped by to send Dennis off. The friends usually drank beer in the old woodshed that was once attached to the house, but had conveniently been moved out-of-site to the northern edge of the farmstead. Today, however, the guys sipped on 16-ounce, long neck, glass bottles of Strohs Bohemian beer, openly, on the house-facing side of the main barn hill. Soon, the five o'clock hour rolled around, the group disbanded, and Dennis and Clair retreated to the stanchion barn for the evening milking chores.

Upon arrival in Detroit the next day, Dennis was assigned service number: US 55 405 469; and, underwent yet another physical exam. The afternoon was filled with several briefing sessions, and the next morning, the new US Army inductees boarded a bus for Fort Knox, Kentucky. The first order of business upon checking in at Fort Knox was attainment of the official U.S. Army haircut.

Basic training at Fort Knox lasted ten weeks. The training was less than memorable, not really much of a task for a farm kid used to rigorous daily labor. More memorable was the constant presence of chocolate cake. It seemed the US Army served the same chocolate cake with most every meal. After leaving the service, it took several years before Dennis regained an appetite for even his own mother's chocolate cake.

One of Dennis' compatriots from the Detroit screening, somehow managed to procure a car which he stashed in a vacant lot not far from the base. The Fort Knox, Kentucky base was about an eight-hour drive from the Lansing area. On the two weekends the basic training cadets were given a full weekend leave, a group of the Detroit crew, including Dennis, would make the drive to Michigan over Friday night, and then head back down to Kentucky on Sunday evening.

During the second weekend leave, Norman told Dennis that Pete Pung had just received his orders to report for active duty. And, he had just been shipped off to Fort Knox! When Dennis returned to complete boot camp, the two neighborhood farm boys located each other for a brief reunion. A little over a year later, the two friends would again briefly cross paths at Fort Hood, Texas.

Pete, a former minor league baseball player, was quickly recruited to play on a travelling Army team. Dennis was able to take in a few games, watching his friend play first base, just like he had many weekends prior in the good old days of their youth back in Westphalia.

At the conclusion of basic training, Dennis was assigned to Fort Lee, Virginia. He had a three-day layover before he needed to report to Fort Lee. Dennis took a bus from Fort Knox to Lansing, spent a day and a half at home, then was able to catch a ride to Virginia with one of his fellow Fort Knox cadets, who lived in the Detroit area and was also reporting to Fort Lee. Public bus transportation and hitching rides to and fro across the country was a routine method of travel for much of the middle-class back in those days, especially for the boys in the military.

The ten-week assignment at Fort Lee, Virginia, encompassed a short Christmas break. Dennis was able to scratch together the bus fare home to spend the Holidays with family and friends. The stint at Fort Lee, known in Army vernacular as Quartermaster School, was almost exclusively for technical training. In Dennis' case the training covered primarily warehousing and radio communications. While at Fort Lee, Dennis settled comfortably into army life and learned to maximize and advantageously use allotted leave time to engage his passion for site-seeing and exploration. He had acquired a 35 mm slide camera, state of the art for the time period, and frequently mailed home slides taken during his occasional, but busy, site seeing trips. At home, Dennis' younger siblings eagerly viewed the slide pictures of scenery and tourist attractions.

In February of '54, Dennis completed the Quarter Master School at Fort Lee, VA, and was assigned to the 805th Signal Depot Company, which was stationed at Fort Sam Houston, Texas. Dennis was elated. Texas, at least to a rural Michigan farm kid, seemed like an exotic travel destination. He looked forward to the experience. The assignment didn't commence until early March, so Dennis was privilege to a couple of weeks of "training holiday" before having to report back for active duty in Texas. Dennis packed up his duffel and boarded the bus from Virginia bound for Michigan. When Dennis returned home for the two week stay, his younger sisters, Virginia now 8 years old, and Linda age 5, kept asking him about the mountain scenery and civil war sites. It seems, they thought their big brother had been away on some extravagant, site-seeing vacation because of the many slide pictures he had been mailing home.

***

The thermometer registered in the teens, accompanied with a raw, biting, west wind, when Dennis and Clair came in for breakfast that bitter cold Michigan morning. It was March 9, and the brothers had finished the morning milking chores early.

"*Ja*, let's get going," Norman said in his usual stoic demeanor.

"I'll get your duffel," Clair said and hoisted the tightly packed, drab green, official Army duffel that more closely resembled a full length boxing gym punching bag than an actual piece of travel luggage.

The two week leave had flown by. It was time for Dennis to head to Fort Sam Houston and report back to active Army duty.

The trio of Dennis, Norman, and Clair, piled into the family's Kaiser for the long trip to the Detroit airport. Norman had acquired a new model Kaiser after WWII had ended. The family now used the old '36 Ford as somewhat of a secondary vehicle that doubled, with the back seat removed, as a farm pickup truck. The generation that had endured the Great Depression never did give up the frugality that enabled their survival. And, despite the relative post-war farm prosperity, Norman and Mary were still very economically minded. If the old Ford still had utility on the farm, they'd find a way to make use of it. With the back seat of the old Ford removed, it was amazing how much cargo the behemoth could haul.

The new Kaiser, purchased at a Kaiser-Frazer dealership in St. Johns after Pauline and Clem Armbrustmacher purchased a similar one, was now the family car. It was used for most of the family transportation needs. The Kaiser-Frazer Corporation had been able to make a quick post-war transition back to automobile production. The relatively small company gained a brief toe-hold in the market by getting a jumpstart on the auto giants, such as General Motors and Ford, in having new cars available for an eager-to-buy public.

Dennis had managed to acquire Army privilege "space available air travel" for the long trip westward to San Antonio, Texas. The challenge was that the only locally available flights for San Antonio, Texas, departed from the Detroit Airport. The trip to Detroit was a long one, and Dennis expected he'd have to catch a bus in Lansing for the trip. However, due to restrictions in the bus schedule, that would have meant leaving the day before the flight, requiring a hotel stay in Detroit. Dennis was glad when Norman agreed to drive him out to the big city. Clair's presence riding shotgun was requested by Norman due to the inherent complexities of the long, pre-freeway trip, to the hitherto unexplored territory of the Detroit Wayne County International Airport.

The flight, the first one ever for Dennis, went off without a hitch. When Dennis' plane touched down in San Antonio, the temperature was a balmy eighty-three degrees, a welcome contrast to the cold damp weather Dennis left behind in Michigan. Dennis was sure he was going to like Fort Sam Houston.

The first week at Fort Sam Houston presented Dennis with an opportunity to address a thorn in his side that had been festering under his skin for the past five years. While still at Fort Lee, Virginia, Dennis learned that the Armed Services, through the United States Armed Forces Institute (USAFI), offered opportunities for soldiers to earn a General Education Development Diploma (GED) recognized nationally as a high school graduate equivalency.

Dennis' first week schedule at Fort Sam Houston, had sufficient breathing room available for him to complete the GED testing. By completing the examination for a single subject area each day, in a matter of a week, Dennis was able to breeze through the testing. At the conclusion of the exams, March 16, 1954 Dennis received the USAFI Military Test Report, indicating that he had passed every subject. His natural inclination for daily reading, and the quality of the ninth grade education he received from the good Sisters at St. Mary's, had adequately prepared him for the high school equivalency. Dennis was elated.

The thorn had been removed, but perhaps there was still somewhat of a stigma to be healed yet. What Dennis really wanted was a bona fide diploma from St. Mary's high school. With a little more leg work, Dennis learned that some schools, would, under the right circumstances, issue high school diplomas when presented with official documentation certifying the successful attainment of high school equivalency. In the evenings after completing his training sessions, Dennis compiled the necessary supporting documents to have USAFI officially forward his test results to St. Mary's School, in Westphalia. Additionally, he wrote his sister Jane with instructions to deliver a second letter to Sister Auxilia, principal at St. Mary's, informing her of the pending notification from USAFI, and with a request to be considered for attainment of a high school diploma from St. Mary's.

On a pleasant, spring Sunday afternoon in late May, Father Aloysious Miller, pastor of St. Mary's, read Dennis' name at the St. Mary's Class of 1954, Commencement Ceremony. Dennis' sister Jane, walked the stage, *in-absentia*, for Dennis, and collected the coveted diploma.

With the GED and diploma out of the way, Dennis got back to the business of being a peace time soldier. The work of the 805th Signal Depot Company involved training in warehousing, and radio communications which essentially involved stringing miles of wire, as the Army was not yet fully reliant on wireless radio communication. When prepping for maneuvers, coils of wires had to be stacked and readied. Then, when maneuvers commenced, the companies would pick them up at the radio depot and also stock up on other radio supplies. Additionally, Dennis would install radios in trucks used for the maneuvers, and then in true military fashion, uninstall them and repack them in the warehouse following the conclusion of the maneuvers.

In addition to the warehousing and radio communications company-specific training, Dennis, like all the other Army regulars, had to continue with general soldier training. Dennis consistently scored well in marksmanship with the standard issue, M-1, rifles used through all of training. The high scores qualified Dennis for specialized sniper training.

During sniper training, Dennis and his soldier contemporaries would regularly ding targets at a distance of 500 yards, with open sights! Physical training, called PT, was a still a daily drudgery, but due to the intensity of the south Texas heat, once a week, PT was held in the relative luxury of one of the many swimming pools on the base.

Fort Sam Houston, located near beautiful, historic, San Antonio, TX, also enabled Dennis to continue his extensive leave-time tourist explorations and site seeing. Back home, the family continued to receive padded manila envelopes stuffed full with 35 mm slide pictures of beautiful botanical gardens, the Alamo, and the historic Menger Hotel and Bar, where Teddy Roosevelt recruited his Rough Riders before heading off to fight in the Spanish-American War.

The steady stream of exciting pictures from exotic destinations, at least exotic from the perspective of the small central Michigan dairy and sheep farm, continued to propagate the notion in the Thelen household that Dennis was, really, pretty much away on vacation. It got to the point where Norman and Mary decided that they wanted in on some of the action. They decided that they would pack up the car and head down to Fort Sam Houston and check out some of the sites for themselves. Mary talked her sister and best friend, Pauline Armbrustmacher and her husband Clem, into accompanying them on the trip.

The trip, over three-thousand miles both ways, without the benefit of freeways, took a little longer than what the travelers had planned. When they finally got there, Dennis showed them around the many shrines, missions, and floral gardens of San Antonio. But the men, especially Uncle Clem, were anxious from being away from their farms for so long. Clem was getting antsy to start the long car ride home. Dennis procured a two-day pass and rode back east with the four of them to Houston where they spent the night. In the morning, Dennis bade the travelers adieu, and then boarded a bus back to the base in San Antonio.

The time passed quickly at Fort Sam Houston. In late 1954, the entire 805th Signal Depot Company, was transferred to Fort Hood, TX, some one-hundred-fifty miles north of Fort Sam Houston. The company packed up their ware into trucks, driving in a convoy across the Texas country side. Dennis had obtained Army certification for driving heavy military trucks, aided in part by his farm experience driving sugar beet trucks for Leo Fedewa and delivering John Deere tractors in Norman's old International. In the convoy, Dennis drove a one-ton truck pulling a trailer. The cooks at Fort Sam Houston prepared a box lunch for the ½ day journey and the convoy stopped briefly on a side road to eat.

Fort Hood had even more swimming pools on the base, which Dennis and the other men used often to avoid the Texas heat. In the extreme heat of the day, the Company watched a lot of training films, some of which were confiscated from the German's during WWII that showed how the Nazi's would attack tanks and other armored vehicles. After evening meal, when the blazing Texas sun relented somewhat, the men played a lot of softball or used the free time to write letters and postcards to family back home.

At the time, the US Army was offering an early out option for soldiers in good standing as a peace-time, cost saving measure. Dennis filed the requisite paper work.

Pfc Dennis J. Thelen was honorably discharged from active military service on June 24, 1955. After receiving his discharge and transfer from Active Duty to Army Reserve status, Dennis jumped into a car with four other of his Fort Hood mates and headed for Chicago. There, he boarded a train back to Lansing. The twenty-two-month adventure was over.

When Dennis returned home, he used his service pay to make a down payment on his first car, a 1955 Fairlane Ford, purchased from Kramer's Ford in nearby Fowler, Michigan.

WORKING GIRL

In May of 1954, Joni graduated St. Mary High School in a class of twenty-nine, twenty-one of which were girls. Her eighth grade graduation consisted of forty-two individuals, evenly split between girls and boys. Most of Joni's male classmates, including Dennis' brother Clair, had left school early due to the demands of farm work. The early exodus from school was still occurring, despite the fact that mechanization of the more labor intensive activities had just begun to occur during the transitional, post WWII period on the farms of rural Michigan.

Additionally, as in most Westphalia, St. Mary's graduating classes of the time, the Catholic seminary had also claimed a few young men from the graduating class, and, in the class of 1954, that number was two individuals.

In the excitement of the commencement ceremony, Joni took note when Father Al Miller, then pastor at St. Mary's, read the name of one Dennis Thelen, the quiet young man who lived down the road and was currently away in the service. And, she looked on and politely clapped as Dennis' sister Jane, a year behind Joni in school, arose from the audience to walk up to the stage and accept Dennis' diploma.

As soon as Joni graduated, she began her job search. St. Mary High School specialized in preparing girls for secretarial/ clerk jobs which were often available in state government and the auto industry in nearby Lansing. With a little help from a family friend, Rita Thelen Witgen, Joni landed a clerk job at

Fisher Body, the coach building division of General Motors in Lansing. Her first day on the job was July 1, 1954, in the Production Control Department, and involved processing body orders for Oldsmobile cars. The pay was competitive, which seemed to Joni at the time to be an astronomical amount. The automobile industry was booming in the early 1950's and Joni was proud to be a part of it.

"Wow, a new TV!," Janice exclaimed with unabashed excitement.

"Yes, I picked it up at Koster Electric in town" Joni said proudly.

After carrying the set into the family room, Raymond stepped back, and, rubbing the small of his back, declared, "I hope the thing doesn't fall through the floor—it probably weighs as much as our biggest steer!"

Joni just smiled. That summer Joni purchased the new TV set for her family. This was the very first set the family ever had. No longer would they need to pile in the car and head over to Grandma Eleanor and the Uncles' house to watch television.

Initially, Joni would catch a ride into work with a neighbor, Vessie Hengesbach's son, Alfred. However, Alfred soon was drafted into the service so Joni stayed in Lansing with her Aunt Celeste, Raymond's sister, for about 2 weeks. Aunt Celeste's house was conveniently located within walking distance, just a few city blocks, away from the Fisher Body offices where Joni worked. While there, she ran into a couple of local girls, Mary Schmidt and Alice Spitzley, who also had jobs in Lansing. Coincidentally, they lived right across the street from Joni's Aunt Celeste. The girls, along with a third young woman, were rent paying boarders of a benevolent childless couple, Ed and Grace Allen. The couple had room for a fourth boarder, and for $5.00 per day, five days a week, Joni had herself a new week-day home.

On weekends Joni would catch a ride back home to the farm. There were lots of options for rides to and from downtown

Lansing, as the upturned local manufacturing economy had lured many young men and women from the farms and village of Westphalia. When Sunday evening, or in some cases, Monday morning, came around again, Joni would catch a ride back out to Lansing, once again joining the weekly migration of young folks from the Westphalia area back to the city of Lansing.

The work was busy but generally enjoyable. Equal rights for women had not totally established itself in the professional workforce in the mid 1950's. The men working in the Fisher Body offices were allowed to smoke at their desks. Woman, however, were required to do their smoking in the ladies' room.

The summer of 1955, which happened to be a very warm summer, was also one of the busiest for Fisher Body and General Motors. Joni had to work lots of overtime. At that time, no air conditioning was available in the office where Joni worked. Instead, they had salt tablets available to keep workers hydrated and alert at their desks. To complicate the business, the unionized workers in the manufacturing plant went on strike once during Joni's tenure at Fisher Body. None of the office workers were unionized at the time and they were expected to cross the picket lines and show up for work as usual. Management did, however, give them special training on how to cross the picket lines in a non-confrontational manner.

The years after high school graduation weren't all work for Joni.

"We're putting together a team in the Lansing City League," Joni's good friend Mary Ellen Thelen-Schneider, told Joni one Friday night when the girls were home for the weekend. "A few girls from the old Pewamo team will be playing," Mary Ellen added. "Jean Kramer, Betty Schafer, and Judy Stump."

The Pewamo girls had been high school basketball rivals of Mary Ellen and Joni, but as often happens, former rivals become good friends once the competitions are over.

Staying true to her childhood tomboy nature, Joni joined up with the girls and they entered a team in the Lansing, Woman's Basketball City League, which was run by Margaret Whitehead, a matriarch of women's sports in the Lansing area. Like high school, Joni, although only five-feet-four-inches tall, played offensive forward for the team which still played in the old six player, split-court format. Conveniently, the games were held during weeknights when Joni was already in Lansing.

The one-time high school rivals played well together and won the City League their very first year of playing together. However, the team was short lived as marriage, and the convent, eventually pulled the players in different directions away from the basketball court.

In the spring of 1956, Joni's sister Janice graduated high school. Janice landed a clerical job at the John Deere Plow Company and moved into the same house as Joni. The two split a bedroom during the week, for which Joni was more than happy to pay the $5.00 weekly rent.

As fate would have it, that summer, on their weekends back home, the two Wieber sisters began dating a couple of young farm boys from the Westphalia area.

SETTLING DOWN

When Dennis returned from his brief, twenty-two-month stint in the Service, the rural Michigan agriculturally based world had noticeably changed. The summer of 1955, marked a decade since the end of WWII. Gradually, and at an ever increasing rate, automation and technology on local farms had progressed to the point where much less manual labor was needed. Many of Dennis' contemporaries were freed to answer the siren song of full time work away from the farm.

The appealing lifestyle of defined hours, weekends off, and, for the time period, exorbitant wages relative to farming, was hard to resist. Just two short years away from the farm had crystallized the changes in the rural community, at least from Dennis' fresh perspective, in a manner that may not have been quite as apparent had he not been privilege to the time away. Dennis still liked the idea of farming for a living, but, he wanted to at least dip his toe into the unknown waters of factory life before, as the old saying goes, "buying the farm."

Within days of stepping off the army bus, Dennis went to General Motors to fill out an application for employment. The place didn't seem too bad. While walking through the application process, Dennis ran into a local acquaintance, Sam Donahue, in one of the GM offices, and stopped to say, "Hi." It seemed like a good omen. Within a couple of days, General Motors came calling, and asked Dennis to report to final assembly at the Main Plant in downtown Lansing.

Dennis' first thought when he reported to the assembly line was, "Man, its loud in here!"

"Over here," a man named Norm, who was Dennis' foreman shouted as he waved Dennis over with his right arm.

Dennis was assigned to a group of men tasked with installing hoods onto car bodies as they passed by on the assembly line. Two men hand carried each individual hood over from the stacked crates of hoods. In choreographed fashion, Dennis would grab the bottom, left hand corner of each hood with his right hand as the two men approached. When the hood was properly positioned over the car's engine compartment, Dennis, with his air wrench grasped firmly in his left hand, would advance a machine screw into a threaded hole on the mounting hardware attached to the car's body.

Dennis' second thought on that first day on the job was, "Man, I'm glad I don't have the little guy's job!"

The little guy, one of Dennis' coworkers, had to tuck himself into a ball and slide under the steering wheel of each car, and reach up through a small access cavity in the chassis. From this severely compromised, ergonomically arrested position, the little guy would then secure a mounting pin into the hood.

Dennis was able to join a carpool with his older cousin and good friend, Jim Armbrustmacher from Fowler, and another neighbor, Don Schmitz. The group would rendezvous at the Riley Township Hall on the corner of Pratt and Francis Roads. At the time, there was only one shift, the day shift.

The factory had its own way of doing things which took some getting used to for a farm boy. Fortunately, the past two years spent in the military helped to lessen the culture shock, somewhat at least. Nevertheless, Dennis was still not used to having restrictions placed on the simple things in life, like going to the bathroom. In the factory, there was one bathroom break before lunch, and one after. In order to keep the assembly line moving, a team of subs would work up and down the line relieving the workers for their ten-minute bathroom break. Lunch was about twenty minutes long.

At home, Dennis was still very much involved in the farm. He helped with chores on a daily basis and, on weekends, helped with the field work.

**

In May of 1955, Dennis' sister Jane graduated high school. The time was bittersweet for the Thelen family. Jane had felt a calling to the religious life since she was a young child, committing to it in her heart already, while still in the seventh grade. At the end of Jane's eighth grade year, the spiritual pull in her heart reached a point where she felt compelled to speak to the Superior at St. Mary's Convent, Sister Adelaide. The good Sister, who had known Jane since her grade school years at St. Mary's school, possessed the spiritual discernment to know that Jane would indeed someday end up in the service of the Lord. Patiently, she counseled young Jane to speak to her parents about her internal callings to religious life.

During the 1950's, St. Mary's Westphalia produced a significant number of vocations to the priesthood and sisterhood. Knowing their daughter's religious conviction and mature spirituality, even at a young age, it can be assumed that Norman and Mary were not totally surprised when Jane approached them about her interior calling. Nevertheless, it's hard to imagine the polarity of emotions the two must have felt hearing their eldest daughter, at the tender age of fourteen, spill her heart out regarding the calling she felt to religious life as a Sister.

On the one hand, having a child with a religious vocation was a tremendous source of pride for a Catholic family. However, the pride would be tempered with an equally powerful sense of loss. Commitment to the religious life, particularly during that early time period, would mean that they would essentially not see their beloved daughter, except on very rare occasions, for the remainder of their lives.

In their wisdom, Norman and Mary counseled Jane that they would really like her to wait until she finished high school before enrolling in the convent. During the early and mid-1900's it was not uncommon for young Catholic boys and girls to begin the seminary and novitiate process while still in middle school.

"Sure, I'll wait," Jane replied obediently with her usual smile.

Neither parent doubted their daughter's sincerity or conviction, and, needless to say, both relished the four years they had remaining with their spiritually blessed, eldest daughter.

In mid-May of 1955, with Jane's high school graduation rapidly approaching, Sister Adelaide took Jane, along with Julia Stump, a Pewamo girl who had also committed to religious life, shopping to buy luggage, one piece each, for their departure. At the convent in Westphalia the Sisters had prepared the clothes, referred to as "habits," that the girls would need for their new life. In addition, the girls were given labels, each with a specific number, to sew onto their habits. Jane's number was 176B. With motherly diligence, Mary helped Jane sew the numbers to each habit.

Later that summer, on Monday, August 29, Jane officially entered the convent of the Sisters of Christian Charity. The morning dawned with the heavy air of a typical late summer August day, and began with a Communion Service at St. Mary Church, in Westphalia for the Thelen family. After Mass the Sisters invited the family to a breakfast of toast, hot dogs, canned peaches and a large sugar cookie, all served by two young nuns at the convent, Sisters Stella and Dolorette.

After breakfast, the family, along with two of the local nuns, Sisters Purmin and Clotilde, headed for Battle Creek to board the train for Chicago. The size of the group required two cars, so Dennis agreed to drive his new Ford Fairlane with half of the group. By the time the group reached Battle Creek, the sultry summer temperature had already peaked at 85 degrees. The Stump family, with their daughter Julia, met up with the Thelen's at the train station. Amidst tearful goodbyes, the two young women boarded the westbound Grand Trunk Western Railway train to Chicago.

To Jane, the train trip seemed to be a long one. The nuns back at St. Mary's had packed a delicious lunch for both Jane and Julia, but every time they tried to eat, their throats refused to swallow. And, each time they looked at each other to talk, tears rolled down their cheeks.

When the Grand Trunk Western train arrived in Chicago, the two were met by Sisters Lucy and Carmel, of the Chicago Sisters of Christian Charity. Their arranged escorts ushered Jane and Julia to a Chicago Transit Authority "L" train. After another hour on the L, the two small-town farm girls, Jane and Julia arrived in Wilmette at Maria Immaculata Motherhouse, where they were welcomed as new candidates for the Sisters of Christian Charity.

Jane's daily routine at the Motherhouse involved classes in scripture and learning about the purpose of religious life and the rules of the Community. In addition, the candidates also began classes at Mallinckrodt College to prepare for future services within the Community. After six months, Jane was accepted to become a Postulant and in another six months, she successfully qualified for the Novitiate.

On August 21, 1956, Jane, Julia, and five other postulants were vested in the Community. At the ceremony, Jane received her new chosen name, Sister Norma. Norman and Mary, as well as Dennis and Virginia, along with uncles and aunts from both sides of the family came to Wilmette, Illinois to celebrate with Jane. Unfortunately, Jane's other siblings were not able to attend as the youngest Thelen, Linda, was still not able to travel due to lingering complications with rheumatic fever.

Jane's heart was filled to the bursting point with happiness and the expression on her face reflected the contentment and peace she had gained in her soul. Jane continued her Novitiate and training over the course of the next eight years, earning a teaching degree while taking classes at Loyola and De Paul University, in Chicago.

Finally, in 1964, Jane was given permission to make her perpetual vows to religious life. Prior to her final vows, an approximately eight-week period from June into August was spent in silence, prayer, and intense preparation. On August 20, together with the five Sisters in her class, Jane proclaimed her perpetual vows in a solemn Holy Mass in Maria Immaculata Chapel. At that time, families were not invited to the perpetual vow Mass and reception. Nevertheless, the family lent their full support through prayers and intercessions offered back home in Michigan.

***

Dennis left the constraints of the Final Assembly job at the first opportunity he had. In fact, after about two weeks on the job, he learned of an opportunity in the General Motor's Parts Department. The warehousing training Dennis had acquired in the Service made him a natural fit for picking parts. As luck would have it, Dennis was able to transfer.

The position involved picking parts for older model cars, and was housed in the old factory of Lansing's Ransom E. Olds, "REO" Motor Car Company. The old REO fully furnished executive offices were still in another wing of the plant even though they had earlier been abandoned. Dennis and his workmates would avail themselves to the plush chairs and fine desks for purposes of eating their lunches.

While in the Parts Department, Dennis had the good fortune of being teamed with a cousin of his from Norman's side, Edgar Schneider. Edgar drove the basket equipped forklift and Dennis would pull the parts off the shelves. Dennis would mark each part off his list as it was picked. The job was decidedly more easy and enjoyable than the final assembly job. However, it didn't last long. After several months, General Motors endured a short downturn in production and Dennis was laid off.

It was still winter, early 1956 now, and Dennis hadn't quite fully scratched the "working off the farm" itch. A similar "picking parts" job was available at the John Bean Factory in Lansing. The John Bean Company manufactured pumps and sprayers for farm use as well as pumps for other applications such as fire trucks. In addition to picking parts, Dennis would also haul to a local scrap yard, using the company dump truck, the daily accumulation of metal tailings from the John Bean manufacturing floor. This kept Dennis quite busy, and he enjoyed the work. However, when his somewhat overzealous foreman also wanted Dennis to pick up new pairs of safety boots for the floor workers, he decided he had had enough of the factory life. Besides, it was now spring, and Dennis was anxious to get back to the business of farming.

That summer, after almost a year of factory work, Dennis returned to full time work back home on the family farm. By now the milking herd had increased to around 30 cows. The farm land base had increased by eighty acres, with Norman and Mary's purchase of the "Dexter Trail Road Farm," a mile and a half east of the main farmstead, purchased when Dennis was about to be discharged from the Service.

DENNIS AND JONI

The summer of 1956, Dennis, now twenty-three years old, decided to commit himself to farming. In addition, that same summer, he began to be smitten by the spry young Wieber girl with the blue eyes, high cheekbones, and wavy brown hair, whom he had grown up a mere mile and half from, but really hadn't gotten to know before. After informally chatting at several of the local social activities and dances, the unobtrusively quiet Dennis finally summoned the courage to ask Joni out on a date.

"Would you like to go to the auto show?" he asked.

"Yes," she replied.

The attraction was mutual and quick-forming between the two. At home, Dennis' siblings noticed a dramatic change in his usual stoic and serious demeanor. He began to laugh more often. Sometimes out loud. The budding attraction also began to affect Dennis' work.

"There's a car parked by the side of the road," Norman said on a Saturday afternoon as he looked out the parlor window towards the field west of the house. Dennis was plowing in the field with the Super M, International Harvester tractor which Norman had purchased in '53.

"Oh, that's Joni Wieber's car," Dennis' ten-year-old sister, Virginia, now called Ginny, piped up.

"Hmmm," Norman mumbled, concerned that the important plowing work might actually be interrupted for a few minutes. With a disgruntled frown, he sat back down in the corner living room chair with his newspaper.

By now, an audience of Ginny, Rosie, Tommy, and the youngest Thelen, seven-year-old Linda, had gathered around the parlor window.

"The tractor stopped," Rosie giggled.

"Hmmm," Norman muttered again, getting up from his chair to see for himself. "Seems strange to be taking a break in the middle of a work day," Norman said aloud, genuinely surprised that Dennis would interrupt plowing for a social call.

As the kids continued their spying out the window, Norman sat back down with his paper. After a few minutes had passed, the children began to disperse from the window.

"Dennis back to plowing?" Norman asked not bothering to look up from the news page of the State Journal.

"No," Ginny said matter-of-factly, "He drove away in the car with Joni."

"HE DID WHAT!" Norman exclaimed as his jaw nearly hit the floor.

By fall, Dennis and Joni were seeing each other every weekend, and they would end each weekend with Dennis taking Joni back out to her weekday house in Lansing. In addition to the local dances, the dates included going to the Lansing Autorama Show, and various country western concerts at the brand new Lansing Civic Center.

In the winter of 1957, during one of the Sunday evening return trips back to Joni's weekday boarding house in Lansing, Dennis popped the big question.

"Will you marry me?" Dennis asked.

"Yes." Joni replied.

***

The predawn sky of October 19, 1957 was punctuated with sparkling starlight and there was a refreshingly crisp cool nip in the still autumn air. Patchy frost laced the lawns at both the Thelen and Wieber farms, and chores were started extra early that morning. Despite the chilly start, the cold night air was no match for the persistent warmth of the rising sun, and the resonant rays of sunshine quickly pushed the day time temperature to sixty degrees. It was a nearly perfect mid-Fall day.

"Stand here and I'll take a picture of your reflection in the mirror," Janice told Joni as the two sisters readied themselves for the wedding in their parents' bedroom.

Joni stepped in front of the waist-high dresser and paused to gaze into her mother's wall mounted mirror. She exhaled and immediately smiled at the beautiful bride that was reflected back at her.

Janice snapped the picture and before she could advance the film for a second shot, Florence called from the kitchen. "*Ja*, make haste girls, it's time to get going."

"I'll get a picture of you leaving the house," Janice offered, and snatched up her carry-all bag as she quickly exited the room.

Joni made a final adjustment to her bridal veil and whirled around in the flowing bridal gown in the general direction of the bedroom door. "This will take some getting used to," Joni thought aloud while picking up the skirt with her hands and forearms as she walked into the living room where her parents were waiting expectantly. Florence smiled, and as the emotion of the moment began to well up inside her, she looked down and quickly stepped into the bedroom from which Joni had just exited. Momentarily she was back in the living room carrying a beautiful white shawl.

"Here, Joni, wear this while you're outdoors," she said, adding, "Your Grandma Eleanor wore it at her wedding."

"Let's go Joni," Raymond said motioning towards the south door with his fine felt, Sunday dress hat, held loosely by the thick fingers of his right hand.

"Let me hold the screen door open so you can fit that dress through," Raymond offered, focusing on something useful to quell the emotions that now had a chokehold on his own throat.

***

At the Thelen household the morning preparations progressed a little more chaotically. When Dennis and Clair returned to the house after morning chores, Mary and Norman were busy tending to last minute reception preparations. Rosie, now sixteen and one of the bridesmaids was upstairs getting ready. Twelve-year-old Tommy was going to be an altar boy at the 9:30 am wedding Mass and Mary was touching up his hair in the family's only bathroom. Ginny and Linda were busy clearing the morning breakfast dishes. Jane, although certainly there in spirit, was ensconced in her novitiate training in Chicago and was not able to physically attend the wedding.

"Did you hide the car," Dennis asked Clair as the two wolfed down a quick after-chores second breakfast of corn flakes.

"Yup, it's hidden over at Uncle Walter's," Clair said not bothering to look up from his cereal bowl.

Locally, it was generally a wise precaution to hide your car on your wedding day. Messing with the groom's car was and still seems to be a most irresistible prank for young men. After a quick bath, Dennis donned his black rental tuxedo and he and his best man, Clair, headed into town for St. Mary's Church, followed closely behind by Norman and Mary and the rest of the family.

At the church, Dennis, Clair, and the other groomsmen, Joni's brother Eddie, on leave from the Service, and Dennis' cousin Joe Armbrustmacher, gathered in the sacristy in the front of the church. Since it was considered taboo for the groom to see the bride before the ceremony, Joni and the bridesmaids, Janice, Mary Ellen Thelen-Schneider, Rosie, and the flower girl, Joni's young cousin, Mary Kay Buaer, readied themselves in the bridal room in the back of the church.

Adjacent to the church in the parish reception hall, Mary Bengal and her crew of helpers were busy preparing the dinner meal, which was served after Mass. In addition, Mary tended to the early preparations for the larger supper meal which was to be held at the onset of the wedding reception. The dinner meal consisted of fried chicken and was attended by the families and wedding party of the bride and groom. The supper meal, which featured roast beef cooked in a large wood-fired cauldron that sat under a lean-to roof on the east side of the hall, was attended by all of the wedding guests.

The wedding Mass at St. Mary's church, was officiated by Father Aloysious Miller. With great joy, Dennis and Joni exchanged marital vows. Thus the two, as well as their two families, were inextricably linked and their long histories were joined together.

Immediately after the wedding ceremony the uncles, aunts, and extended family headed over to the adjacent reception hall to tap into the kegged beer and wait for the noon meal to be served. Back at the church, the wedding party and immediate family had to pose for the requisite wedding pictures before being excused to the hall for dinner. Finally, the chicken and potato dinner was served to the hungry congregation.

After dinner, Dennis and Joni, and their parents, went over to the Wieber's house to freshen up and relax until the reception started at about five o'clock in the afternoon. Some of the closer relatives, aunts and uncles who attended the Mass and dinner, stayed behind at the hall to help prepare the dining area for the coming evening reception. Once that work was done, the relatives would tap into the beer kegs and break out the playing cards for a few games of euchre.

The bride and groom, and their parents, generally used the time between the noon meal and the start of the reception as a time to relax and enjoy some family time together. However, that wasn't always the case. Joe Fedewa, the local farm boy who was engaged to marry Janice just eight months after Dennis and Joni's wedding, had to go home and bale hay between the wedding Mass and reception—on his own wedding day!

**

"Let's go see ol' Johnny Geller," Eddie said to Clair after they had finished the noon meal. Neither of the two young men particularly wanted to go back to the Wieber's house to just sit and relax and wait for the evening reception to start.

"OK," Clair eagerly agreed.

The Wieber family friend's old shack of a house was only a few hundred feet from the St. Mary's Reception Hall.

"Let me grab a bottle first," Eddie said as he walked into the hall kitchen to retrieve one of the bottles of whiskey Raymond and Norman had put away to be opened up for mixed drinks later on during the evening reception.

About an hour later when the two returned to the hall, Clair and Eddie had big smiles on their faces. Upstairs in the hall, Clair's cousins and good friends the Armbrustmachers were playing the piano and singing songs as they liked to do during family gatherings. Clair made his way over and squeezed in behind the rear of the group of singers who happened to be getting dangerously close to the four-tiered wedding cake, precariously perched on a small folding table.

The cake was made by a locally famous farm wife cake baker, Bertha Simon, who annually dominated the cake baking competition at the Ionia Free Fair. She even once had her picture taken at the Fair's Cake Baking Competition receiving congratulations, a peck on the cheek and a first place blue ribbon from then governor of Michigan, George W. Romney.

As Jim Armbrustmacher rollicked the piano into a chorus of Old Susanna, the singing crowd gathered around him began to swing back and forth to the rhythm of the song. Caught up in the spirit of the moment, and perhaps the spirits imbibed at Johnny Geller's, Clair momentarily lost his balance. Reflexively, he stiffened his arms to catch himself on the card table supporting the wedding cake immediately behind him. Needless to say, Clair, being a robust, twenty-one-year-old, healthy farm boy, was more than the feeble card table could handle. The lone table leg closest to the singing group buckled and folded under the weight of the hefty farm boy struggling to break his fall. The tiered wedding cake initially wobbled, but swiftly gave way to the forces of gravity, and slid towards the corner of the table lagging from the compromised table leg.

As mentioned earlier, the kitchen crew was headed by Mary Bengal who, for many years, cooked for all the weddings and funerals hosted at St. Mary's. She was known far and wide for the amazing roast beef dinners she cooked in the wood fired, outdoor cauldron adjacent to the hall. Over the years, she had developed a keen, sixth sense for impending kitchen and food service disasters. From the corner of her eye, she had been watching the singing group, suspicious that a disaster might be looming. And, when she saw Clair amble over to join the group, she instinctively readied herself into a defensive position. With all the inherent strength and quickness afforded a woman of industrial German-American stock, Mary Bengal quickly and adroitly righted the table before the sliding cake could topple over the edge. The speedy move saved the cake, and likely the hide, of young Clair.

***

The afternoon activities in the hall eventually quieted down and the tables upstairs were reset for hosting the reception supper. The old St. Mary's Hall had two levels. The upper level was well lit with windows along the north and south walls that flooded the hall with light during the day. Similarly, several banks of electric lights along the ceiling fully illuminated the hall during the evening hours. The upstairs featured a hardwood dance floor, and in addition to serving as the dining area, it was also where the band set up for the evening entertainment and dancing.

At the bridal table, Father Al Miller rose and began the evening reception supper with the standard meal prayer. Dennis and Joni clinked their wine glasses together at the conclusion of the ceremonial toast, and the wedding feast began.

"Oh, look, there's Grandma Eleanor, and my uncles" Joni said as she squeezed her new husband's hand.

Off to the couple's right, the widowed Eleanor was seated with her sons and daughter-in-law. Isadore and his wife, along with Joni's three bachelor uncles, Harold; Leon; and Art filled out the table. Leon proudly sported a corsage on his lapel, put there by virtue of his being Joni's godfather. Glancing to his left, Dennis acknowledged his many uncles and aunts, seated expectantly with their own respective families.

When the roast beef supper was finished and the wedding cake had been served, many of the guests retreated to the basement for lively conversation served up with glasses of frothy draft beer. The hall basement was poorly lit, for the most part windowless, had low ceilings, a concrete floor, and as such, provided an excellent pub-type environment. A sturdy hardwood bar stretched along the south wall where glasses of cold Strohs beer were served from pressurized kegs to thirsty wedding patrons.

Meanwhile, the women friends and family members quickly did the dishes upstairs while the men in the family tore down and stored away the upstairs tables. Raymond and Norman had procured the local wedding band known as the Thelen Orchestra for the reception and while the floor transition from dining room to dance hall was ongoing, Gregor, the band leader, and his bandmates set up on the west end of the hall.

Gregor Thelen called out several square dances among other dance songs played during the evening. A good time was had by all and the evening entertainment progressed without incident. The consumption of beer was significant at area rural weddings in the mid 1950's but bad comportment was held in check by a strong individual constitution and tolerance for alcohol, and minimal social tolerance for intoxicated behavior. People knew how to have a good time, but, with exceptions of course, most generally knew how to celebrate responsibly. During that particular time period, the Parish Hall was expected to be emptied out and closed up by around eleven o'clock, and the people respectfully complied. Clean up was done the following morning.

As the evening wound down, Dennis and Joni began saying their thanks and goodbyes to friends and family and readied themselves to depart from the reception. Because Dennis' car was hidden in his Uncle Walter's garage, they had to catch a ride with their soon to be brother-in-law, Joe Fedewa. Dennis helped Joni maneuver her dress train through the St. Mary's Hall door while Joe fired up the engine of the get-away car.

Outside the hall, the refreshing air of the cool autumn night offered a brief, but welcome respite from the crowded air inside. Soon, the couple's parents joined them outside to impart their blessings and goodbyes.

With their tired feet planted firmly on the ground, Raymond, Florence, Norman, and Mary watched with a sense of pride and sadness as Dennis and Joni stepped into the waiting car.

"Ja," Mary sighed, "It's been a good day."

"Ja," the other three nodded in agreement.

As the wedding car pulled away, an abrupt late evening breeze rustled across the sidewalk in front of the four happy parents, randomly scattering the yellow and red leaves that had collected at their feet.

ACKNOWLEDGEMENTS

The author and illustrator thank Dennis and Joni for telling their stories and for putting up with all the questions and constant requests for more and more details. We also thank family and friends, particularly Aunt's Janice, Sr. Norma, Rosie, Virginia, and Linda; and, Uncles Clair, Tom, and Eddie for their input during the writing of the book and during the chance encounters of the many years prior. We also acknowledge the help in editing from Renee Owen, and Rochelle Thelen.